EX LIBRIS

VINTAGE CLASSICS

ROBERTO BOLAÑO

Roberto Bolaño was born in Santiago, Chile, in 1953. He grew up in Chile and Mexico City, where he was a founder of the Infrarealism poetry movement. Described by the *New York Times* as 'the most significant Latin American literary voice of his generation', he was the author of over twenty works, including *The Savage Detectives*, which received the Herralde Prize and the Rómulo Gallegos Prize when it appeared in 1998, and *2666*, which posthumously won the 2008 National Book Critics Circle Award for Fiction. Bolaño died in Blanes, Spain, at the age of fifty, just as his writing found global recognition.

ALSO BY ROBERTO BOLAÑO

NOVELS

The Savage Detectives

2666

Nazi Literature in the Americas

The Skating Rink

The Third Reich

Woes of the True Policeman

The Spirit of Science Fiction

NOVELLAS

By Night in Chile

Distant Star

Amulet

Antwerp

Monsieur Pain

A Little Lumpen Novelita

Cowboy Graves

STORIES

The Insufferable Gaucho

The Return

POETRY

The Romantic Dogs

Tres

The Unknown University

ROBERTO BOLAÑO

LAST EVENINGS ON EARTH

TRANSLATED FROM THE SPANISH BY
Chris Andrews

VINTAGE CLASSICS

1 3 5 7 9 10 8 6 4 2

Vintage Classics is part of the Penguin Random House
group of companies whose addresses can be found
at global.penguinrandomhouse.com

Penguin
Random House
UK

This edition published in Vintage Classics in 2024
These stories were first published in Spain in *Llamadas telefónicas* and *Putas
asesinas* by Editorial Anagrama in 1997 and 2001 respectively
First published in Great Britain with the title *Last Evenings on Earth*
by Harvill Secker in 2007

This work has been published with a subsidy from the
Directorate-General of Books, Archives and Libraries of the
Spanish Ministry of Culture

penguin.co.uk/vintage-classics

Printed and bound in Great Britain by Clays Ltd, Elcograf S.p.A.

The authorised representative in the EEA is
Penguin Random House Ireland,
Morrison Chambers, 32 Nassau Street, Dublin D02 YH68

A CIP catalogue record for this book is available from the British Library

ISBN 9781784879570

Penguin Random House is committed to a sustainable future
for our business, our readers and our planet. This book is made
from Forest Stewardship Council® certified paper.

CONTENTS

Sensini   1

Henri Simon Leprince   23

Enrique Martín   32

A Literary Adventure   52

Phone Calls   67

The Grub   74

Anne Moore's Life   91

Mauricio 'The Eye' Silva   131

Gómez Palacio   150

Last Evenings on Earth   163

Days of 1978   198

Vagabond in France and Belgium   216

Dentist   237

Dance Card   266

Sensini

THE WAY IN WHICH MY FRIENDSHIP WITH
Sensini developed was somewhat unusual. At the
time I was twenty-something and poorer than a
church mouse. I was living on the outskirts of Girona, in
a dilapidated house that my sister and brother-in-law had
left me when they moved to Mexico, and I had just lost
my job as a night watchman in a Barcelona campsite, a
job that had exacerbated my tendency not to sleep at night.
I had practically no friends and all I did was write and
go for long walks, starting at seven in the evening, just
after getting up, with a feeling like jet lag: an odd sensa-
tion of fragility, of being there and not there, somehow
distant from my surroundings. I was living on what I had
saved during the summer, and although I spent very little,
my savings dwindled as autumn drew on. Perhaps that
was what prompted me to enter the Alcoy National
Literature Competition, open to writers in Spanish, whatever their nationality or place of residence. There were

three categories: for poems, stories, and essays. First I thought about going in for the poetry prize, but I felt it would be demeaning to send what I did best into the ring with the lions (or hyenas). Then I thought about the essay, but when they sent me the conditions, I discovered that it had to be about Alcoy, its environs, its history, its eminent sons, its future prospects, and I couldn't face it. So I decided to enter for the story prize, sent off three copies of the best one I had (not that I had many), and sat down to wait.

When the winners were announced I was working as a vendor in a handicrafts market where absolutely no one was selling anything hand-crafted. I won fourth prize and 10 000 pesetas, which the Alcoy Council paid with scrupulous promptitude. Shortly afterwards I received the anthology, with the winning story and those of the six finalists, liberally peppered with typographical errors. Naturally my story was better than the winner's, so I cursed the judges and told myself, Well, what can you expect? But the real surprise was coming across the name Luis Antonio Sensini, the Argentine writer, who had won third prize with a story in which the narrator went away to the countryside where his son had died, or went to the country because his son had died in the city – it was hard to tell – in any case, out there in the countryside, on the bare plains, the narrator's son went on dying, that much was clear. It was a claustrophobic story, very much in Sensini's manner, set in a world where vast geographical spaces could suddenly shrink to the dimensions of a coffin, and it was better than the winning story and the one that came second, as well as those that came fourth, fifth, and sixth.

I don't know what moved me to ask the Alcoy Council for Sensini's address. I had read one of his novels and some of his stories in Latin American magazines. The novel was the kind of book that circulates by word of mouth. Entitled *Ugarte*, it was about a series of moments in the life of Juan de Ugarte, a bureaucrat in the Viceroyalty of the Río de la Plata at the end of the eighteenth century. Some (mainly Spanish) critics had dismissed it as Kafka in the colonies, but gradually the novel had made its way, and by the time I came across Sensini's name in the Alcoy anthology, *Ugarte* had recruited a small group of devoted readers, scattered around Latin America and Spain, most of whom knew each other, either as friends or as gratuitously bitter enemies. He had published other books, of course, in Argentina, and with Spanish publishers who had since gone to the wall, and he belonged to that intermediate generation of Argentine writers, born in the twenties, after Cortázar, Bioy Casares, Sábato, and Mújica Laínez, a generation whose best known representative (to me, back then, at any rate) was Haroldo Conti, who disappeared in one of the special camps set up by Videla and his henchmen during the dictatorship. It was a generation (although perhaps I am using the word too loosely) that hadn't come

3

to much, but not for want of brilliance or talent: followers of Roberto Arlt, journalists, teachers and translators; in a sense they foreshadowed what was to come, in their own sad and sceptical way, which led them one by one to the abyss.

I had a soft spot for those writers. In years gone by, I had read Abelardo Castillo's plays and the stories of Daniel Moyano and Rodolfo Walsh (who was killed under the dictatorship, like Conti). I read their work piecemeal, whatever I could find in Argentine, Mexican, or Cuban magazines, or the second-hand bookshops of Mexico City: pirated anthologies of Buenos Aires writing, probably the best writing in Spanish of the twentieth century. They were part of that tradition, and although, of course, they didn't have the stature of Borges or Cortázar, and were soon overtaken by Manuel Puig and Osvaldo Soriano, their concise, intelligent texts were a constant source of complicit delight. Needless to say, my favourite was Sensini, and the fact that I had been his fellow runner-up in a provincial literary competition – an association that I found at once flattering and profoundly depressing – encouraged me to make contact with him, to pay my respects and tell him how much his work meant to me.

The Alcoy Council sent me his address without delay – he lived in Madrid – and one night, after dinner or a light meal or just a snack, I wrote him a long letter, which rambled from *Ugarte* and the stories of his that I had read

4

in magazines to myself, my house on the outskirts of Girona, the competition (I made fun of the winner), the political situation in Chile and in Argentina (both dictatorships were still firmly in place), Walsh's stories (along with Sensini, Walsh was my other favourite in that generation), life in Spain, and life in general. To my surprise, I received a reply barely a week later. He began by thanking me for my letter; he said that the Alcoy Council had sent him the anthology too but that, unlike me, he hadn't found time to look at the winning story or those of the other finalists (later on, in a passing reference, he admitted that it wasn't so much a lack of time as a lack of 'fortitude'), although he had just read mine and thought it well done, 'a first-rate story', he said (I kept the letter), and he urged me to persevere, not, as I thought at first, to persevere with my writing, but to persevere with the competitions, as he intended to do himself, so he assured me. He went on to ask me which competitions were 'looming on the horizon', imploring me to notify him as soon as I heard of one. In exchange he sent me the conditions of entry for two short-story competitions, one in Plasencia and the other in Écija, with prizes of 25,000 and 30,000 pesetas respectively. He had tracked these down, as I later discovered, in Madrid newspapers or magazines whose mere existence was a crime or a miracle, depending on your point of view. There was still time for me to enter both competitions, and Sensini finished his letter on a curiously enthusiastic note, as if the pair of us were on our marks for a race that, as well as being hard and meaningless, would have no end. 'Pen to paper now, no shirking!' he wrote.

I remember thinking, What a strange letter. I remember reading a few chapters of *Ugarte*. Around that time the book dealers came to Girona to set up their stalls in the square where the cinemas are, displaying their mostly unsaleable stock: remaindered books published by firms that had recently gone bankrupt, books printed during the Second World War, romantic fiction and wild west novels, collections of postcards. At one of the stalls I found a book of stories by Sensini and bought it. It was as good as new – in fact it *was* new, one of those titles that publishers sell off to the book dealers when no one else can move it, when there's not a bookshop or a distributor left who's willing to take it on – and for the following week I lived and breathed Sensini. I read his letter over and over, leafed through *Ugarte*, and when I wanted a little action, something new, I turned to the stories. Although the themes and situations varied, the settings were usually rural, and the protagonists were the fabled horsemen of the pampas, that is to say armed and generally unfortunate individuals, either loners or men endowed with a peculiar notion of sociability. Whereas *Ugarte* was a cold book, written with neurosurgical precision, the collection of stories was all warmth: brave and aimless characters adrift in landscapes that seemed to be gradually drawing away from the reader (and sometimes taking the reader with them).

I didn't manage to submit an entry for the Plasencia competition, but I did for the Écija one. As soon as I had posted off the copies of my story (under the pseudonym Aloysius Acker), I realised that sitting around waiting for the results could only make things worse. So I decided to look for more competitions; that way at least I'd be able to comply with Sensini's request. Over the next few days, when I went down to Girona, I spent hours looking through back copies of newspapers in search of announcements. Some papers put them in a column next to the society news; in others, they came after the crime reports and before the sports section; the most serious paper had them wedged between the weather and the obituaries. They were never in the book pages, of course. In my search I discovered a magazine put out by the Catalonian government, which, along with advertisements for scholarships, exchanges, jobs, and postgraduate courses, published announcements of literary competitions, mostly for Catalans writing in Catalan, but there were some exceptions. I soon found three for which Sensini and I were eligible, and they were still open, so I wrote him a letter.

As before, I received a reply by return of post. Sensini's letter was short. He answered some of my questions, mainly about the book of stories I had recently bought, and included photocopies of the details for three more

7

short-story competitions, one of which was sponsored by the National Railway Company, with a tidy sum for the winner and 50,000 pesetas per head (as he put it) for the ten finalists: no prize for dreaming, you have to be in it to win it. I wrote back saying I didn't have enough stories for all six competitions, but most of my letter was about other things (in fact I got rather carried away): travel, lost love, Walsh, Conti, Francisco Urondo . . . I asked him about Gelman, whom he was bound to have known, gave him a summary of my life story, and somehow ended up going on about the tango and labyrinths, as I always do with Argentines (it's something Chileans are prone to).

Sensini's reply was prompt and extensive, at least as far as writing and competitions were concerned. On one sheet, recto and verso, single-spaced, he set out a kind of general strategy for the pursuit of provincial literary prizes. I speak from experience, he wrote. The letter began with a blessing on the prizes (whether in earnest or in jest, I have never been able to tell), those precious supplements to the writer's modest income. He referred to the sponsors – local councils and savings banks – as 'those good people with their touching faith in literature' and 'those disinterested and dutiful readers'. He entertained no illusions, however, about the erudition of the 'good people' in question, who presumably exercised their touching faith on these ephemeral anthologies (or not). He told me I should compete for as many prizes as possible, although he suggested

8

I take the precaution of changing a story's title if I was entering it for, say, three competitions that were due to be judged around the same time. He cited the example of his story 'At Dawn', a story I didn't know, which he had used to test his method, as a guinea pig is used to test the effects of a new vaccine. For the first competition, with the biggest prize, 'At Dawn' was entered as 'At Dawn'; for the second, he changed the title to 'The Gauchos'; for the third, it was called 'The Other Pampa'; and for the last, 'No Regrets'. Of these four competitions, it won the second and the fourth, and with the money from the prizes he was able to pay a month and a half's rent (in Madrid the rents had gone through the roof). Of course, no one realised that 'The Gauchos' and 'No Regrets' were the same story with different titles, although there was always the risk that one of the judges might have read the story in another competition (in Spain the peculiar occupation of judging literary prizes was obstinately monopolised by a clique of minor poets and novelists, as well as former laureates). The little world of letters is terrible as well as ridiculous, he wrote. And he added that even if one's story did come before the same judge twice, the danger was minimal, since they generally didn't read the entries or only skimmed through them. Furthermore, who was to say that 'The Gauchos' and 'No Regrets' were not two different stories whose singularity resided precisely in their respective titles? Similar, very similar even, but different. Towards the end of the letter he said that of course, in a perfect world, he would be otherwise occupied, living and writing in Buenos Aires, for example, but the way things were, he had to earn a crust somehow (I'm not sure they say that in Argentina; we do in Chile) and, for the time being, the competitions were helping him to get by. It's like a lesson in Spanish geography, he wrote. At the end, or maybe in a post-script, he declared: I'm getting on for sixty, but I feel as if I were twenty-five. At first this struck me as very sad, but when I read it for the second or third time I realised it was his way of asking me: How old are you, kid? I remember I replied immediately. I told him I was twenty-eight, three years older than him. That morning I felt not exactly happy again, but more alive, as if an infusion of energy were reanimating my sense of humour and my memory.

Although I didn't follow Sensini's advice and become a full-time prize-hunter, I did enter for the competitions he and I had recently discovered, without success. Sensini pulled off another double in Don Benito and in Écija, with a story originally called 'The Sabre', renamed 'Two Swords' for Écija and 'The Deepest Cut' for Don Benito. And in the competition sponsored by the Railways he was one of the finalists. As well as a cash sum, he won a ticket that entitled him to travel free on Spanish trains for a year.

Little by little I learnt more about him. He lived in a flat in Madrid with his wife and his daughter, Miranda, who was seventeen years old. He had a son, from his first marriage, who had gone to ground somewhere in Latin America, or that was what he wanted to believe. The son's name was Gregorio; he was thirty-five and had worked as a journalist. Sometimes Sensini would tell me about the enquiries he was making through human rights organisations and the European Union in an attempt to determine Gregorio's whereabouts. When he got on to this subject, his prose became heavy and monotonous, as if he were trying to exorcise his ghosts by describing the bureaucratic labyrinth. I haven't lived with Gregorio, he once told me, since he was five years old, just a kid. He didn't elaborate, but I imagined a five-year-old boy and Sensini typing in a newspaper office: even then it was already too late. I also wondered about the boy's name and somehow came to the conclusion that it must have been an unconscious homage to Gregor Samsa. Of course I never mentioned this to Sensini. When he got on to the subject of Miranda, he cheered up. Miranda was young and ready to take on the world, insatiably curious, pretty too, and kind. She looks like Gregorio, he wrote, except that (obviously) she's a girl and she has been spared what my son had to go through.

Gradually, Sensini's letters grew longer. The district where he lived in Madrid was run down; his flat had two bedrooms, a dining room-cum-living room, a kitchen and a bathroom. At first I was surprised to discover that his place was smaller than mine; then I felt ashamed. It seemed unfair. Sensini wrote in the dining room, at night, 'when the wife and the girl are asleep', and he was a heavy smoker. He earned his living doing some kind of work for a publisher (I think he edited translations) and by sending his stories out to do battle in the provinces. Every now and then he received a royalty cheque for one of his many books, but most of the publishers were chronically forgetful or had gone broke. The only book that went on selling well was *Ugarte*, which had been published by a firm in Barcelona. It didn't take me long to realise that he was living in poverty: not destitution, but the genteel poverty of a middle-class family fallen on hard times. His wife (her name was Carmela Zadjman, a story in itself) did freelance work for publishers and gave English, French, and Hebrew lessons, although she had occasionally been obliged to take on cleaning jobs. The daughter was busy with her studies and would soon be going to university. In one of my letters I asked Sensini whether Miranda wanted to be a writer too. He wrote back: No, thank God, she's going to study medicine.

One night I wrote and asked for a photo of his family. Only after putting the letter in the post did I realise that what I really wanted was to see what Miranda looked like. A week later I received a photo, no doubt taken in the Retiro, which showed an old man and a middle-aged woman next to a tall, slim adolescent girl with straight hair and very large breasts. The old man was smiling happily, the middle-aged woman was looking at her daughter, as if saying something to her, and Miranda was facing the photographer with a serious expression that I found both moving and disturbing. Sensini also sent me a photocopy of another photo, showing a young man more or less my age, with sharp features, very thin lips, prominent cheekbones and a broad forehead. He was strongly built and probably tall, and he was gazing at the camera (it was a studio photo) with a confident and perhaps slightly impatient air. It was Gregorio Sensini, at the age of twenty-two, before he disappeared, quite a bit younger than me, in fact, but he had an air of experience that made him seem older.

The photo and the photocopy lived on my desk for a long time. I would sit there staring at them or take them to the bedroom and look at them until I fell asleep. Sensini had asked me to send a photograph of myself. I didn't have a recent one, so I decided to go to the photo booth in the station, which at the time was the only photo booth in the whole of Girona. But I didn't like the way the photos came out. I thought I looked ugly and skinny and scruffy-haired. So I kept putting off sending any of them and went back to spend more money at the photo booth. Finally I chose one at random, put it in an envelope with a postcard, and sent it to him. It was a while before I received a reply. In the meantime I remember I wrote a very long, very bad poem, full of voices and faces that seemed different at first, but all belonging to Miranda Sensini, and when, in the poem, I finally realised this and could put it into words, when I could say to her, Miranda it's me, your father's friend and correspondent, she turned around and ran off in search of her brother, Gregorio Samsa, in search of Gregorio Samsa's eyes, shining at the end of a dim corridor in which the shadowy masses of Latin America's terror were shifting imperceptibly.

The reply, when it came, was long and friendly. Sensini and Carmela's verdict on my photo was positive: they thought I looked nice, as they imagined me, a bit on the skinny side maybe, but fit and well, and they liked the postcard of Girona cathedral, which they hoped to see for themselves in the near future, as soon as they had sorted out a few financial and household problems. It was clear that they were hoping to stay at my place when they came. In return they offered to put me up whenever I wanted to go to Madrid. It's a modest flat, and it isn't clean either, wrote Sensini, imitating a comic-strip gaucho who was famous in South America at the beginning of the seventies. He didn't say anything about his literary projects. Nor did he mention the competitions.

At first I thought of sending Miranda my poem, but after much hesitation and soul-searching I decided not to. I must be going mad, I thought, if I sent her that poem, there'd be no more letters from Sensini, and who could blame him? So I didn't send it. For a while I applied myself

14

to the search for new literary prizes. In one of his letters Sensini said he was worried that he might have run his race. I misunderstood; I thought he meant he was running out of competitions to enter.

I wrote back to say they must come to Girona; he and Carmela were most welcome to stay at my house. I even spent several days cleaning, sweeping, mopping, and dusting, having convinced myself (quite unreasonably) that they might turn up at any moment, with Miranda. Since they had one free pass they would only have to buy two tickets, and Catalonia, I stressed, was full of wonderful things to see and do. I mentioned Barcelona, Olot, the Costa Brava, talked about the happy days we could spend together. In a long reply, thanking me for my invitation, Sensini said that for the moment they couldn't leave Madrid. Unlike any of the preceding letters, this one was rather confused, although in the middle he returned to the theme of prizes (I think he had won one again) and encouraged me not to give up, to keep on trying. He also said something about the writer's trade or profession, and I had the impression that his words were meant partly for me and partly for himself, as a kind of reminder. The rest, as I said, was a muddle. When I got to the end I had the feeling that someone in his family wasn't well.

Two or three months later Sensini wrote to tell me that one of the bodies in a recently discovered mass grave was probably Gregorio's. His letter was restrained. There was no outpouring of grief; all he said was that on a certain day, at a certain time, a group of forensic pathologists and members of human rights organisations had opened a mass grave containing the bodies of more than fifty young people, etc. For the first time, I didn't want to reply in writing. I would have liked to ring him, but I don't think he had a telephone, and if he did I didn't know his number. My letter was brief. I said I was sorry, and ventured to point out that they still didn't know for sure that the body was Gregorio's.

Summer came and I took a job working in a hotel on the coast. In Madrid that summer there were numerous lectures, courses and all sorts of cultural activities, but Sensini didn't participate in any of them, or if he did, it wasn't mentioned in the newspaper I was reading.

At the end of August I sent him a card. I said that maybe that when the season was over I would visit him. That was all. When I got back to Girona, in the middle of September, among the small pile of letters that had been slipped under the door, I found one from Sensini dated August 7. He had written to say goodbye. He was going back to Argentina; with the return of democracy he would be safe now, so there was no point staying away any longer. And it was the only way he would be able to find out for sure what had happened to Gregorio. Carmela, of course, is returning with me, he said, but Miranda will stay. I wrote to him immediately, at the only address I had, but received no reply.

Gradually I came to accept that Sensini had gone back to Argentina for good and that, unless he wrote to me again, our correspondence had come to an end. I waited a long time for a letter from him, or so it seems to me now, looking back. The letter, of course, never came. I tried to tell myself that life in Buenos Aires must be hectic, an explosion of activity, hardly time to breathe or blink. I wrote to him again at the Madrid address, hoping that the letter would be sent on to Miranda, but a month later it was returned to me marked 'not known at this address'. So I gave up and let the days go by and gradually forgot about Sensini, although on my rare visits to Barcelona I would sometimes spend whole afternoons in second-hand bookshops looking for his other books, the ones I knew by their titles but was destined never to read. All I could find in the shops were old copies of *Ugarte* and the collection of stories published in Barcelona by a company that had recently gone into receivership, almost as if a message were being sent to Sensini (and to me).

One or two years later I discovered that he had died. I think I read it in a newspaper, I don't know which one. Or maybe I didn't read it; maybe someone told me, but I can't remember talking to anyone who knew him around that time, so I probably did read the obituary somewhere. It was brief, as I remember it: the Argentinean writer Luis

Antonio Sensini, who lived for several years in exile in Spain, had died in Buenos Aires. I think there was also a mention of *Ugarte* at the end. I don't know why, but it didn't come as a surprise. I don't know why, but it seemed logical that Sensini would go back to Buenos Aires to die.

Some time later, when the photo of Sensini, Carmela and Miranda, and the photocopied image of Gregorio were packed away with my other memories in a cardboard box that I still haven't committed to the flames for reasons I prefer not to expand upon here, there was a knock at the door of my house. It must have been about midnight, but I was awake. It gave me a shock all the same. I knew only a few people in Girona and none of them would have turned up like that unless something out of the ordinary had happened. When I opened the door there was a woman with long hair, wearing a big black overcoat. It was Miranda Sensini, although she had changed a good deal in the years since her father had sent me the photo. Next to her was a tall young man with long blond hair and an aquiline nose. I'm Miranda Sensini, she said to me with a smile. I know, I said, and invited them in. They were on their way to Italy; after that they planned to cross the Adriatic to Greece. Since they didn't have much money they were hitch-hiking. They slept in my house that night. I made them something to eat. The young man was called Sebastian Cohen and he had been born in Argentina too, although he had lived in Madrid since he was a child. He helped me prepare the meal while Miranda looked around the house. Have you known her for long? he asked. Until a moment ago, I'd only seen her in a photo, I replied.

After dinner, I prepared one of the rooms for them and said they could go to bed whenever they wanted. I thought about going to bed myself, but realised it would be hard, if not impossible, to sleep, so I gave them a while to get settled, then went downstairs, put on the television with the volume down low, and sat there thinking about Sensini.

Soon I heard someone on the stairs. It was Miranda. She couldn't get to sleep either. She sat down beside me and asked for a cigarette. At first we talked about their trip, about Girona (they had been in the city all day, but I didn't ask why they had come to my house so late), and the cities they were planning to visit in Italy. Then we talked about her father and her brother. According to Miranda, Sensini never got over Gregorio's death. He went back to look for him, although we all knew he was dead. Carmela too? I asked. He was the only one who hadn't accepted it, she said. I asked her how things had gone in Argentina. Same as here, same as in Madrid, said Miranda, same as everywhere. But he was well known and loved in Argentina, I said. Same as here, she said. I got a bottle of cognac from the kitchen and offered her a drink. You're crying, she said. When I looked at her she turned away. Were you writing? she asked. No, I was watching TV. No, I mean when we arrived. Yes, I said. Stories? No, poems.

Ah, said Miranda. For a long time we sat there drinking in silence, watching the black and white images on the television screen. Tell me something, I said, Why did your father choose the name Gregorio? Because of Kafka, of course, said Miranda. Gregor Samsa? Of course, she said. I thought so, I said. Then Miranda told me the story of Sensini's last months in Buenos Aires.

He was already sick when he left Madrid, against the advice of various Argentine doctors, who never billed him and had even arranged hospital treatment on the National Health a couple of times. Returning to Buenos Aires was a painful and happy experience. In the first week he started taking steps to locate Gregorio. He wanted to go back to his job at the university, but what with the bureaucracy and the inevitable jealousies and bitterness, it wasn't going to happen, so he had to make do with translating for a couple of publishing houses. Carmela, however, got a teaching position and towards the end they lived exclusively on her earnings. Each week Sensini wrote to Miranda. He knew he didn't have long to live, she said, and sometimes he seemed to be impatient, as if he wanted to use up the last of his strength and get it over with. As for Gregorio, there was nothing conclusive. Some of the pathologists thought his bones might have been in the pile exhumed from the mass grave, but they would of course have to do a DNA test, and the government didn't have the money or didn't really want the tests done, so they kept being postponed. Sensini also went searching for a girl who had probably been Greg's girlfriend when he was in hiding, but he couldn't find her either. Then his health deteriorated and he had to go into hospital. He didn't even write after that, said Miranda. It had always been very important to him, writing every day, whatever else was happening. Yes, I said, that's the way he was. I asked her if he'd found any literary competitions to enter in Buenos Aires. Miranda looked at me and smiled. Of course! You were the one he used to enter the competitions with; he met you through a competition. Then it struck me: the reason she had my address was simply that she had all her father's addresses, and she had only just realised who I was. That's me, I said. Miranda poured me out some more cognac and said there was a year when her father used to talk about me quite a lot. I noticed she was looking at me differently. I must have annoyed him so much, I said. Annoyed him? You're joking; he loved your letters. He always read them to Mum and me. I hope they were funny, I said, without much conviction. They were really funny, said Miranda, my mother even gave you guys a name. A name? Which guys? Dad and you. She called you the gun-slingers or the bounty hunters, I can't remember now, something like that, or the buccaneers. I see, I said, but the real bounty hunter was your father. I just passed on some information. Yes, he was a professional, said Miranda, suddenly serious. How many prizes did he win all told? I asked her. About fifteen, she said with an absent look. And you? So far just the one, I said. A short-listed place in the Alcoy competition, that's how I got to know your father. Did you know that Borges once wrote to him in Madrid, to say how much he liked one of his stories? No, I didn't know, I said. And Cortázar wrote about him, and Mújica Laínez too. Well, he was a very good writer, I said. Jesus! said Miranda, then got up and went out on to the terrace as if I had said something to offend her. I let a few seconds go by, picked up the bottle of cognac and followed her. Miranda was leaning on the balustrade, looking at the lights of Girona. You have a good view, she said. I filled her glass, then my own, and we stood there for a while looking at the moonlit city. Suddenly I realised that we were at peace, that for some mysterious reason the two of us had reached a state of peace, and that from now on, imperceptibly, things would begin to change. As if the world really was shifting. I asked her how old she was. Twenty-two, she said. I must be over thirty then, I said, and even my voice sounded different.

Henri Simon Leprince

THE EVENTS RECOUNTED HERE TOOK PLACE
in France shortly before, during, and shortly after
the Second World War. The protagonist, whose
name, Leprince, is oddly appropriate, although he is quite
the opposite of a prince (middle-class, well educated,
respectable friends, but downwardly mobile and short of
money) – is a writer.

Naturally, he is a failed writer, barely scraping a living
in the Paris gutter press, and his stories and poems (which
the bad poets regard as bad and the good poets don't even
read) are published in provincial magazines. Publishing
houses and their accredited readers (that execrable sub-
caste) seem for some mysterious reason to detest him.
His manuscripts are invariably rejected. He is middle-
aged, single, and accustomed to failure. In his own way,
he is a stoic. He reads Stendhal with a kind of defiant
pride. He reads certain surrealists whom deep down he
utterly despises (or envies). He reads the balsamic prose

of Alphonse Daudet, and out of fidelity to the father he also reads the deplorable Léon Daudet, a stylist of some distinction.

1940: France capitulates, and in the aftermath of the storm, the writers, who until then have been divided into scores of pullulating schools, gather to form two bands opposed by a mortal enmity: on the one hand, those who are prepared to resist, including the few partisans of active resistance and the advocates of passive resistance (the majority) as well as mere sympathisers and others who resist by omission, or are moved by suicidal urges, or the lure of transgression or by a sense of fair play or decency, and so on, and, on the other hand, those who are prepared to collaborate, similarly subdivided into various categories, all of them under the gravitational sway of the seven deadly sins. For many, the political reprisals provide an opportunity to settle literary scores. The collaborationists take control of various publishing houses, magazines, and newspapers. Leprince would seem to be stranded in a no-man's-land, or so he thinks until it dawns on him that his place, his natural habitat, is among the hacks, the embittered, the third-rate.

In due course he is approached by the collaborationists, who regard him, justifiably, as one of their kind. It is a friendly and no doubt generous gesture on their part. The recently appointed editor of the newspaper that he works for calls him, explains the new editorial policy, in line with the new direction that Europe is taking, offers him a better position, more money, prestige: minimal rewards that Leprince has never enjoyed.

That morning he finally comes to a realisation. Never before has he fully grasped the abjection of his place in the pyramidal hierarchy of literature. Never before has he felt so important. After a night of soul-searching and exaltation, he rejects the offer.

The following days are a test. Leprince tries to go on with his life and his work as if nothing had happened, knowing all the while that the attempt is vain. He tries to write but nothing comes. He tries to return to his favourite authors, but the pages seem to have gone blank, or to conceal mysterious signals that spring out from every paragraph. He tries new books but, unable to concentrate, he can find no instruction or enjoyment in reading. He has nightmares; sometimes he talks to himself without realising. Whenever he can, he goes for long walks through familiar parts of the city, which, to his amazement, look just the same, impervious to the occupation and the changes. Shortly afterwards he makes contact with a number of malcontents, people who listen to the BBC broadcasts from London and believe that conflict is unavoidable.

At first his participation in the Resistance is minimal; he is simply present at its birth. A discreet and calm figure (although opinions differ as to his calmness), he generally goes unnoticed. Nevertheless, those to whom responsibilities have fallen (none belong to the guild of writers) soon single him out and place their trust in him, perhaps because there are so few willing to take risks. In any case, Leprince joins the Resistance, and his diligence and composure soon qualify him for increasingly delicate missions (although these short errands and minor skirmishes are of little significance beyond literary circles).

For the writers, however, Leprince is something of an enigma and a surprise. Those who enjoyed a certain notoriety before the capitulation and never deigned to notice Leprince find themselves running into him everywhere they go, and worse, depending on him for protection and safe passage. Leprince seems to have emerged from limbo; he helps them, puts the meagre sum of his possessions at their disposal; he is cooperative and diligent. The writers talk to him. The conversations take place at night, in dark rooms or corridors, and are always conducted in whispers. One writer suggests he try his hand at composing stories, verse or essays. Leprince assures him that he has been doing precisely that since 1933. The nights of waiting are long and anxious, and some of the writers are talkative; they ask where he has published his works. Leprince mentions mouldering magazines and newspapers whose mere names provoke nausea or sadness. These conversations generally end at daybreak: Leprince leaves his charge in a safe house, with a hearty handshake or a brisk hug followed by a few words of thanks. And the words are sincere, but once the episode is over the writers avoid Leprince and he fades from their minds like an unpleasant but forgettable dream.

There is something elusive, something indefinable about him that people find repellent. They know he is there to help, but deep down they simply cannot warm to him. Perhaps they sense that Leprince is tainted by the years he has spent in the underworld of sad magazines and the gutter press, from which no man or beast escapes, except the exceedingly strong, brilliant, and bestial.

Needless to say, Leprince has none of these qualities. He is not a fascist, or a card-carrying Party member, nor does he belong to any society of authors. The authors with whom he is in contact regard him, perhaps, as a paradoxical *parvenu* or reverse opportunist (since for him the obvious thing would be to denounce and insult them, to help the police in their interrogations and devote himself heart and soul to the collaborationist cause) who, in one of those fits of madness to which the literary journalist is prone, happened to choose the right side, as unconsciously as bacteria infecting a host.

The flamboyant novelist from Languedoc, Monsieur D., for example, notes in his diary that Leprince reminds him of a Chinese shadow puppet, but does not elaborate. The others ignore him, with one or two exceptions; there is the odd mention of Leprince the man, but nothing about his writing. Nobody can be bothered to look up the works of the writer who saved their life.

Utterly detached, Leprince goes on working at the newspaper office (where he is regarded with increasing suspicion) and drafting poems. The daily risks he runs are considerably superior to the minimum required for the preservation of self-respect. He is often courageous to the point of recklessness. One night he shelters a surrealist poet hunted by the Gestapo, who is destined to end his days (through no fault of Leprince's) in a German concentration camp. The poet leaves without a word of thanks; for him, Leprince is simply a comrade doing what he himself would do in the same situation, not a colleague (to use that appalling term) or a fellow member of his demanding profession. One weekend Leprince escorts a critic to a village near the Spanish border. The critic once poured scorn (perhaps with good reason) on a book penned by his guide, a book which, at this crucial moment, he has completely forgotten, so negligible, so insubstantial is Leprince's work and public stature.

Sometimes Leprince suspects that his face, his education, his attitude or the books he has read are to blame for this rejection. Between articles for the newspaper and clandestine missions, he throws himself into the composition of a long poem: over 600 lines exploring the mystery and the martyrdom of minor poets. When the poem is finished, after three months of strenuous and painful effort, he realises, to his astonishment, that he is not a minor poet. Any other writer would have pursued his investigations, but Leprince is devoid of curiosity about himself. He burns the poem.

In April 1943 he loses his job. In the months that follow he lives from hand to mouth, on the run, pursued by the police, informers, and destitution. One night, as chance would have it, he is given shelter by a young lady novelist. Leprince is anxious and the novelist is an insomniac, so they stay up talking for hours.

That night, deep inside Leprince, a mechanism is released; he openly confesses all his frustrations, all his dreams and ambitions. The young novelist, who frequents literary circles as only a Frenchwoman can, recognises Leprince or thinks she does. Over the previous months she has seen him on hundreds of occasions, always in the shadow of some famous writer wanted by the authorities, or waiting outside the room of a playwright involved in the Resistance, always in the role of messenger, secretary, or valet. You were the only one I didn't know, says the young novelist, and I kept wondering what you were doing there. You were like the invisible man, she adds, always waiting silently, ready to help.

Encouraged by the young woman's frankness, he opens his heart. He talks about his work and she is hugely surprised. Naturally, they broach the subject of Leprince's obscurity. After some hours of conversation, the young woman believes that she has identified the problem and its solution. She speaks bluntly: there is something about

29

him, she says, something in his face, his way of speaking, his gaze, that most people find repellent. The solution is obvious: he has to disappear, go under cover, try not to let his face show in his writing. The solution is so child-ishly simple, it is bound to work. Leprince listens in amaze-ment and agrees. He knows he is not going to follow the young novelist's advice; he feels surprised and perhaps slightly offended, but he also knows it is the first time that someone has listened to him and understood him.

The following morning a Resistance car comes to pick him up. Before he leaves, the young novelist shakes him by the hand and wishes him luck. Then she kisses him on the lips and starts to cry. Leprince doesn't understand what is happening. Confused, he mumbles a few words of thanks and walks away. The novelist watches him from the window: Leprince gets into the car without looking back. She spends the rest of that morning thinking of him (as Leprince will somehow sense or dream, perhaps in a pas-sage of his uneven work), fantasising about him, telling herself she is in love with him, until weariness finally over-comes her and she falls asleep on the sofa.

They will never see each other again.

Modest and repellent, Leprince survives the war, and in 1946 retires to a small village in Picardy where he takes a job as a teacher. His contributions to the press and cer-tain literary magazines are regular if not numerous. In his heart, Leprince has finally accepted his lot as a bad writer, but he has also come to understand and accept that good writers need bad writers if only to serve as readers and stewards. He also knows that by saving (or helping) several good writers he has earned the right to sully clean sheets of paper and make mistakes. He has also earned the right to publish in two or maybe three magazines. At some point, of course, he tries to locate the young novelist, to find out about her. But when he goes back to her house, other people are living there and nobody knows where she has gone. Leprince, of course, searches for her, but that is another story. In any case he never sees her again.

He does, however, see the Parisian writers. Not as often as he would really like to, but he sees them, and talks to them and they know who he is (vaguely in most cases); there are even one or two who have read a couple of his prose poems. For some, his presence, his fragility, his terrifying sovereignty serve as a spur or reminder.

Enrique Martín

for Enrique Vila-Matas

A POET CAN ENDURE ANYTHING. WHICH amounts to saying that a human being can endure anything. Except that it's not true: there are obviously limits to what a human being can endure. Really endure. A poet, on the other hand, *can* endure anything. We grew up with this conviction. The opening assertion is true, but that way lie ruin, madness, and death.

I met Enrique Martín a few months after arriving in Barcelona. He was born in 1953, like me, and he was a poet. He wrote in Castilian and Catalan with results that were fundamentally similar, though formally different. His Castilian poetry was well meaning, affected, and quite often clumsy, without the slightest glimmer of originality. His model (in Castilian) was Miguel Hernández, a good poet whom, for some reason, bad poets seem to adore (my explanation, though it's probably simplistic, is that Hernández

writes about pain, impelled by pain, and bad poets generally suffer like laboratory animals, especially during their
protracted youths). Enrique's Catalan poetry, by contrast,
was about real things and daily life, and only his friends
ever read or heard it (although to be perfectly frank, the
same is probably true of what he wrote in Castilian; the
only difference, in terms of audience, was that he published
the Castilian poems in magazines with tiny circulations,
seen only, I suspect, by his friends, if at all, while he read
the Catalan poems to us in bars or when he came round
to visit). Enrique's Catalan, however, was bad (how he managed to write better poems in a language he hadn't mas-
tered than he did in his mother tongue must, I suppose,
be numbered among the mysteries of youth). In any case
Enrique had a very shaky grasp of the rudiments of Catalan
grammar and it has to be said that he wrote badly, whether
in Castilian or in Catalan, but I still remember some of his
poems with a certain emotion, coloured no doubt by nos-
talgia for my own youth. Enrique *wanted* to be a poet, and
he threw himself into this endeavour with all his energy
and willpower. He was tenacious in a blind, uncritical way,
like the bad guys in westerns, falling like flies but perse-
vering, determined to take the hero's bullets, and in the end
there was something likable about this tenacity; it gave him
an aura, a kind of literary sanctity that only young poets
and old whores can appreciate.

At the time I was twenty-five and thought I had seen

33

everything. Enrique was the opposite: there were so many things he wanted to do, and, in his own way, he was preparing to take on the world. His first step was to bring out a literary magazine, or fanzine, really, which he financed with his savings (he had been working in some obscure office near the port since he was fifteen). At the last minute, Enrique's friends (and one of mine among them) decided not to include my poems in the first issue, an incident which, I am ashamed to admit, led to an interruption of our friendship. According to Enrique, it was the fault of another Chilean, an old friend of his, who had opined that two Chileans was one Chilean too many for the first issue of a little magazine devoted to Spanish writing. I was in Portugal at the time, and when I got back, I decided that was it: I would have nothing more to do with the magazine and it would have nothing more to do with me. I refused to listen to Enrique's explanations, partly because I couldn't be bothered, partly to assuage my wounded pride, and I washed my hands of the whole business.

We didn't see each other for a while. But in the bars of the Gothic Quarter I would sometimes run into mutual acquaintances, and they kept me laconically informed of Enrique's latest adventures. That's how I found out that the magazine (prophetically named *White Rope*, although I'm sure it wasn't his idea) had folded after the first issue, that the first performance of a play he had tried to put on at a cultural centre in the Nou Barris district had been

34

greeted with boos and jeers, and that he was planning to launch another magazine.

One night he turned up at my flat. He was carrying a folder full of poems and he wanted me to read them. We went out to dinner at a restaurant in the Calle Costa and over coffee he read me a few of the poems. He awaited my judgment with a mixture of a self-satisfaction and fear. I realised that if I said they were bad, I would never see him again, as well as getting myself into an argument that could easily continue into the small hours. I said I thought they were well written. I wasn't overly enthusiastic, but carefully avoided the slightest criticism. I even said I thought one of them was very good, in the manner of León Felipe, a nostalgic poem about the landscapes of Extremadura, where Enrique had never lived. I don't know if he believed me. He knew I was reading Sanguinetti at the time and subscribed (though not exclusively) to the Italian's views on modern poetry, so I could hardly be expected to admire his verses about Extremadura. But he pretended to believe me; he pretended to be glad he had read me the poems and then, revealingly, he started talking about the magazine that had perished after the first issue, and that's when I realised that he didn't believe me but wasn't going to say so.

That was it. We talked a while longer, about Sanguinetti and Frank O'Hara (I still like Frank O'Hara but I haven't read Sanguinetti for ages), about the new magazine he was planning to launch (he didn't invite me to contribute), and then we said goodbye in the street, near my house. It must have been a year or two before I saw him again.

At the time I was living with a Mexican woman and it looked as if the relationship would be the death of her, and me, and the neighbours, and sometimes even the people who ventured to pay us a visit. Once was enough for our unfortunate visitors, and soon we were hardly seeing anyone. We were poor (although the woman came from a well-off family in Mexico City, she absolutely refused all their offers of financial assistance); our battles were Homeric and a dark cloud seemed to be looming over us day and night.

That's how things were when Enrique Martín reappeared. As he crossed the threshold with a bottle of wine and some French pâté, I had the impression he had come as a spectator, to watch the final act of a major crisis in my life (although in fact I felt fine, it was my girlfriend who was feeling rotten), but later, when he invited us to dinner at his flat, and was so keen to introduce us to his girlfriend, I realised that he hadn't come to observe but, probably, to be observed, or possibly even because, in a sense, my opinion still mattered to him. I know I didn't appreciate this at the time. For a start, I was annoyed by his sudden appearance, and tried to make my greeting sound ironic or cynical, though it probably just sounded apathetic. To be honest, I wasn't fit company for anyone in those days. This was common knowledge: people avoided me or fled my presence. But Enrique wanted to see me and, for some mysterious reason, the Mexican woman liked Enrique and his girlfriend, so we ended up having a series of meals together, five in all.

Naturally, by the time we resumed our friendship – though the term is no doubt excessive – we disagreed about almost everything. My first surprise came when I saw his flat (when our ways had parted he was still living with his parents and although I later heard that he was sharing a place with three friends, for one reason or another I never went there). Now he had a loft in the Barrio de Gracia, full of books, records and paintings, a large though perhaps rather dim dwelling that his girlfriend had decorated with eclectic taste, and they had some interesting things: objects picked up on recent trips to Bulgaria, Turkey, Israel, and Egypt, some of which were more than tourist souvenirs or imitations. My second surprise came when he told me that he had stopped writing poetry. He said this after dinner, in the presence of my girlfriend and his, although in fact the confession was directed specifically at me (I was playing with an enormous Arab dagger, with ornamental working on both sides of the blade; it can't have been very practical to use), and when I looked up he was smiling as if to say, I've grown up, I've realised you can enjoy art without making a fool of yourself, without keeping up some pathetic pretence of being a writer.

The Mexican woman (who was forthright to a fault) thought it was a shame he had given up; she made him tell the story of the magazine in which my poems hadn't appeared, and in the end she judged the arguments that Enrique had marshalled in defence of his renunciation to be sound and sensible, predicting that before too long he would be writing again with renewed vigour. Enrique's girlfriend agreed with her completely, or almost. Both women seemed to think (although Enrique's girlfriend, for obvious reasons, held this opinion more strongly than mine) that his decision to concentrate on his job – he'd been promoted, which meant he had to travel to Cartagena and Málaga for reasons I didn't care to ascertain – and spend his spare time looking after his record collection, his flat, and his car was far more poetic than wasting his time imitating León Felipe or at best (so to speak) Sanguinetti. I was totally non-committal when Enrique asked my opinion (as if it might be an irreparable loss for lyric poetry in Spanish or Catalan, for God's sake). I told him I was sure he had made the right decision. He didn't believe me.

That night, or at one of the other four dinners, the conversation turned to children. It was inevitable: poetry and children. I remember (and this I remember with absolute clarity) Enrique confessing that he would like to have a child. The experience of childbirth, those were his words. Not to share it with a woman, no, he wanted it for himself: carrying the child for nine months inside him and then giving birth. I remember, as he said this, I felt a chill in my blood. The two women looked at him tenderly, but I had an intimation, and this was what chilled me, of what would happen years later, and not many years, unfortunately. When the feeling faded – it was brief, just a twinge – Enrique's declaration struck me as a quip, unworthy of reply. Predictably, the others all wanted to have children, and I, predictably, didn't, and in the end, of the four who were present at that dinner, I am the only one who has a child. Life is mysterious as well as vulgar.

It was during the last dinner, when my relationship with the Mexican woman was on the point of exploding, that Enrique told us about a magazine that he contributed to. Here we go, I thought. He corrected himself immediately: That *we* contribute to. The plural puzzled me momentarily, but then the penny dropped: he and his girlfriend. For once (and for the last time) the Mexican woman and I were in agreement: we asked to see the magazine straight away. It turned out to be one of the numerous periodicals sold at newsstands, with stories on subjects ranging from UFOs and ghosts to apparitions of the Virgin, little known pre-Columbian civilisations and, generally, any kind of paranormal event. It was called *Questions & Answers*, and I think it's still being published. I asked – we asked – how exactly they contributed. Enrique (his girlfriend said practically nothing during this last dinner) explained: on weekends they went to places where there had been sightings of flying saucers; they interviewed the people who had seen them, examined the surroundings, looked for caves (that night Enrique affirmed that many mountains in Catalonia and the rest of Spain were hollow); they stayed up all night, snug in their sleeping bags, with a camera at the ready, sometimes just the two of them, more often in a group of four, five, or six. It was a nice way to spend the night, out in the open, and when it was over, they wrote a report, part of which was published (so what happened to the rest of it?) with photos in *Questions & Answers*.

That night, after dinner, I read a couple of the articles that Enrique and his girlfriend had contributed to the magazine. They were badly written, dull, pseudo-scientific – the word *science*, in any case, was used several times – and insufferably arrogant. He wanted to know what I thought of them. I realised that my opinion no longer mattered to him in the least, so, for the first time, I was absolutely frank. I suggested changes; I told him he should learn how to write. I asked him if they had editors at the magazine.

Once we got out of the flat, the Mexican woman and I burst into uncontrollable laughter. I think it was later that week that we split up. She went to Rome; I stayed on in Barcelona for another year.

For a long time I had no news of Enrique. In fact I think I forgot all about him. I went to live on the outskirts of a village near Girona with five cats and a dog (a bitch, actually). I rarely saw my old friends and acquaintances, although from time to time one of them would drop in and stay with me, never for more than a couple of days. Whoever the visitor happened to be, we would end up talking about friends from Barcelona or Mexico, but I can't remember any of them mentioning Enrique Martín. I only went down to the village once a day, with the dog, to buy food and rummage through my post office box, where I would often find a letter from my sister in Mexico City, which seemed to have changed beyond recognition. The other letters, few and far between, were from South American poets adrift somewhere in South America, with whom I engaged in desultory exchanges, tetchy and melancholic by turns, just like me and my correspondents, coming to the end of youth, coming to accept the end of our dreams.

One day, however, I received a different sort of letter. Actually, it wasn't, strictly speaking, a letter. On the backs of two cards – invitations to a kind of cocktail party thrown by a Barcelona publisher to launch my first novel, a party which I did not attend – someone had sketched a rather rudimentary map, next to which were written the following numbers:

$$3860 + 429777 - 469993? + 51179 -$$
$$588904 + 966 - 39146 + 498207856$$

Unsurprisingly, this missive was not signed. The anonymous sender had evidently attended the launch. I made no attempt to decipher the numbers, although I guessed it was an eight-word sentence, no doubt dreamt up by one of my friends. There was nothing particularly mysterious about it, except, perhaps, for the sketched map. It showed a winding path, a tree beside a house, a river dividing into two, a bridge, a mountain or a hill, a cave. On one side, a simple compass rose indicated north and south. Beside the path, in the opposite direction to the mountain (in the end I decided it must be a mountain), an arrow pointed the way to a village in Ampurdán.

That night, back at my house, while I was preparing dinner, it struck me that it must have been sent by Enrique Martín. I imagined him at the launch, talking to some of my friends (one of whom must have given him the number of my post office box), making scathing remarks about the book, working the room with a glass of wine in his hand, saying hello to everyone, loudly enquiring whether or not I would put in an appearance. I think I felt something like contempt. I think I remembered my exclusion from *White Rope*, which was ancient history by then.

A week later I received another anonymous letter. Again it was written on one of the invitations to my book launch (he must have picked up several), but this time I noticed some differences. Under my name he had written out a line by Miguel Hernández, about happiness and work. And on the other side, the same numbers and a map, radically different from the first one. To begin with, I thought it was just scribble: tangled, intersecting, broken, dotted lines, exclamation marks, drawings rubbed out and superimposed. Finally, after scrutinising it for the umpteenth time and comparing it with the original cards, I cottoned on: the new map was a continuation of the first one; it was a map of the cave.

I remember thinking we were too old for this sort of joke. One afternoon I leafed through an issue of *Questions & Answers* at a newsstand. I didn't see Enrique's name among the contributors. After a few days I forgot all about him and his letters.

Some months went by, three, maybe four. One night I heard the sound of a car pulling up outside my house. I thought it must have been someone who had got lost. I went out with the dog to see who it was. The car had stopped next to some brambles, with the motor running and the lights on. For a while, nothing happened. From where I was standing I couldn't see how many people were in the car, but I wasn't scared; with that dog at my side I was hardly ever scared. She was growling, keen to hurl herself at the strangers. Then the lights went off, the motor stopped, and the car's single occupant opened the door and greeted me like an old friend. It was Enrique Martín. I'm afraid I didn't reciprocate. The first thing he asked me was whether I had received his letters. I said yes. No one had interfered with the envelopes? The envelopes were still properly sealed? I replied in the affirmative and asked him what was going on. Problems, he said, looking back at the lights of the village and the curving road, beyond which there was a stone quarry. Let's go inside, I said, but he didn't budge. What's that? he asked, meaning the lights and the noises from the quarry. I told him what it was and explained that at least once a year, I had no idea why, they kept working till after midnight. That's strange, said Enrique. Again I said, let's go in, but either he didn't hear me or he pretended not to. I don't want to bother you, he said, after my dog had sniffed him. Come in, we'll have a drink, I said. I don't drink alcohol, said Enrique. I was at your book launch, he added. I imagined you'd come. No, I didn't go, I said. Now he's going to start criticising my book, I thought. I was hoping you could look after something for me, he said. That was when I realised that he was holding a kind of package in his right hand; it looked like a bundle of A4 sheets. He's gone back to writing poetry, I thought. He seemed to guess what I was thinking. It isn't poetry, he said with a smile that was at once forlorn and brave, a smile I hadn't seen for many years, not on his face, at any rate. What is it, I asked? Nothing, just some stuff. I don't want you to read it; I only want you to look after it. All right, let's go inside, I said. No, I don't want to bother you, and anyway I haven't got time; I have to get going straight away. How did you know where I live? I asked. Enrique named a mutual friend, the Chilean who had decided that one Chilean was enough for the first issue of *White Rope*. He's got a nerve, giving out my address, I said. You're not friends any more? asked Enrique. I guess we are, I said, but we don't see each other much. Anyway I'm glad he did; it's been really nice to see you, said Enrique. I should have said: and to see you, but I just stood there. Well, I'm off, said Enrique. Then there was a series of very loud noises, like explosions, coming from the quarry, which made him jumpy. I reassured him. It's nothing, I said, but in fact it was the first time I had heard explosions at that time of night. Well, I'm off, he said. Take care, I said. Can I give you a hug? he asked. Of course, I said. What about the dog, he won't bite me? It's a she, I said, and no, she won't.

For the next two years, while I lived in that house outside the village, I complied with Enrique's request and kept his packet of papers intact, fastened with sticky tape and string, among old magazines and my own papers, which, it doesn't go without saying, multiplied at an alarming rate during that period. The only news I had of Enrique was supplied by the Chilean from *White Rope*; one day we talked about the magazine and the old days, and he clarified his role in the elimination of my poems, which was non-existent, so he said, and so I concluded after listening to his account, not that it mattered to me by then. He told me that Enrique had a bookshop in the Barrio de Gracia, near his old flat, which, years before, I had visited five times with the Mexican woman. He told me that

45

Enrique and his wife had split up and no longer contributed to *Questions & Answers*, and that his ex was working with him in the bookshop. They weren't living together any more, he said, they were just friends, and Enrique gave her the job because she was out of work. And how's his bookshop going? I asked. Really well, said the Chilean, apparently he got good severance pay from the company where he'd been working since he was a teenager. He lives on the premises, he said. Behind the bookshop, in two smallish rooms. The rooms, I later found out, gave on to an interior courtyard, where Enrique grew geraniums, ficus, forget-me-nots and lilies. There were two doors in the shopfront and a metal screen that he pulled down every night and locked, as well as a little door that opened on to the building's entrance hall. I didn't feel like asking the Chilean for the address. I didn't ask him whether or not Enrique was writing either. But shortly afterwards I received a long letter from the man himself, signed this time, informing me that he had been in Madrid (I think he was writing from Madrid, but I'm not sure any more) for the famous International Science Fiction Writers' Convention. No, he wasn't writing science fiction (I think he used the expression SF); he had been sent as a special correspondent by *Questions & Answers*. The rest of the letter was muddled. He talked about some French writer whose name didn't ring a bell, according to whom we are all aliens, 'we' meaning every living creature on planet

46

earth; exiles, all of us, wrote Enrique, or outcasts. Then he explained just how it was that the French writer had reached this hare-brained conclusion. But that part was incomprehensible. He mentioned the 'thought police', speculated about 'hyper-dimensional tunnels', and went gabbling on in the way he used to in his poems. The letter ended with a enigmatic sentence: 'all who know are saved'. Then there were the conventional closing formulae. It was the last letter he wrote to me.

Again it was our mutual Chilean friend who filled me in and told me the latest news. We were having a meal together, during one of my increasingly frequent trips to Barcelona, and in the course of the conversation he let it drop, casually, without dramatising the facts.

Enrique had been dead for two weeks. It had happened more or less like this: one morning his ex-wife, now his employee at the bookshop, arrived and found the premises still locked. This surprised her, but she was not alarmed, because Enrique sometimes slept in. For such occasions she had her own key, with which she proceeded to unlock the metal screen and then the glass door in the shopfront. She went straight to the flat at the back, and there she found Enrique hanging from a rafter in his bedroom. The sight almost gave her a heart attack, but she pulled herself together, called the police, shut the shop and waited outside, sitting on the curb, crying, I suppose, until the first patrol car pulled up. When she went back inside, she was surprised to find Enrique still hanging from the rafter. While the police were asking her questions, she noticed that the walls of the room were covered with numbers, big and small, some painted with a stencil, others with a spray-can. She remembered the policemen taking photos of the numbers (659983 + 779511 − 336922, that sort of thing: incomprehensible) and Enrique looking down at them dismissively. The ex-wife turned employee thought the numbers represented debts he had run up. Yes, Enrique was in debt, not much, not enough for anyone to want to kill him, but he did have debts. The policemen asked her whether the numbers had been on the walls the previous day. She said no. Then she said she didn't know. She didn't think so. She hadn't been into that room for a while.

They checked the doors. The one that opened on to the entrance hall was locked from the inside. They found no indication that any of the doors had been forced. There were only two sets of keys: she had one, and they found the other next to the cash register. When the magistrate arrived, they took Enrique's body down and removed it from the premises. The findings of the autopsy were conclusive: he had died almost instantly, by his own hand, another one of Barcelona's frequent suicides.

Night after night, in the solitude of my house in Ampurdán, which I would soon be leaving, I thought about Enrique's suicide. I found it hard to believe that the man who had wanted to have a child, who had wanted to give birth to it himself, could have been so thoughtless as to let his employee and ex-wife find his body hanging – naked? clothed? in pyjamas? – and possibly still swinging from a rafter in the middle of the room. The business with the numbers was more believable. I had no trouble imagining Enrique busy at his cryptography all night long, from eight o'clock, when he shut the bookshop, until four in the morning, a good time to die. Naturally I elaborated various hypotheses in an attempt to explain the manner of his death. The first was directly related to the last letter I had received from him: suicide as a ticket home to the planet of his birth. According to the second hypothesis, he had been murdered in one of two ways. But both strained credibility. I remembered our last meeting, in front of my house, how nervous he had been, as if he were being followed, or hunted.

On my subsequent visits to Barcelona, I compared notes with Enrique's other friends. No one had noticed any significant change in him; he hadn't given sketch maps or sealed packets to anyone else. Concerning one aspect of his life, however, the information was contradictory or incomplete: his work for *Questions & Answers*. Some said that his association with the magazine had come to an end long ago. According to others, he had been a regular contributor up to his death.

One afternoon when I had nothing to do, after sorting out a few things in Barcelona, I went to the office of

Questions & Answers. The editor received me. Had I been expecting a shady character, I would have been disappointed. He could have been an insurance salesman, pretty much like any magazine editor. I told him Enrique Martín was dead. He didn't know, said he was sorry to hear it, and waited. I asked if Enrique had been a regular contributor to the magazine and, as I expected, he replied in the negative. I mentioned the International Science Fiction Writers' Conference, which had been held recently in Madrid. He told me that his magazine had not sent anyone to cover the event. Fiction, he explained, was not their domain; they were investigative journalists. Although personally, he added, he was a science fiction fan. So Enrique went on his own account, I thought aloud. He must have, said the editor, in any case he wasn't working for us.

Before everyone forgot about Enrique, before his friends grew accustomed to his definitive absence, I obtained his ex-wife and ex-employee's phone number and called her. She didn't remember me at first.

'It's me,' I said, 'Arturo Belano. I went to your flat five times; I was living with a Mexican woman.'

'Ah yes,' she said.

Then there was a silence and I thought there was a problem with the line. But she was still there.

'I rang to say how sorry I was to hear what happened.'

'Enrique went to your book launch.'

'I know, I know.'

'He wanted to see you.'

'We did see each other.'

'I don't know why he wanted to see you.'

'I'd also like to know.'

'Well it's too late now, isn't it?'

'I guess so.'

We talked for a while more, about her nerves, I think, and the state she was in, then I ran out of coins (I was calling from Girona) and we got cut off.

A few months later I left the house. I took the dog with me. I gave the cats to some neighbours. The night before leaving I opened the package that Enrique had given me to look after. I thought I'd find numbers and maps, maybe some sign that might explain his death. There were fifty A4 sheets, neatly bound. There were no maps or coded messages on any of them, just poems, mainly in the style of Miguel Hernández, but there were also some imitations of León Felipe, Blas de Otero, and Gabriel Celaya. That night I couldn't get to sleep. Now it was my turn to escape.

A Literary Adventure

B WRITES A BOOK IN WHICH HE MAKES FUN OF certain writers, variously disguised, or, to be more precise, certain *types* of writers. In one of his stories there is a character not unlike A, a writer of about B's age, but who, unlike B, is famous, well-off and has a large readership; in other words he has achieved the three highest goals (in that order) to which a man of letters can aspire. B is not famous, he has no money and his poems are published in little magazines. Yet A and B are not entirely dissimilar. They both come from lower-middle-class or upwardly mobile working-class families. Politically, both are left wing; they have in common a keen intellectual curiosity and a deficient formal education. With A's meteoric rise, however, a sanctimonious tone has crept into his writing, and B, who is a slave to print, finds this particularly irritating. In his newspaper articles, and with increasing frequency in his books, A has taken to pontificating on all things great and small, human or divine, with a leaden pedantry, like a man who, having used literature as a ladder to social status and respectability, now safely ensconced in his nouveau-riche ivory tower, snipes at anything that might tarnish the mirror in which he contemplates himself and the world. For B, in short, A has become a prig.

B, as I said, writes a book, and in one of the chapters he makes fun of A. The portrait is not especially cruel (and it is confined to one chapter of a sizeable volume). He creates a character, Álvaro Medina Mena, a successful writer, who happens to express the same opinions as A. The contexts are transposed: where A rails against pornography, Medina Mena attacks violence; where A criticises the commercialism of contemporary art, Medina Mena marshals his arguments against pornography. The story of Medina Mena doesn't stand out from the others in the book, most of which are better (in terms of composition, though perhaps no better written). B's book is published – it is the first time he has been taken on by a major publishing house – and reviews begin to appear. Very slowly at first. Then, in one of the country's leading newspapers, A publishes a review positively glowing with enthusiasm, which convinces the remaining critics and turns B's book into a minor bestseller. Naturally, B feels uncomfortable. Initially, at least. Then, as is often the way, it strikes him as natural (or at least logical) that A should praise his book; after all, it is an interesting book in a number of ways, and A is not a bad critic, after all.

But two months later, in an interview published in another (less prestigious) newspaper, A mentions B's book again, in extremely laudatory terms, wholeheartedly giving it his stamp of approval: 'an untarnished mirror'. There is something about A's tone, however, that makes B wary, as if there were a message to be read between the lines, as if the famous writer were saying to him, Don't think you've fooled me; I know you put me in your book; I know you made fun of me. He's praising my book to the skies, thinks B, so he can let it drop back to earth later on. Or he's praising my book to make sure no one will identify him with Medina Mena. Or he hasn't even realised, and it was a case of genuine appreciation, a simple meeting of minds. None of these possibilities seems to bode well. B doesn't believe that minds can meet in a simple (or innocent) way and he resolves to do all he can to make A's acquaintance. Deep down he knows that A has recognised himself in Medina Mena. He is at least reasonably sure that A has read his book in its entirety with due attention. So why would he refer to it like this? Why praise a book that makes fun of you? (By now B is beginning to think that the caricature was not only exaggerated but also perhaps a little unfair.) He can't figure it out. The only half-plausible explanation is that A hasn't, in fact, identified himself, which, given his advancing cretinism, might just be the case (B reads his articles systematically; he has read every one since the glowing review, and some mornings he longs to plant his fist in A's increasingly prudish face, oozing self-assurance and righteous anger, as if he thought he were the reincarnation of Unamuno or something).

So B does everything he can to meet A face to face, but does not succeed. They live in different cities. A travels a good deal and B can't be sure of finding him at home. His telephone is almost always engaged or the answering-machine is on, in which case B hangs up immediately because he is terrified of answering-machines.

After a while B gives up the idea of contacting A. He tries to forget the whole business and almost succeeds. He writes another book. When it is published, the first review to appear is by A. So soon does it appear in fact that B cannot see how even the most assiduous reader could have finished the book so quickly. It was sent out to the critics on a Thursday and A's review was published the following Saturday; a long review, at least five pages of typescript, considered and insightful too, a lucid, illuminating reading, even for B, to whom it reveals aspects of the book that had escaped his notice. At first B is grateful and flattered. Then he is frightened. It strikes him that A could not possibly have read the book between the day the publisher sent it out and the review's publication date. The way the post works in Spain, if a book is sent on

Thursday, you'd be lucky to receive it the following Monday. The first explanation that occurs to B is that A wrote the review without reading the book, but that is untenable. A has obviously read the book and read it carefully. There is, however, a more credible explanation: A obtained the book directly from the publishing house. B phones the marketing manager. He asks how it is possible that A has already read his book. The marketing manager has no idea (although he has read the review and is very pleased). He promises to look into it. B almost gets down on his knees (in so far as one can transmit such a posture via the telephone) and begs him to ring back that night. Predictably enough, he spends the rest of the day coming up with increasingly absurd scenarios. At nine that evening he rings the marketing manager from home. There is, of course, a perfectly logical explanation: A happened to visit the publishing house some days before the copies were sent out; he took one with him, and so was able to read it at his leisure and write the review. Having heard this, B calms down. He tries to put a meal together but there's nothing in the fridge so he decides to go out for dinner. He takes along the newspaper with the review in it. At first he walks aimlessly through the empty streets. Then he finds a little restaurant that he has never patronised and goes in. All the tables are empty. B sits down next to the window, in a corner away from the fireplace, which is feebly warming the room. A girl asks him what he would like. B says he would like to have dinner. The girl is very pretty. Her hair is long and messy, as if she just got out of bed. B orders soup, and a meat and vegetable dish to follow. While he is waiting he reads the review again. I have to see A, he thinks. I have to tell him I'm sorry, I should never have started this game. There is, however, absolutely nothing offensive about the review: the other reviewers will end up saying all the same things, though perhaps not as well (A does know how to write, thinks B reluctantly or perhaps resignedly). The food tastes like earth, decay, and blood. The chill in the restaurant is seeping into his bones. That night he has serious stomach trouble and the next morning he staggers to the outpatients' department of the nearest hospital. The doctor who sees him prescribes antibiotics and bland food for a week. Lying in bed, and inclined to stay there, B decides to ring a friend; he needs to tell someone the whole story. But he can't decide who to ring. What if I rang A and told him, pretending it was all about someone else, he wonders. But no, at best, A would think it was a coincidence; he would go back and read B's books in a different light, then tear him to shreds in public. At worst, A would pretend not to have understood him. In the end, B doesn't ring anyone and soon another kind of fear begins to grow in him: what if someone, some anonymous reader, has realised that Álvaro Medina Mena is A in disguise? The situation is already horrible; if someone else found out, he reflects, it could become intolerable. But who would be able to identify the model for Álvaro Medina Mena? In theory, any of the 3,500 readers of the novel's first edition; in practice, a handful of individuals: A's devoted fans, literary sleuths or people like B who are exasperated by the rising tide of millennial moralising and pontification. What can B do to keep the secret? He doesn't know. He runs through various possibilities, from enthusiastically reviewing A's next opus or even writing a book-length study of his work to date (including the unfortunate newspaper articles) to ringing him up and laying his cards (whatever they might be) on the table, or paying him a visit one night, cornering him in the hallway of his flat and forcing him to confess why he is doing this, why he has fastened on to B's work like a limpet, what kind of redress he is seeking in this roundabout way.

In the end, B doesn't do anything.

His new book is favourably reviewed but sells poorly. No one is surprised that A has endorsed it. Except when he is judging Spanish letters (and politics) from his high horse, like Cato the Censor, A is reasonably generous in his treatment of newcomers to the literary scene. After a while, B forgets the whole business. Perhaps, he tells himself, it was all a figment of his feverish imagination, overexcited by having two books come out with major publishers; perhaps it was a delusion spawned by his secret fears, or a symptom of nervous exhaustion after so many years of hard labour and obscurity. So he puts it out of his mind and after a while the incident begins to fade, like any other memory, though perhaps it remains more vivid than most. Then, one day, he is invited to a conference on new writing to be held in Madrid.

B is delighted to attend. He is about to finish another book and the conference, he thinks, will serve as a platform for pre-publicity. The trip and the hotel have been paid for, of course, and B wants to take advantage of his time in the capital to visit galleries and relax. The conference will last two days; B is participating in the first day's proceedings and will be a member of the audience on the second day. When it is all over, the writers are to be transported *en masse* to the residence of the Countess of Bahamontes, woman of letters and patron of various cultural programmes and organisations, including a writer's fellowship bearing her name and a poetry magazine, probably the best of those published in the capital. B, who knows no one in Madrid, joins the group going to round off the evening at the Countess's house. After a light but delicious supper, liberally washed down with wines from the family vineyards, the party continues into the small hours. At the start there are no more than fifteen people present, but as the hours go by, the festivities are enlivened by the arrival of a variegated array of arts personalities, including several writers, but also film makers, actors, painters, television presenters, and bullfighters.

At one point, B has the privilege of being introduced

to the Countess and the honour of being taken aside by her, and led to a corner of the terrace, where there is a view over the garden. There's a friend waiting for you down there, says the smiling Countess, gesturing with her chin towards a wooden arbour surrounded by palms, pines, and plane trees. B looks at her uncomprehendingly. Once, he thinks, long ago, she must have been pretty, but now she is a jumble of flesh and twitchy sinews. B doesn't dare ask who the 'friend' is. He nods, assures her he will go down immediately, but doesn't move. The Countess doesn't move either and for a moment they both stand there in silence, looking into each other's eyes as if they had known each other (or loved and hated each other) in another life. Then other guests commandeer the Countess and B is left alone, fearfully gazing at the garden and the arbour, in which, after a while, he is sure he can see someone, or the fleeting movement of a shadow. It must be A, he thinks, from which he immediately deduces: he must be armed.

B's first thought is to flee. But then he realises that the only way out, as far as he knows, is past the arbour, so the best escape plan would be to stay in one of the mansion's innumerable rooms and wait for dawn. But maybe it's not A, thinks B, maybe it's the editor of some magazine, or a publisher, or a writer who would like to meet me. Barely conscious of what he is doing, B withdraws from the terrace, picks up a drink, goes down the stairs and out into the garden. There he lights a cigarette and approaches the arbour, taking his time. When he gets there, he finds it empty, but he is sure he saw someone, so he decides to wait. An hour later, bored and tired, he returns to the house. He asks the few remaining guests, who are wandering about like sleepwalkers or actors in a terribly slow play, where the Countess is, but none of them can give him a coherent answer. A waiter (who could just as well be a guest) tells him that the lady of the house has no doubt retired for the night, as it is past her usual bed-time; you know what old people are like. B nods and thinks: fair enough, at her age she can't afford to overdo things. Then he says goodbye to the waiter, they shake hands and he walks back to his hotel. It takes him more than two hours to get there.

The next day, instead of catching the plane back to the city where he lives, B spends the morning moving to a cheaper hotel and settling in, as if he intended to spend a long time in the capital, and then devotes the whole afternoon to ringing A's home number. To begin with, he keeps getting the answering-machine. A's voice and the voice of a woman, saying, one after another, in cheerful tones, that they aren't in, but will be back soon, so leave a message, and if it's important, leave a number so we can ring back. By the time he has listened to this invitation several times, without leaving a message, B has formed some hypotheses about A and his partner and the mysterious entity they constitute. First, the woman's voice. She is young, much younger than A and B, energetic by the sound of it, determined to carve out her place in A's life and make sure that place is respected. Poor fool, thinks B. Then A's voice. Supremely serene, the voice of Cato. This guy is a year younger than me, thinks B, but he sounds fifteen or twenty years older. Finally, the message: why the joyful tone? Why do they suppose that if it's important the caller is going to stop trying and be content to leave his or her number? Why do they take turns, as if they were reading out a play? To make it clear that two people live there? Or to show the world what a wonderful couple they make? All these questions remain unanswered, of course. But B keeps calling, roughly once every half-hour, and finally, at ten that night, ringing from a pay phone in a cheap restaurant, he gets through and a woman's voice answers. B is so surprised that at first he doesn't know what to say. Who is it? asks the woman. She asks several times, then remains silent, without hanging up, as if she were giving B time to gather his courage and speak. Then, slowly and thoughtfully (so he imagines), the woman hangs up. Half an hour later, B calls again, from a telephone booth. Again it is the woman who picks up the phone, asks who it is and waits for an answer. I want to see A, says B. He should have said: I want to *speak* to A. Or at least that is what the woman assumes he meant, and she says so. After a moment of silence, B says sorry, but what he wants is to *see* A. And who may I say is calling? It's B, says B. The woman hesitates for a few seconds, as if she were won-dering who B is, then says: very well, wait a moment. Her tone of voice hasn't changed, thinks B, not the slightest hint of fear or aggression. B can hear voices; she must have left the receiver on a table or a chair, or hanging from the wall in the kitchen. Although what they are saying is com-pletely unintelligible, he can distinguish the voices of a man and a woman: A and his young partner, thinks B, but then a third voice joins in, a man's voice, much deeper. At first it seems they are engaged in a conversation of such riveting interest that A cannot tear himself away from it, even for a moment. Then B thinks it sounds more like they are arguing. Or trying to reach agreement on an urgent question that must be settled before A can pick up the phone. And in this suspense or uncertainty someone shouts, maybe A. Suddenly there is silence on the line, as if the woman had sealed B's ears with wax. And then (several five-peseta coins later), quietly, gently, someone hangs up.

B doesn't sleep that night. He plans to call again, but, impelled by superstition, decides to change booths. The next two phones he tries are out of order (surprising how run down and dirty the capital is) and when he finally finds one that is working and goes to put the coins in the slot, his hands start shaking as if he were having some kind of attack. The sight of his shaking hands distresses him so much he almost bursts into tears. The best thing to do, he thinks sensibly, would be to calm down and collect himself, and for that, what better place than a bar. So he starts walking and after a while, having rejected several bars for various and sometimes contradictory reasons, he enters a small establishment with excessively bright lighting, into which more than thirty people are packed. The atmosphere, as he promptly realises, is one of unrestrained and noisy camaraderie. He soon finds himself talking to perfect strangers who, in normal circumstances (back home, in his day-to-day life), he would avoid. They are celebrating someone's last night as a bachelor, or the victory of a local football team. He returns to his hotel at dawn, feeling vaguely ashamed and cursing himself for not having persisted with his calls.

The next day, instead of looking for somewhere to eat (he is not particularly surprised to discover that his appetite has disappeared), B goes into the first phone booth he can find, in a fairly noisy street, and calls A. Once again, the woman answers. He doesn't expect her to recognise him straight away, but she does. A's not in, says the woman, but he wants to see you. And after a silence: we're very sorry about what happened yesterday. What happened yesterday? asks B in all sincerity. We kept you waiting, and then we hung up. I mean, I hung up. A wanted to talk to you, but I didn't think it was a good time. Why not? asks B, who has now cast aside all semblance of discretion. For a number of reasons, says the woman . . . A hasn't been well lately . . . When he talks on the phone he tends to get overexcited . . . He was working, and I don't like to interrupt him . . . She doesn't sound as young as she did before. She is definitely lying and not even taking the trouble to come up with convincing lies, on top of which she hasn't mentioned the man with the deep voice. But in spite of all this, B is charmed. She's lying like a spoilt little girl, secure in the knowledge that I will forgive her lies, he thinks. And the way she is protecting A makes her all the more irresistible. How long are you going to be in the city? asks the woman. Just until I see A, then I'll go, says B. Uh huh, says the woman (sending a shiver down B's spine), then she thinks for a while in silence. During those seconds or minutes B imagines her face. The image is vague but haunting. The best thing would be for you to come tonight, says the woman. Do you have the address? Yes, says B. Good, we'll expect you for dinner at eight. All right, says B in a faltering voice and hangs up.

B spends the rest of the day wandering around like a vagabond or a lunatic. He doesn't visit a single gallery, of course, although he does go into a couple of book-shops, in one of which he buys A's latest book. He finds a spot in a park and sits down to read it. The book is fascinating, although every page is steeped in sadness. He is such a good writer, thinks B. He considers his own work, blemished by satire and rage, and compares it unfavourably to A's. Then he falls asleep in the sun, and when he wakes up the park is full of beggars and junkies who seem, at first glance, to be moving around, but are not, in fact, although to say they are still would also be inaccurate.

B goes back to his hotel, takes a shower, shaves, puts on his cleanest set of clothes, the ones he wore on his first day in Madrid, and sets off. A lives in the centre of the city, in an old five-storey building. B presses the intercom button and a woman's voice asks who it is. It's B, he says. Come in, says the woman, and the buzzing noise that the security door makes when it is unlocked continues until B reaches the lift. B even thinks he can hear it as he goes up to A's flat, as if the lift were dragging a long tail, like that of a lizard or a snake.

A is waiting for him on the landing, by the open door. He is tall, pale, and slightly fatter than in the photos. There is a certain shyness in his smile. For a moment B feels as if the energy that brought him to A's door has suddenly drained away. He pulls himself together, tries to smile, holds out his hand. If I can just get through this without violence or melodrama, he thinks. At last, says A. How are you? Very well, says B.

Phone Calls

B IS IN LOVE WITH X. UNHAPPILY, OF COURSE. There was a time in his life when B would have done anything for X, as people generally say and think when they are in love. X breaks up with him. She breaks up with him over the phone. At first, of course, B suffers, but eventually he gets over it, as people generally do. Life, as they say in the soap operas, goes on. The years pass.

One night when he has nothing to do, B manages to get through to X after ringing a couple of times. Neither of them is young any more and age is audible in their voices transmitted from one side of Spain to the other. They renew their friendship and after a few days decide to meet again. Both have been through divorces, suffered new illnesses and frustrations. When B gets on the train and sets off for the city where X lives, he is not yet in love. They spend the first day holed up in X's flat, talking about their lives (in fact X does all the talking, B listens

67

and asks a question now and then). That night X invites him to share her bed. B doesn't really want to sleep with X, but he accepts. When he wakes up in the morning, he is in love again. But is he in love with X or with the idea of being in love? The relationship is difficult and intense: X is on the brink of suicide every day; she is having psychiatric treatment (pills, lots of pills, but they don't seem to be helping at all), she often bursts into tears for no apparent reason. So B looks after X. His attentions are loving and diligent, but awkward too. They mimic the attentions of a man who is truly in love, as B soon comes to realise. He tries to show X a way out of her depression, but all he does is steer her into a dead end, or what she considers a dead end. Sometimes, when he is on his own or watching X sleep, he thinks it is a dead end too. As a kind of antidote, he tries to remember his former loves, he tries to convince himself that he can live without X, that he can survive on his own. One night X asks him to go away, so B takes a train and leaves the city. X goes to the station to see him off. Their farewell is tender and hopeless. B has booked a sleeper but he can't get to sleep until very late. When he finally falls asleep, he dreams of a snowman walking through the desert. The snowman is following a border, and probably headed for disaster. But he presses on regardless, arming his will with cunning: he walks at night, when freezing starlight sweeps the desert. When B wakes up (the train has already arrived at the

68

Sants Station in Barcelona), he thinks he understands the meaning of the dream (if it has a meaning) and finds some degree of solace in it as he makes his way home. That night he rings X and tells her the dream. X says nothing. The next day he rings X again. And the day after. X's attitude is increasingly cold, as if B were receding further into the past with each phone call. I'm disappearing, thinks B. She's rubbing me out and she knows just what she's doing and why she's doing it. One night B threatens to catch a train and turn up at X's flat the next day. Don't even think about it, says X. I'm coming, says B, I can't stand these phone calls any more, I want to see your face when I'm talking to you. I won't open the door, says X, and then hangs up. B simply can't understand. For a long time he wonders how it is possible for the feelings and desires of a human being to swing from one extreme to the other like that. Then he gets drunk or tries to lose himself in a book. The days go by.

One night, six months later, B calls X. X recognises his voice immediately. Ah, it's you, she says. Her lack of warmth is positively chilling. Yet B senses that X wants to tell him something. She's listening to me as if no time had passed, he thinks, as if we had spoken yesterday. How are you? asks B. What's new? After a few monosyllabic replies, X hangs up. Perplexed, B dials her number again. When he gets through, however, he decides to remain silent. At the other end X's voice says: Well, who is it? Silence. Then

69

she says: I'm listening, and waits. The telephone line is transmitting time – the time that came between B and X, that B could not understand – compressing and stretching it, revealing a part of its nature. Without realising, B starts to cry. He knows that X knows who is calling. Then, silently, he hangs up.

Up to this point the story is banal; unfortunate, but banal. It is clear to B that he should never ring X again. One day there is a knock at the door; it is A and Z. They are policemen and they want to ask him some questions. In connection with what, B would like to know. A is reluctant to say; but Z, after clumsily beating around the bush, comes out with it. Three days ago, on the other side of Spain, someone killed X. At first B is shattered; then he realises that he is a suspect and his instinct for survival puts him on his guard. The policemen ask him about his movements on two days in particular. B can't remember what he did or whom he saw on those days. Naturally he knows that he didn't leave Barcelona – in fact he didn't leave his neighbourhood or even his flat – but he can't prove it. The policemen take him away. B spends the night at the police station. At one point during the questioning he thinks they are going to take him to the city where X used to live and, strangely, this prospect appeals to him, but in the end it doesn't happen. They take his fingerprints and ask if he will agree to a blood test. He agrees. The next morning they let him go home. Officially, B has not been under arrest; he has only been helping the police in a murder inquiry. When he gets back to his flat, he collapses on his bed and falls asleep immediately. He dreams of a desert and of X's face. Shortly before waking, he realises that they are one and the same. From which it is fairly simple for him to infer that he is lost in the desert.

That night he puts some clothes in a bag, goes to the station and takes a train to the city where X used to live. The journey, from one side of Spain to the other, lasts the entire night. Unable to sleep, he thinks about all the things he could have done, but didn't do; all the things he could have given X, but didn't. He also thinks: If I had died, X wouldn't be travelling right across Spain in the other direction. Then he thinks: and that is precisely why I am the one who is still alive. For the first time, during that sleepless trip, he sees X's true worth; he feels love for her again, and, for the last time, half-heartedly, he despises himself. When he arrives, very early in the morning, he goes straight to X's brother's flat. X's brother is surprised and confused, but invites him in and offers him a coffee. He is half dressed and his face is wet. B notices that he hasn't had a shower; he has only washed his face and wet his hair a bit. B accepts the offer of coffee, then says that he just found out about the murder of X, explains that he has been questioned by the police, and asks what happened. The whole thing's been awful, says X's brother, making coffee in the kitchen, but I can't see what you've got to do with it. The police think I might be the killer, says B. X's brother laughs. You've always been unlucky, haven't you, he says. Odd you should say that, thinks B, when I'm the one who's still alive. But he is also grateful not to have his innocence doubted. Then X's brother goes to work, leaving B in the flat. Exhausted, B soon falls into a deep sleep. Unsurprisingly, X appears in his dreams.

When he wakes, he thinks he knows who the killer is. He has seen his face. That night he goes out with X's brother. They go to various bars and talk about this and that and although they do their best to get drunk, they can't. Walking back to the flat through the empty streets, B says he once rang X but didn't speak. What the fuck for? says X's brother. I only did it once, says B, but I realised that X got lots of calls like that. And she thought they were from me, you see? says B. You mean the murderer is the anonymous caller? Exactly, says B, and X thought it was me. X's brother frowns. I think it was one of her exes; there were quite a few of them, you know. B says nothing in reply (it's as if X's brother hadn't understood at all) and they continue in silence until they reach the flat.

In the lift B thinks he is going to throw up. He says: I'm going to throw up. Hold on, says X's brother. They walk quickly down the passage, X's brother unlocks the door and B rushes in looking for the bathroom. But when he gets there, his nausea has subsided. He is sweating and his stomach aches, but he can't throw up. The toilet with the lid up looks like a toothless mouth laughing at him. Or laughing at someone, anyway. After washing his face, he looks at himself in the mirror: his face is white as a sheet. He spends what is left of the night dozing fitfully, trying to read and listening to X's brother snore. The next day they say goodbye and B returns to Barcelona. I'll never go back to that city again, thinks B, because X doesn't live there any more.

A week later, X's brother calls to tell him that the police have caught the killer. The guy was harassing her with anonymous phone calls, he says. B doesn't answer. An ex, says X's brother. Well, it's good to know, says B. Thanks for calling. Then X's brother hangs up and B is alone.

The Grub

H E LOOKED LIKE A WHITE GRUB, WITH HIS
straw hat and a Bali cigarette hanging from
his bottom lip. Each morning when I went
to the Librería de Cristal to browse I would see him sitting on a bench in the Alameda. The bookshop, as its
name suggests, was glass-fronted, and when I looked up,
there he was, sitting still among the trees, staring into
nothingness.

I guess we got used to each other's presence. I would
arrive at eight-thirty in the morning, and he would already
be there, sitting on a bench, doing nothing except smoking
and keeping his eyes open. I never saw him with a newspaper or a sandwich, a beer or a book. I never saw him
speak to anyone. Once, noticing him there as I glanced
up from the French literature shelves, I thought he must
sleep in the Alameda, on a bench, or in a doorway in one
of the neighbouring streets, but then I realised he was too
clean and tidy to be sleeping in the street and must have

a room in some boarding-house nearby. He was, I noticed, a creature of habit, like myself. My routine consisted of getting up early, having breakfast with my mother, father, and sister, pretending to go to school, then catching a bus to the centre of the city, where I would devote the first part of my morning to books and walking around, and the second part to movies and, more surreptitiously, to sex.

I generally bought my books at the Librería de Cristal or the Librería del Sótano. If I was short of cash, I'd pick over the special offers table at the Cristal, but if I was sufficiently solvent, I'd go to the Sótano for the new titles. If I had no money at all, which was often the case, I would steal from one or the other, indiscriminately. But in any case, I would invariably pay a visit to both the Librería de Cristal and the Librería del Sótano (located, as the name suggests, in a basement, across from the Alameda). If I arrived before the shops opened, I'd look for a street vendor, buy myself a ham sandwich and a mango juice and wait. Sometimes I'd sit on a bench in the Alameda, tucked away in the shrubbery, and write. All this lasted until about ten in the morning, which is when the cinemas began to open up for their first screenings. I preferred European films, though if I was feeling particularly inspired, I wasn't averse to New Mexican Erotic or New Mexican Horror, which were pretty much the same thing, anyway.

The film I saw most often was French, I think. It was

about two girls who live alone in a house outside town. One is blonde and the other's a redhead. The blonde's boyfriend has left her, and as well as having to deal with that, she is going through a personality crisis: she thinks she is falling in love with her housemate. The redhead is younger, more innocent, more irresponsible; in other words, she's happier (although, when I saw this film, I was young, irresponsible, and innocent and believed myself to be deeply wretched). One day a criminal on the run sneaks into their house and holds them hostage. By an odd co-incidence this happens on the very night the blonde, after making love with the redhead, has decided to commit sui-cide. The fugitive climbs in through a window, creeps around the house, knife in hand, goes into the redhead's room, overpowers her, ties her up, interrogates her, asks her how many other people live there (just her and the blonde, she replies), then he gags her. But the blonde is not in her room and the fugitive goes searching through the house, getting more and more nervous, until finally he finds her lying unconscious on the floor of the cellar, having obviously swallowed the contents of the medicine cabinet. The fugitive, who is not a killer (he wouldn't kill a woman, anyway) saves the blonde: he makes her vomit, brews a litre of coffee, makes her drink milk, etc.

As the days go by, the women and the fugitive start to get to know one another. The fugitive tells them his story: he is an ex-bank robber, who has escaped from jail, and his former associates have killed his wife. The women are cabaret artists, and one afternoon or one night (it's hard to tell since they keep the curtains closed the whole time) they put on a show for him: the blonde slips into a magnificent bear skin and the redhead pretends to be the trainer. At first the bear is obedient, but then he rebels and claws at the redhead's clothes, tearing them off piece by piece. Finally, naked, she collapses in defeat and the bear leaps on to her. No, he doesn't kill her; he makes love to her. And the strangest thing of all is that, having watched this performance, the fugitive falls in love not with the redhead but with the blonde, that is, with the bear.

The ending is predictable but not without a certain poetry: one rainy night, after killing his two former associates, the fugitive flees with the blonde to an unknown destination leaving the redhead sitting in an armchair, reading, giving them time before she calls the police. The book she is reading – I realised this the third time I saw the film – is *The Fall* by Camus. I also saw some Mexican films more or less in the same style: women kidnapped by villains who turn out to have hearts of gold; fugitives who take rich young ladies hostage and get themselves shot to pieces after a night of passion; beautiful servants who, starting from nothing, climb the tall ladder of crime to reach the pinnacle of wealth and power. In those days most of the films produced by the Churubusco studios were erotic thrillers, although there were quite a few erotic horror films and erotic comedies too. The horror films basically followed the pattern set by Mexican Horror in the fifties, which is as much a part of the national culture as the mural painting of Rivera, Siqueiros, and company. The innovations were limited to supplementing the stock of timeless icons – Saint, Mad Scientist, Cowboy Vampire, Ingénue – with contemporary nudes, preferably played by unknown North American, European, or occasionally Argentine actresses, slipping in scenes of a more or less overtly sexual nature, and treading a line between the laughable and the intolerable in the depiction of violence. I wasn't so keen on the erotic comedies.

One morning, while I was looking for a book in the Librería del Sótano, I noticed that a film was being shot in the middle of the Alameda and I went over to see what I could see. I recognised Jaqueline Andere straight away. She was on her own, gazing at a row of trees to her left, hardly moving, as if waiting for a signal. Spotlights had been set up around her. I don't know what possessed me to ask for her autograph; I've never been interested in autographs. I waited till they had finished shooting. A man approached her and they talked (was it Ignacio López Tarso?). He gesticulated irritably, then walked off, and after a few moments of hesitation Jaqueline Andere chose a different path. She was coming directly towards me. I started walking too and we met halfway. It was one of the simplest things that has ever happened to me: no one stopped me, or said anything, or came between Jaqueline and me. No one asked me what I was doing there. Before our paths crossed, Jaqueline stopped and turned back to look at the crew, as if she were listening to something, although none of them had spoken. Then she kept walking with the same carefree air towards the Palacio de Bellas Artes, and all I had to do was stop, greet her, ask for an autograph, and hide my surprise at how short she was, even wearing high heels. For a moment we were alone together and it struck me that if I had wanted to kidnap her, I could have. The mere thought made the hair stand up on the back of my neck. She looked at me from head to toe, with her ash-blonde hair (I didn't remember it being that colour – maybe she had dyed it), her big brown almond eyes, so soft, no, soft is not the word, calm, astonishingly calm, as if she were sedated or brain dead or an alien, and she said something to me, but I didn't catch it at first.

A pen, she said, a pen to sign with. I found a biro in the pocket of my jacket and got her to sign the first page of *The Fall*. She took the book from me and looked at it for a few seconds. Her hands were small and very delicate. How would you like me to sign? As Albert Camus or Jaqueline Andere? Whichever you prefer, I said. Although she didn't look up from the book I could tell she was smiling. Are you a student? she asked. I replied in the affirmative. So how come you're here instead of in class? I don't think I'll ever go back to school, I said. How old are you?

she asked. Seventeen, I said. And do your parents know you're not going to class? No, of course not, I said. You still haven't answered my question, she said, looking up and into my eyes. Which question? I asked. What are you doing here? When I was young, kids used to hang out in pool halls or bowling alleys when they skipped classes. Well, I read books and go to the movies, I said. Anyway, I'm not skipping a class. No, you leave that to the amateurs, she said. Now it was my turn to smile. And what movies can you see at this time of the day? All sorts, I said, some of yours. She didn't seem to like that; she looked at the book again, bit her bottom lip, looked at me and blinked as if her eyes were hurting. Then she asked my name. Well, let's get this signed, she said. She was left-handed. Her handwriting was large and hard to read. I have to go, she said, handing me the book and the biro. She held out her hand, shook mine and went back across the Alameda towards the film crew. I stood still, watching her. When she was about fifty metres away two women approached her, dressed as missionary nuns, two Mexican missionary nuns who escorted Jaqueline to the shade of an ahuehuete tree. Then a man went over to her, they talked, and the four of them walked away down one of the paths that lead out of the Alameda.

On the first page of *The Fall*, she had written: 'For Arturo Belano, student at large, with a kiss from Jaqueline Andere.'

Suddenly I had no desire to browse in a bookshop, walk around, read, or least of all go to a matinée session. The prow of an enormous cloud appeared over the centre of Mexico City, while to the north the first thunderclaps resounded. I realised that the shooting of Jaqueline's film had been suspended because of the imminent rain and I felt lonely. For a few seconds I didn't know what to do, where to go. Then the Grub said hello to me. Having seen me so many times, I suppose he had begun to recognise me too. I turned around and there he was, sitting on the same bench as always, a clear-cut presence, absolutely real, with his straw hat and his white shirt. The scene, as I was troubled to discover, had undergone a subtle but decisive transformation with the departure of the film crew: it was as if the waters had parted to reveal the sea floor. The empty Alameda was the sea floor, and the Grub its most precious treasure. I said hello, probably made some banal remark, and it began to pour. We left the Alameda together and headed for the Avenida Hidalgo; then we walked down Lázaro Cárdenas to the corner with Perú.

What happened next is hazy, as if seen through the rain that was lashing the streets, yet perfectly natural. The bar was called Las Camelias and it was full of mariachis and chorus girls. I ordered enchiladas and a beer, the Grub ordered a Coke and a bit later on he bought three turtle eggs from a vendor. He wanted to talk about Jaqueline Andere. I soon realised, to my astonishment, that he didn't know she was a film star. I pointed out that she was there for a film shoot, but he simply didn't remember the crew or the equipment they had set up. Jaqueline's apparition on his path, near his bench, had obliterated all the rest. When it stopped raining, the Grub pulled a bunch of notes from his back pocket, paid, and left.

We saw each other again the next day. From the expression on his face when he saw me I thought he couldn't remember who I was or didn't want to say hello. I went over to him anyway. He seemed to be asleep, although his eyes were open. He was thin, but his flesh, except on his arms and legs, gave the impression of being soft, even flaccid, like the flesh of an athlete no longer in training. His flaccidity, however, was not so much physical as psychological. His bones were small and strong. I soon discovered that he was from the north, or had lived there a long time, which comes to the same thing. I'm from Sonora, he said. By coincidence, that was where my grandfather came from. This intrigued the Grub and he wanted to know what part of Sonora. From Santa Teresa, I said. I'm from Villaviciosa, said the Grub. One night I asked my father if he knew Villaviciosa. Of course I do, said my father, it's a few kilometres from Santa Teresa. I asked him to describe it for me. It's a very small town, said my father, wouldn't be more than a thousand people (later I found out there weren't even five hundred), pretty poor, not many jobs, and no industry at all. It'll disappear sooner or later, he said.

How do you mean disappear? I asked him. Emigration, he said, the people will leave and to go to Santa Teresa or Hermosillo or the United States. When I reported this to the Grub he didn't agree, although it would be an exaggeration to say that he ever agreed or disagreed with anything. The Grub never argued or expressed opinions, but not out of any particular respect for others; he simply listened and stored things away, or maybe he just listened and forgot it all, off in a world of his own. His speech was soft and monotonous, although occasionally he would raise his voice, and then he sounded like a madman imitating a madman. I never knew whether those outbursts were intentional, part of some private game, or beyond his control, cries from hell. His conviction that Villaviciosa would endure was founded on the town's long history, but also (though I only came to understand this later) on the tenuous nature of its existence, threatened from all quarters, which is precisely what doomed it to extinction, according to my father.

Although the Grub was not a curious man, few things escaped his notice. He once examined the books I was carrying, one by one, as if he could barely read or couldn't read at all. After that he never showed the slightest interest in my books, although I had a new one every morning. Sometimes, perhaps because he considered me a fellow countryman of sorts, we talked about Sonora, which I hardly knew: I had been there only once, for my grandfather's funeral. He would speak of towns like Nacozari,

Bacoache, Fronteras, Villa Hildalgo, Bacerac, Bavispe, Agua Prieta, Naco, names that were pure gold to my imagination. He would mention forsaken villages in the districts of Nacori Chico and Bacadéhuachi, near the border with Chihuahua state, and then, I don't know why, he would cover his mouth as if he were about to sneeze or yawn. He seemed to have roamed over all the mountain ranges, on foot, camping out: the Sierra Las Palomas and the Sierra La Cieneguita, the Sierra Guijas and the Sierra La Madera, the Sierra San Antonio and the Sierra Cibuta, the Sierra Tumacacori and the Sierra Sierrita right up into Arizona, the Sierra Cuevas and the Sierra Ochitahueca in the north-east, near Chihuahua, the Sierra La Pola and the Sierra Las Tablas in the south, towards Sinaloa, the Sierra La Gloria and the Sierra El Pinacate, up in the north-east, on the way to Baja California. He knew the whole of Sonora, from Huatabampo and Empalme on the Gulf coast to the remote one-horse towns in the desert. He could speak Yaqui and Pápago (a language that straddles the Sonora–Arizona border) and he understood Seri, Pima, Mayo, and English. His Spanish was dry, with a slightly oratorical tone from time to time, undercut by the look in his eye. Like a soul in torment, I have wandered all over your grand-father's country, may he rest in peace, he said to me once.

We met each morning. Sometimes I tried not to notice him and go back to my solitary walks and matinées, but he was always there, sitting on the same bench in the

Alameda, very still, with a Bali cigarette hanging from his lip, and his straw hat half covering his grub-like forehead; and inevitably, looking up from the books in the Librería de Cristal, I would see him, watch him for a while, and end up going over to sit beside him.

I soon discovered that he always carried a gun. At first I thought maybe he was a policeman or someone was out to get him, but he couldn't have been a policeman (or not any more, if he ever had been) and I have rarely seen anyone so unconcerned by the presence of others; he never looked behind him, or to the side, and he hardly ever looked down. When I asked him why he carried a gun, the Grub said, Habit, and I didn't doubt him for a moment. He carried it in the back of his trousers. Have you used it much? I asked him. Yes, lots of times, he said, as if in a dream. For several days I was obsessed with the Grub's gun. Sometimes he would take it out, remove the clip and hand it to me so I could inspect it. It looked old and felt heavy. Generally I gave it back to him after a few seconds and asked him to put it away. Sometimes it made me nervous to be sitting on a bench in the Alameda talking to (or at) a man with a gun, not because of what he might have done to me – I knew from the start that the Grub and I would always be friends – but because I was worried the Mexico City police might see us there, search us, find the Grub's gun, and dump us both in some dark prison cell.

One morning he was unwell and that was when he told

me about Villaviciosa. I saw him from the Librería del Cristal and he looked the same as ever, but when I went over to him, I noticed that his shirt was crumpled, as if he had slept in it. When I sat down beside him I could see that he was trembling. Soon he began to tremble more violently. You've got a fever, I said, you should go to bed. I accompanied him to the boarding-house where he lived, although he insisted there was no need. Lie down, I said. The Grub took off his shirt, put the pistol under his pillow, and seemed to fall asleep immediately, though with his eyes open and fixed on the ceiling. In the room there was a narrow bed, a bedside table and a decrepit wardrobe. Inside the wardrobe I found three perfectly folded white shirts like the one he had just taken off and two pairs of matching trousers on hangers. Under the bed I noticed a very classy leather suitcase, the sort that has a lock like a safe. I couldn't see a single newspaper or magazine. The room smelt of disinfectant, like the boarding-house stairs. Give me some money so I can go to the chemist and buy you something, I said. He pulled a bundle of notes from his trouser pocket, gave it to me, and lay still again. Every now and then a shudder ran down his body from head to foot as if he were about to die. But only every now and then. For a moment I thought I really should call a doctor, but then I realised that the Grub wouldn't like that. By the time I returned, bearing medicine and bottles of Coke, he really had fallen asleep. I gave him a hefty dose of antibiotics and pills to bring his temperature down. Then I made him drink half a litre of Coke. I had also bought a pasty, which I left on the bedside table in case he got hungry later on. As I was getting ready to go, he opened his eyes and started talking about Villaviciosa.

For a man of so few words, it was a detailed description. He said the village had seventy houses, no more, two bars and a general store. He said the houses were made of adobe and some had cement patios. He said the patios gave off a bad and sometimes unbearable smell. Unbearable, he said, for anyone with a soul, or even without a soul, even without senses. He said that was why some of the patios had been cemented. He said the village was between two and three thousand years old and its native sons worked as hired killers or security guards. He said a killer never hunted a killer, how could he, it would be like a snake biting its own tail. He said that snakes had been known to bite their own tails. He said that snakes had even been known to swallow themselves whole and if you see a snake in the process of swallowing itself you better run because sooner or later something bad is going to happen, some dislocation of reality. He said the village was near a river, called Río Negro because its water was black, and as it flowed past the cemetery it spread out in a delta and sank into the dry earth. He said that sometimes the people would stare for hours at the horizon and the sun setting behind a mountain called El Lagarto, and the horizon was the colour of flesh, like the back of a dying man. And what do they expect to see? I asked. The sound of my own voice frightened me. I don't know, he said. Then he said: a shaft. And then: wind and dust, maybe. Then he calmed down and after a while he seemed to be asleep. I'll come back tomorrow, I murmured, take the medicines and don't get out of bed.

I left quietly.

The next morning, before going to the Grub's boarding-house, I spent a while as usual at the Librería de Cristal. When I was about to leave, I looked out through the shop window and saw him. He was sitting on the same bench, wearing a clean, loose white shirt and a pair of perfectly white trousers, his face half covered by his straw hat, and a Bali cigarette hanging from his lower lip. He was gazing straight ahead, as normal, and he seemed well. At noon, as we were about to say goodbye, he held out several notes with a sullen expression on his face and said something about the trouble he'd caused me the previous day. It was a lot of money. I told him he didn't owe me anything, I would have done the same for any friend. The Grub insisted I take the money. You can use it to buy some books, he said. I've got lots, I replied. Well you can stop stealing them for a while, he said. In the end I took the money. It's a long time ago and I can't remember exactly how much it was, the Mexican peso has been devalued over and over again, but I remember it was enough to buy twenty books and two Doors records, and for me that was a fortune. The Grub wasn't short of cash.

He never talked to me again about Villaviciosa. For a month and a half, or maybe two months, we met each morning and at midday went our separate ways, when it was time for me to catch a bus back home to La Villa for lunch. Once I invited the Grub to see a movie, but he didn't want to. He liked to talk to me, either sitting on his bench in the Alameda or wandering around the neighbouring streets, and every now and then he deigned to go into a bar, where he would always look for the turtle-egg vendor. I never saw him touch alcohol. A few days before he disappeared for good he got me to talk about Jaqueline Andere for some reason. I realised it was his way of remembering her. I talked about her ash-blonde hair and compared it favourably or unfavourably to the honey-blonde colour it was in her films, and the Grub nodded almost imperceptibly, looking straight ahead as if the image of Jaqueline Andere were imprinted on his retinas or as if he were seeing her for the first time. Once I asked him what kind of women he liked. It was a stupid question, asked by an adolescent looking for something to say. But the Grub took it seriously and considered his reply for a long time. Finally he said, Calm women. And then he added, But only the dead are really calm. And after a while, Not even the dead, come to think of it.

One morning he gave me a knife. On the bone handle

the word 'Caborca' had been inscribed in fine letters of nickel silver. I remember thanking him effusively. That morning, as we talked in the Alameda or walked through the busy streets of the city centre, I kept opening the blade and shutting it again, admiring the handle, feeling its weight in the palm of my hand, marvelling at its perfect proportions. Otherwise, that day was identical to all the others. The next morning the Grub was gone.

Two days later I went to his boarding-house to look for him and they told me he had gone up north. I never saw him again.

Anne Moore's Life

ANNE MOORE'S FATHER SERVED HIS COUNTRY and the free world aboard a hospital ship in the Pacific from 1943 to 1945. His first daughter, Susan, was born while he was at sea off the Philippines, just before the end of the Second World War. Soon after, he returned to Chicago, where Anne was born in 1948. But Dr Moore didn't like Chicago, so three years later, he and his family moved to Great Falls, in the state of Montana.

That is where Anne grew up. Her childhood was peaceful, but it was also strange. In 1958, when she was ten years old, she glimpsed for the first time what she would later call the ashen (or the dirty) face of reality. Her sister had a boyfriend called Fred, who was fifteen. One Friday Fred came to the Moores' house and said that his parents had gone on a trip. Anne's mother said it wasn't right, he was just a boy, he shouldn't be left alone in the house like that. Anne's father reckoned that Fred was old enough to look after himself. That night Fred had dinner at the Moores' house, then sat on the porch chatting to Susan and Anne until ten. Before leaving he said good-bye to Mrs Moore. Dr Moore had already gone to bed.

The next day Fred took Susan and Anne for a drive around the park in his parents' car. According to what Anne told me, Fred's state of mind was noticeably different from the night before. He was preoccupied and hardly spoke, as if he and Susan had argued. For a while they just sat there in the car, in silence, Fred and Susan in the front and Anne in the back, then Fred proposed that they go to his house. Susan didn't answer. Fred started the car and drove to a poor neighbourhood where Anne had never been; it was as if he was lost or, deep down, didn't really want to take them to his house, even though he was the one who had suggested it. Anne remembers that as they drove around Susan didn't look at Fred once; she spent the whole time looking out of the window, as if the houses and the streets slowly filing past were part of a never to be repeated show. And Fred, gazing fixedly straight ahead, didn't once look at Susan. Neither of them said a word or turned to look at the young girl in the back seat, although at one point, momentarily, she caught Fred's eye in the rear-view mirror, staring at her, hard and bright.

When they finally arrived at Fred's house, neither Fred nor Susan made a move to get out. Even the way Fred parked the car in the street instead of in the garage seemed provisional, a way of breaking the flow. As if by parking like that, he was giving us and himself extra time to think, says Anne in hindsight.

After a while (Anne doesn't remember how long) Susan got out of the car, ordered her sister to do the same, took her by the hand, and they walked away without saying goodbye. When they were several yards away, Anne turned and saw the back of Fred's neck; he hadn't moved, he was still at the wheel, as if still driving, staring straight ahead, says Anne, although by then he may have closed or half-closed his eyes; he may have been looking down, or crying.

They walked back home and Susan refused to explain her behaviour, in spite of Anne's questions. She wouldn't have been surprised to find Fred in the garden that afternoon. It wasn't the first time he and her sister had fought, and they always made up soon afterwards. But Fred didn't come round that Saturday, or on Sunday, and he wasn't in class on Monday, as Susan was later to confess. On Wednesday the police arrested Fred for drunken driving in a poor neighbourhood of Great Falls. After questioning him, they went to his house and found the bodies of his parents: his mother's in the bathroom and his father's in the garage. His father's body was partly wrapped in blankets and cardboard, as if Fred had been intending to dispose of it in the coming days.

As a result of this crime, Susan, who seemed at first to be coping remarkably well, had a mental breakdown and was in therapy for several years with a series of psychologists. Anne, by contrast, was unaffected, although the incident, or the shadow it cast, would revisit her intermittently in later years. But at the time she didn't even dream about Fred, or if she did, she sensibly forgot the dreams as soon as she emerged from sleep.

At the age of seventeen, Anne went to college in San Francisco. Susan had gone there two years earlier, to study medicine at Berkeley, and was sharing an apartment with two other students in the southern part of Oakland, near San Leandro. Her letters home were infrequent. When Anne arrived she found her sister in a terrible state. Susan was not studying; she slept during the day, disappeared at night and wouldn't come back until well into the next morning. Anne began a degree in English Literature and took a course in Impressionist Painting. She found an afternoon job at a cafeteria in Berkeley. To begin with she lived in the same room as her sister. In fact they could have gone on like that indefinitely. During the day, while Anne was at college, Susan was at home sleeping, and since she was hardly ever there at night, they could make do with one bed. But after a month Anne moved to a place in Hackett Street, near the café where she was working, and stopped seeing her sister, although she would sometimes call her (it was always one of her housemates who answered the phone) to see how she was, pass on news about Great Falls and find out if she needed anything. Susan was drunk the few times Anne got through to her. One morning they told her that Susan had moved out. For two weeks she searched all over Berkeley but couldn't find her. Finally, one night she rang her parents in Great Falls, and it was her sister Susan who answered the phone. Anne couldn't believe it. She felt somehow cheated and betrayed. Susan had given up her studies for good and now she wanted to start all over again in a nice, quiet town, she said. If that's what you want to do, I'm sure that's best, said Anne, although in fact she felt her sister was in a mess and was throwing her life away.

Not long after this, Anne met Paul, a painter, grandson of Russian-Jewish anarchists, and moved in with him. Paul had a little two-storey house. His studio, full of large, permanently unfinished pictures, occupied the ground floor, and on the first floor there was a big space that served as bedroom, living room and dining room, as well as a tiny kitchen and bathroom. Of course he wasn't the first man she had slept with. She had gone out with a classmate from the Impressionist Painting course – he was the one who introduced her to Paul – and back in Great Falls she had had two boyfriends: a basketball player and a boy who worked in a bakery. For a while she thought she was in love with the boy from the bakery. His name was Raymond and the bakery belonged to his father. In fact, Raymond came from a long line of bakers, going back several generations. He was studying and working at the same time, but when he graduated he decided to become a full-time baker. He wasn't an outstanding student, according to Anne, but he wasn't bad either. And what she especially remembered about Raymond, in those years, was how proud he was of his trade, the family trade, in a place where people pride themselves on all sorts of things, but not, as a rule, on baking bread for a living.

Anne and Paul's relationship was unusual. Anne was seventeen going on eighteen and Paul was twenty-six. They had problems in bed from the start. In summer Paul was often impotent, in winter he was prone to premature ejaculation, and in spring and autumn he wasn't interested in sex. That's according to Anne; she also says that he was the most intelligent person she had ever met. Paul knew about everything: painting, art history, literature, music. Sometimes he was insufferable, but he could tell when it was coming on and knew to shut himself up in his studio and paint until he had stopped being insufferable and reverted to his normal self – charming, chatty, and loving – at which point he would stop painting and take Anne to the movies, or the theatre, or one of the many talks and readings that were happening at Berkeley, preparing people's minds for the decisive years to come. At first they lived off Anne's wages from the cafeteria and a scholarship that Paul had. Then one day they decided to travel to Mexico and Anne quit her job.

They went to Tijuana, Hermosillo, Guaymas, Culiacán,

and Mazatlán, where they rented a beach house. They went swimming every morning; in the afternoon Paul painted while Anne read, and at night they went to a North American bar, the only one in town, called The Frog, frequented by tourists and Californian students. They stayed there late into the night, drinking and talking to people they would normally have ignored. Outside The Frog they bought marijuana from a thin Mexican guy who always wore white and wasn't allowed into the bar. He waited for clients in his car, parked opposite, next to a dead tree.

The thin guy was called Rubén, and sometimes he would exchange marijuana for cassettes, which he played straight away in the car. They soon made friends with him. One afternoon, while Paul was painting, Rubén turned up at the beach house and Paul asked him to pose. From that day on, they never had to pay for their marijuana. But Rubén would sometimes arrive in the morning and stay well into the night, which annoyed Anne, not just because she had to cook for an extra person, but also because, the way she saw it, the Mexican was intruding on the idyllic life they had planned to lead, just the two of them.

At first Rubén talked only to Paul, as if he could tell that Anne resented his presence, but as the days went by they became friends. Rubén spoke a little English and Paul and Anne practised their rudimentary Spanish with him. One afternoon, while they were swimming, Anne felt Rubén touching her legs under the water. Paul was on the beach, watching them. When Rubén came up to the surface he looked her in the eyes and said he was in love with her. That day, as they later found out, someone drowned: a boy who used to go to The Frog; they had chatted with him a couple of times.

Shortly afterwards they went back to San Francisco. It was a good time for Paul. He had two exhibitions, sold some paintings, and his relationship with Anne was steadier than ever. At the end of the year they both travelled to Great Falls and spent Christmas with Anne's parents. Paul didn't like Anne's mother and father, but he got on well with Susan. One night Anne woke up alone in bed. She went looking for Paul and heard voices in the kitchen. When she went downstairs she found Paul and Susan talking about Fred. Paul was listening and asking questions, and Susan was telling him about the last day she had spent with Fred, driving around the poorest neighbourhoods of Great Falls. She told the story over and over, from different points of view. Anne remembers that there was something oddly artificial about this conversation between her lover and her sister, as if they were assessing the plot of a film, not something that had happened in real life.

The following year Anne quit her studies and devoted herself to looking after Paul. She bought his canvases, stretchers, and paint; she cooked, washed, swept, mopped the floors, did the washing-up, and generally tried to make their home a haven of peace and creativity. But their relationship was far from perfect. As a lover Paul kept getting worse. Sex with him did nothing for Anne and she began to wonder if she might be a lesbian. Around that time they met Linda and Marc. Linda sold drugs for a living, like Rubén in Mazatlán, and occasionally she wrote children's stories, which kept getting rejected by publishers. Marc was a poet, or at least that was what Linda said. At that stage he usually spent most of the day shut up in his apartment, listening to the radio or watching television. In the morning he would go out and buy three or four newspapers, and on rare occasions he went to the university, where he met up with old friends or attended the classes of some famous poet who was doing a stint as a visiting professor at Berkeley. But, according to Anne, the rest of the time, he stayed in his apartment, or in his room if Linda had visitors, listening to the radio, watching television and waiting for the declaration of the Third World War.

It came as a surprise to Anne when Paul's career suddenly stalled. Everything happened too quickly. First he lost his scholarship, then the galleries in the Bay area stopped exhibiting his work, and in the end he gave up painting and started studying literature. In the afternoons, Paul and Anne would go to Linda and Marc's apartment and talk for hours about the Vietnam war and about travel. Although Paul and Marc were never really close, they could

99

spend hours on end reading each other poems and drinking (around that time, Anne remembers, Paul began to write poems in the style of William Carlos Williams and Kenneth Rexroth, whom they had once heard give a reading in Palo Alto). Anne's friendship with Linda, on the other hand, deepened imperceptibly but surely, although it seemed to lack a firm base. Anne liked Linda's self-assurance, her independence, her eclectic way of life, the way she flouted certain social conventions while respecting others.

When Linda got pregnant, her relationship with Marc came to a sudden end. She went to live in an apartment in Donaldson Street and kept working until a few days or maybe (Anne can't remember) a few hours before the birth. Marc stayed on in the old apartment and became even more reclusive. At first Paul continued to visit Marc, but he soon realised they had nothing to say to each other, so he stopped. The two women, however, grew closer, and Anne would sometimes even sleep over at Linda's apartment, mainly at weekends, to help her look after the baby when she was busy with her clients.

A year after their first trip to Mexico, Paul and Anne went back to Mazatlán. This time it was different. Paul wanted to rent the beach house, but it was taken, so they had to make do with a sort of bungalow three blocks away. As soon as they arrived in Mazatlán, Anne fell ill. She had diarrhoea and a fever and couldn't get out of bed for three days. The first day Paul stayed in the bungalow and looked after her, but then he started disappearing for hours, and once he stayed out all night. Rubén, however, came to see her. Anne realised that Paul had been out on the town with Rubén and at first she hated the Mexican. But on the third night, when she was starting to feel a bit better, Rubén turned up at the bungalow at two in the morning to enquire about the state of her health. They talked until five and then made love. Anne was still feeling weak. The door was ajar, and at one point she was sure that Paul was behind it, watching them, or looking through the window, but Rubén was so tender and it went on so long that she forgot about everything else, she says.

When Paul appeared the next day, Anne told him what had happened. Paul said 'Shit!' but didn't elaborate. For a couple of days he tried to write something in a notebook with a black cover that Anne was never allowed to read, but he soon gave up and applied himself to sleeping on the beach and drinking. Sometimes he went out with Rubén as if nothing had happened; other nights he stayed at the bungalow and twice they tried to make love, with less than satisfactory results. She slept with Rubén again. Once, at night, on the beach, and another time in the bedroom at the bungalow, while Paul was sleeping on the sofa next door. As the days went by, Anne noticed that Rubén was becoming jealous of Paul. But this only happened when the three of them were together, or when Anne and Rubén were alone, not when Paul and Rubén went out at night to visit the bars of Mazatlán. They were like brothers then, Anne remembers.

When the day came to leave, Anne decided to stay in Mexico. Paul understood and said nothing. It was a sad goodbye. She and Rubén helped Paul pack his bags and put them in the car and then they gave him presents: an old book of photos from Anne and a bottle of tequila from Rubén. Paul didn't have any presents for them, but he gave Anne half the money he had left. When Paul was gone, Anne and Rubén shut themselves in the bungalow and spent three days in a row making love. Anne's money soon ran out and Rubén went back to selling drugs outside The Frog. Anne left the bungalow and went to live at Rubén's house in a suburb from which you couldn't see the ocean. The house belonged to Rubén's grandmother, who lived there with her eldest son, Rubén's uncle, an unmarried fisherman, about forty years old. Things soon took a turn for the worse. Rubén's grandmother didn't like the way Anne walked around the house half-naked. One afternoon, when Anne was in the bathroom, Rubén's uncle came in and propositioned her. He offered her money. Anne, of course, refused the offer, but not firmly enough (she didn't want to offend him, she remembers) and the next day Rubén's uncle offered her money again in return for her favours.

Without realising what she was about to unleash, Anne told Rubén. That night Rubén took a knife from the kitchen and tried to kill his uncle. The shouting was loud enough to wake the whole neighbourhood, Anne remembers, but strangely nobody seemed to hear. Luckily, Rubén's uncle, who was a stronger and more experienced fighter, soon disarmed him. But Rubén wasn't about to give in, and threw a vase at his uncle's head. As bad luck would have it, just at that moment his grandmother was coming out of her room, wearing a very bright red nightdress, the likes of which Anne had never seen. Rubén's uncle ducked and the vase struck his grandmother on the chest. The uncle gave Rubén a beating, then took his mother to hospital. When they returned, the uncle and the grandmother marched straight into the room where Anne and Rubén were sleeping and gave them two hours to get out of the house. Rubén had bruises all over his body and could hardly move, but he was so scared of his uncle that before the two hours were up, they had packed all their gear into the car.

Rubén had relatives in Guadalajara, so that's where they went. They ended up staying only four days. The first night they slept in Rubén's sister's house, which was small, stiflingly hot, and crowded. They shared a room with three small children and the next day Anne decided to find a hotel. They had no money, but Rubén still had some marijuana and acid tablets he could sell, or so he thought. His first attempt was a failure. He didn't know Guadalajara well; he didn't know where to deal, and he came back to the hotel tired and empty-handed. That night they talked until very late and in a moment of frustration Rubén asked Anne what they would do if they couldn't get money to pay for the hotel or buy petrol for the car. Anne said (she was joking, of course) that she could sell her body. Rubén didn't get the joke and slapped her. It was the first time a man had ever hit her. I'd rob a bank before I let you do that, he said, and threw himself on her. Anne remembers what followed as some of the weirdest sex of her life. It was as if the walls of the hotel room were made of meat. Raw meat and grilled meat, bits of both. And while they were fucking she looked at the walls and she could see things moving, scurrying over that irregular surface, like something from a John Carpenter horror movie, though I can't remember that actually happening in any of his films.

The next day Rubén sold the drugs and they headed for Mexico City. They lived with Rubén's mother, in a suburb near La Villa, pretty close to where I was living at the time. If I'd seen you then, I would have fallen in love with you, I told Anne many years later. Who knows, said Anne. Then she added: If I'd been a teenage boy, I wouldn't have fallen in love with me.

For some time, two or three months, Anne thought she was in love with Rubén and envisaged spending the rest of her life in Mexico. But one day she rang her parents, asked them for money to buy an air ticket, said goodbye to Rubén and went back to San Francisco. She moved into

Linda's apartment and found a job as a waitress. Sometimes when she came home from work, Linda was still up and they would talk until late. Some nights they talked about Paul and Marc. Paul was living on his own and had started painting again, though much less than before, and with no prospect of exhibiting. According to Linda the problem with Paul's paintings was that they were very bad. Marc was living like a recluse in his apartment, listening to the radio and watching all the news broadcasts on television. He had hardly any friends left. Anne remembers that a few years later, Marc published a book of poems, which was something of a success in the Berkeley student community, and he gave readings and took part in some conferences. It seemed like the ideal moment for him to start a new relationship and share his life with someone, but after the initial buzz, he retreated to his apartment and she never heard anything more about him.

When a guy called Larry moved in with Linda, Anne rented a little apartment in Berkeley, near the café. Things seemed to be going well, but Anne knew they were about to fall apart. She could tell from her dreams, which were increasingly strange, from her state of mind, drifting towards melancholy, from her unpredictable mood swings. She went out with a couple of guys, but in both cases it was a disappointment. Sometimes she went to see Paul, but she soon stopped, because although the visits would begin well enough they almost always ended in tears, self-reproach, and sadness, or in violent outbursts (Paul would tear up sketches, even destroy paintings). Sometimes she thought about Rubén and laughed at how naïve she had been. One day she met a guy called Charles and they became lovers.

Charles seemed to be the opposite of Paul, Anne remembers, although deep down they were very similar. He was black and had no source of income. He liked to talk and he knew how to listen. Sometimes they spent the whole night making love and talking. Charles liked talking about his childhood and his adolescence, as if he sensed there was a secret there that he had overlooked. Anne, on the other hand, preferred to talk about what was happening to her at that precise moment in her life. She would also talk about her fears, the catastrophe looming ahead, lurking in some apparently normal day. In bed, Anne remembers, things were as unsatisfactory as ever. For a little while, maybe because of the novelty, it was pleasant, maybe even magical on occasions, but then it went back to being like it always was. And that was when Anne made what, from a certain point of view at least, she regards as a monumental error. She told Charles what it was like for her in bed, with all the men she had slept with, including him. At first Charles didn't know what to say, but several days later he suggested that since she didn't feel anything, she might as well use the situation to her advantage. It took Anne a few days to realise that Charles was talking about prostitution.

Maybe she accepted because at the time she was fond of him. Or because it seemed an exciting thing to try. Or because she thought it would bring on the catastrophe. Charles bought her a red dress and matching high-heeled shoes, and he bought himself a gun, because, as he said to Anne, no one respects a pimp without a gun. Anne first saw the gun when they were driving from San Francisco to Berkeley and she opened the glove box to look for something, cigarettes maybe. She got a fright. Charles assured her there was no reason to be frightened; the gun was like an insurance policy, for her and for him. Then he showed her the hotel where she was to take the clients, drove around the neighbourhood a couple of times and dropped her at the entrance to a bar where guys used to go looking for women. He went off, possibly to another bar, to hang out with his friends, although he told Anne he was going to be on the lookout the whole time.

Never in her life had she felt so ashamed, Anne remembers, as when she went in and sat down on a bar stool, knowing she was there to pick up her first client, knowing that everyone else in the bar could tell. She hated the red dress, the red shoes; she hated Charles's gun and the catastrophe that was always about to happen but never did. And yet she managed to collect herself, order a double martini and begin a conversation with the barman. They talked about boredom. The barman seemed to be an expert on the subject. Soon they were joined by a man of about fifty, who looked like her father, but shorter and fatter, whose name Anne has forgotten or maybe she never knew it; in any case I will call him Jack. Jack paid for Anne's drink and proposed they continue their conversation elsewhere. As Anne was about to get down from her stool, the barman came over and said he had something important to tell her. She thought maybe it was a reflection on boredom, for her ears only. The barman leant across the bar and whispered in her ear, Don't you ever set foot in this bar again. When he had resumed his normal posture, he and Anne looked each other in the eye and Anne said, OK and left. The man who looked like her father was waiting on the sidewalk. They got into his car and went to the hotel Charles had pointed out. For the duration of the short trip, Anne stared out at the streets as if she were a tourist. She vaguely hoped to catch a glimpse of Charles in a doorway or an alley, but there was no sign of him and she thought, I bet he's in some bar.

Anne's contact with the man who looked like her father was brief, though not devoid of tenderness, surprisingly for her. When he left, Anne took a taxi home. The next day she told Charles it was all over, she didn't want to see him again. Charles was very young, Anne remembers, and his fondest dream, apparently, was to have a whore, but he took it well, although he nearly burst into tears. Some time later, when Anne was working nights in another café in Berkeley, she saw him again. He was with friends and they laughed at her. This hurt Anne much more than all their fights. Charles was wearing cheap clothes, so perhaps he hadn't made his way in the world of prostitution, though Anne preferred not to think about that.

The following years, as Anne remembers them, were fairly restless. For a while she lived with some friends in a cabin near Lake Martis; she slept with Paul again; she took a course in creative writing at the university. Sometimes she would ring her parents in Great Falls. Sometimes her parents would come to San Francisco and spend two or three days with her. Susan had married a pharmacist and was living in Seattle. Paul had become a computer salesman. Sometimes Anne asked why he didn't start painting again, but Paul wouldn't answer that question. She travelled outside the United States. She went to Mexico a couple of times. With some friends, she drove a station wagon down to Guatemala, where she was held overnight by the police, and one of her friends was beaten up. She went to Canada about five times to stay with a friend who wrote children's stories, like Linda, and had bought a house in the country near Vancouver to get away from it all. But she always came back to San Francisco and that was where she met Tony.

Tony was Korean, from South Korea, and he worked in a clothing factory where most of the employees were illegal immigrants. He was friends with Paul, or Linda, or one of her workmates from the café at Berkeley, Anne can't remember, all she remembers is that it was love at first sight. Tony was very gentle and very sincere, the first truly sincere man Anne had met, so sincere that, the first time they went to the movies together (to see an Antonioni film), as they came out of the cinema he confessed without the slightest embarrassment that he had found the film boring and that he was a virgin. When they slept together for the first time, however, Anne was surprised by Tony's sexual know-how; he was far better than any of her previous lovers.

Before long they got married. Anne had never really thought about marriage, but she did it so Tony could get a green card. Instead of getting married in California, they went all the way to Taiwan, where Tony had relatives, and held the wedding there. Then Tony went to Korea to see his family and Anne travelled to the Philippines to visit a friend from college who was married to a successful Filipino lawyer and had been living in Manila for two years. When they went back to the United States they settled down in Seattle (Tony had relatives there too) and with his savings, and Anne's, and money from his parents, Tony set up a fruit shop.

Living with Tony, Anne remembers, was like living in a protective cocoon. Outside, storms raged every day, people lived in constant fear of a private earthquake, everyone was talking about collective catharsis, but she and

Tony had found a refuge where they could be at peace. And we were, says Anne, though not for long.

A curious aside: Tony loved pornographic films and he used to take Anne to watch them, something she would, of course, never have thought of doing on her own. She was shocked by the fact that in the films the men always ejaculated on to, rather than in, their partners: on their breasts, buttocks, or face. Going to those cinemas made her feel ashamed, unlike Tony, who couldn't see what there was to be ashamed of, given that the films were legal. In the end she decided not to go with him, so Tony went on his own. Another aside: Tony was very hard working; he worked harder (by far) than any of Anne's previous lovers. And another: Tony never got angry, never argued, as if he could see absolutely no point in trying to make someone else agree with him, as if, for him, everyone was lost, so how could one lost person presume to show another the way. Especially since the way, as well as being hidden from everyone, probably didn't even exist.

One day Anne's love for Tony ran out and she left Seattle. She went back to San Francisco, where she slept with Paul again and with other men. For a while she stayed in Linda's apartment. Tony was devastated. Night after night he called her, trying to find out why she had left him. Night after night Anne explained it to him: that was just the way things had turned out, love comes to an end, maybe it hadn't even been love that had brought them together in the first place, she needed a change. For several months Tony went on calling her and asking what it was that had made her break off their marriage. One night, Anne remembers, one of Tony's sisters telephoned and begged her to give him a second chance. She told Anne she had rung her parents in Great Falls and didn't know what else she could do. Anne was taken aback by this, yet it struck her as extraordinarily caring. In the end Tony's sister started crying, apologised for having called (it was after midnight) and hung up.

Tony travelled to San Francisco twice in the hope of convincing Anne to come back. They had countless phone conversations. Finally, Tony seemed to accept the inevitable, but still he kept calling her. He liked talking about their trip to Taiwan, their marriage, the things they had seen; he asked Anne what it was like in the Philippines and he told her about South Korea. Sometimes he was sorry he hadn't gone to the Philippines with her and Anne had to remind him that she had wanted to go alone. When Anne asked about the fruit shop, how the business was going, Tony replied in monosyllables and quickly changed the subject. One night Tony's sister rang again. At first all Anne could hear was a murmur and she asked to her speak up. Tony's sister raised her voice, but only a little, and said that Tony had committed suicide that morning. Then, without a trace of bitterness in her voice, she asked if Anne would be attending the funeral. Anne said yes. But the next morning, instead of catching a plane to Seattle, she took one that landed a couple of hours later in Mexico City. Tony had died at the age of twenty-two.

During the days Anne spent in Mexico City, our paths might have crossed again; again I might have fallen in love with her, although Anne doubts it. She remembers those days as unreal and dreamlike, yet in spite of everything she had time for sight-seeing. She went to visit the city's museums and almost all of the pre-Columbian ruins still standing among the buildings and the traffic. She tried to find Rubén, but couldn't. After two months, she took a plane to Seattle and visited Tony's grave. She almost fainted in the cemetery.

The following years went by too quickly. There were too many men, too many jobs; there was too much of everything. One night, working in a cafeteria, she made friends with two brothers, Ralph and Bill. That night she went to bed with both of them, though while she was making love to Ralph, she looked into his brother's eyes, and when she made love to Bill, she shut her eyes but could still see his. The next night Bill came round, on his own this time. They slept together, but spent longer talking than making love. Bill was a construction worker and his outlook on life was brave and melancholic, more or less the same as Anne's. Both of them had one older sibling, both had been born in 1948 and they were even physically alike. Within a month they had decided to live together.

Around that time Anne received a letter from Susan; she had got divorced and was having treatment for her alcoholism. She said in her letter that once a week, sometimes more often, she went to an Alcoholics Anonymous meeting and it was opening up a new world for her. Anne replied on the back of a tourist postcard of San Francisco, saying things she didn't really feel, but when she finished writing the card she thought of Bill and herself and felt that she had finally found something in life, her own private Alcoholics Anonymous, something solid, something she could hold on to, like a high branch she could swing from and balance on.

The only thing she didn't like about her relationship with Bill was his brother. Sometimes Ralph would turn up at midnight, completely drunk, and get Bill out of bed to talk about the strangest things. They talked about a town in North Dakota where they had been when they were teenagers. They talked about death and what comes after death: nothing according to Ralph, less than nothing according to Bill. They talked about how a man's life consists of learning, working, and dying. Sometimes, but less and less often, Anne participated in these conversations, and she had to admit she was impressed by Ralph's intelligence or his aptitude for finding the weak points in other people's arguments. But one night Ralph tried to sleep with her and from then on she kept her distance, until he finally stopped coming around.

After living together for six months Anne and Bill moved to Seattle. Anne found a job in a company that distributed electrical appliances and Bill went to work on a thirty-floor building that was under construction. For once, they had money to spare and Bill suggested they buy a house and settle down in Seattle for good, but Anne didn't feel ready, so for the time being they rented one floor of a big house occupied by three families, with a wonderful garden they all shared. In the garden, Anne remembers, there was an oak tree, a beech, and a creeper that covered the walls of the house.

Those were perhaps the calmest years of her life in the United States, says Anne, but one day she fell ill and the doctors diagnosed a serious condition. She became irritable and couldn't stand Bill's conversation, or his friends, or even the sight of him coming home each day from the construction site in his overalls. She couldn't stand her own job either, so one day she quit, put some clothes in a suitcase and went to Seattle airport without a clear idea of where she was heading. She had thought about going home to Great Falls and talking to her father, asking his advice as a doctor, but by the time she got to the airport, it all seemed so pointless. She spent five hours sitting there thinking about her life and her illness, and both seemed empty, like a horror film with a subtle twist, one of those films that doesn't seem scary at first, but by the end you're either screaming or shutting your eyes. She would have liked to cry, but couldn't. She turned around, went back to her house in Seattle and waited for Bill to come home. When he arrived, she told him everything that had happened that day and asked him what he thought. Bill said he really couldn't understand, but she could count on his support.

After a week, however, things started going wrong again. She and Bill got drunk, argued, made love, and drove around neighbourhoods they didn't know, but which somehow seemed vaguely familiar to Anne. They came close to having an accident several times that night, Anne remembers. From then on it only got worse. A few months later Anne had an operation but the result was not conclusive. For the moment the illness was in remission, but Anne had to stay on medication and have frequent checkups. A relapse was possible and could have been fatal, according to Anne.

Not much else worthy of note happened during those months. Anne and Bill went to Great Falls for Christmas. Susan started drinking again. Linda kept selling drugs in San Francisco and her finances were sound although her love-life was unstable. Paul bought a house and sold it shortly afterwards. Sometimes, mainly at night, he and Anne would talk on the phone, like two strangers, coldly, without ever mentioning what, for Anne, were the really important things. One night, while they were making love, Bill suggested they have a child. Anne's reply was brief and calm, she simply said no, she was still too young, but inside she could feel herself starting to scream, or rather, she could feel, and see, the dividing line between not-screaming and screaming. It was like opening your eyes in a cave bigger than the earth, Anne remembers. It was around then that she had a relapse and the doctors decided to operate again. Her spirits fell, and Bill's too; they were like a pair of zombies some days. The only activity that gave Anne any pleasure was reading; she read anything she could get her hands on, mostly North American novels and essays, but also poetry and history. She couldn't sleep at night and would usually stay awake until six or seven in the morning. When she did sleep, it was on the sofa; she couldn't bear to get into bed with Bill. Not that she wanted to reject him, or found him repulsive, not at all – Anne even remembers going into the bedroom sometimes and staying there a while to watch him sleep – she just couldn't feel calm lying beside him.

After the second operation Anne put her clothes and books in a pair of suitcases, and this time she did leave Seattle. First she went to San Francisco and then she took a plane to Europe.

When she arrived in Spain she had barely enough money to last two weeks. She spent three days in Madrid, then went to Barcelona, where one of Paul's friends lived. She had his address and phone number, but when she rang there was no answer. She stayed in Barcelona for a week, ringing Paul's friend morning, afternoon, and night, going for long walks around the city, always on her own, or sitting on a bench in the Parque de la Ciudadela and reading. She slept in a hotel on the Ramblas and ate, irregularly, in cheap restaurants in the old part of the city. Little by little, her insomnia relented. One afternoon she tried to make a reverse charge call to Bill, but he wasn't there. Then she rang her parents, who were out too. After leaving the long-distance office, she stopped at a telephone booth and rang Paul's friend: no answer. It occurred to her that maybe she was dead, but she dismissed the thought immediately. Solitude is one thing, death is quite another. That night, Anne remembers, she tried to stay up late reading a book about the life of Willa Cather that Linda had given her before she left, but sleep overcame her.

The following day she rang Paul reverse charges and he was in. She told him she hadn't been able to get in touch with his friend in Barcelona, but didn't mention her financial situation. Paul thought for a few seconds and then had an idea: she could try ringing another friend, or at least an acquaintance of his, a woman who lived in Mallorca but also had a house near Girona. Gloria was her name; she had started studying music at the age of forty-something, and now she was playing with the Palma Symphony Orchestra, or something like that. You probably won't get her either, said Paul, or that is what Anne remembers anyway. Next she rang Susan in Great Falls and asked her to send money to Barcelona. Susan promised she would do it that same day. Her voice sounded strange, as if she had been asleep or was drunk. The second possibility worried Anne, because it might mean that Susan would forget to send the money.

That night she rang Gloria twice from a telephone booth in the Ramblas. She reached her the second time and explained her situation in detail. They talked for fifteen minutes, and then Gloria told Anne that she could go and live in her house in Vilademuls, a village near Banyoles, where the famous lake is; no need to worry about money, she could pay later when she got a job. Anne asked how she would be able to get into the house, and Gloria said she would be sharing the house with two other Americans, one of whom was bound to be there when she arrived. There was no warmth in Gloria's voice, Anne remembers, but no pretence either. She had a slight New England accent, although Anne knew straight away she wasn't from New England; it was an objective voice, like Linda's (though less nasal), the voice of a woman who walks alone, which sounds like something from a Western, though very few women in Westerns walk alone; in any case that was the image that occurred to Anne.

So she spent two more days in Barcelona until Susan's money arrived, paid the bill at the hotel and went to Vilademuls, a village with no more than fifty inhabitants in winter and two hundred and something in summer. As

Gloria had assured her, one of the Americans was there at the house, waiting for her. He was called Dan and he taught English in Barcelona, but every weekend he went up to Vilademuls to work on his detective novels. The only time Anne left the village that winter was to see a doctor in Barcelona. Dan and sometimes Christine, the other American, would arrive on Friday night. Very occasionally they brought friends, Americans too for the most part, but as a rule they came to the house to be alone: Dan worked on his drafts and Christine wove at her loom. Anne spent the weekdays writing letters, reading (she found a large collection of books in English in Gloria's room), cleaning, or doing the minor repairs that the ancient house often required. When spring came, Christine found her a job teaching in a language school in Girona, and, to begin with, Anne shared a flat with an English and an American woman; but then, since she had a steady income, she decided to rent a flat of her own, although she still spent the weekends at Vilademuls.

Around that time Bill came to visit her. It was the first time he had been out of the States and he spent a month travelling around Europe. He didn't like it. Nor did he like the atmosphere at Vilademuls, Anne remembers, although Dan and Christine were straightforward people, and in fact Dan was not unlike Bill: he had worked in construction for a while and had similar experiences; he also liked to think of himself, wrongly, as a tough guy. But Bill didn't like Dan and Dan probably didn't like Bill either, although he took care not to let it show. According to Anne, seeing Bill again was beautiful and sad, though the words hardly begin to convey something deeper and indefinable. It was around then that I saw her for the first time. I was in a bar called La Arcada, on the Rambla de Girona. I saw Bill walk in and she came in after him. Bill was tall, his skin was tanned and his hair was completely white. Anne was tall and slim, with high cheekbones and very straight brown hair. They sat at the bar and I could hardly take my eyes off them. I hadn't seen such a beautiful man and woman for a long time. They were so sure of themselves. So distant and disconcerting. I thought all the other people in the bar should have knelt before them.

Shortly afterwards I saw Bill again. He was walking along a street in Girona and this time, not surprisingly, he didn't seem quite so beautiful. In fact he seemed tired and flustered. A few days later, as I was coming down the hill from my house in La Pedrera, I saw Anne. She was going the other way and for a second or two we looked at each other. At that stage, Anne remembers, she had left the language school and was giving private English lessons and making a fair bit of money. Bill had left and she was living in the old part of Girona, opposite a bar called Freaks and a cinema called the Opera.

From then on our paths began to cross quite often, as I remember. And although we didn't talk, we recognised each other. I guess at some point we started to say hello, as people do in smaller cities.

One morning I was in the Rambla chatting with Pep Colomer, an old painter who lives in Girona, when Anne stopped and talked to me for the first time. I can't remember what we said, maybe our names and where we came from. At the end of the conversation I invited her to dinner at my house that evening. It was Christmas time, or nearly, and I made a pizza and bought a bottle of wine. We talked until very late. That was when Anne told me she'd been to Mexico several times. Overall, her adventures were very similar to mine. Anne thought this was because the lives or the youths of any two individuals would always be fundamentally alike, in spite of the obvious or even glaring differences. I preferred to think that somehow she and I had both explored the same map, fought the same doomed campaigns, received a common sentimental education. At five in the morning, or perhaps later, we went to bed and made love.

Anne immediately became an important part of my life. After the first two weeks I realised that sex was a pretext; what really drew us together was friendship. I got into the habit of going to her flat at about eight at night, when she had finished her last lesson, and we would talk until one or two in the morning. At some point, she would make sandwiches and we'd open a bottle of wine. We'd listen to some music or go down to Freaks to continue drinking and talking. A fair few of Girona's junkies used to gather outside that bar, and the local toughs were often to be seen cruising around, but Anne would reminisce about the toughs of San Francisco, who were seriously tough, and I would reminisce about the toughs of Mexico City, and we'd laugh and laugh, although now, to be honest, I can't remember what was so funny, perhaps just the fact that we were alive. At two in the morning we'd say goodnight and I would go back to my house in La Pedrera, up on the hill.

Once I went with her to the doctor, at the Dexeus Clinic in Barcelona. By then I was going out with another girl and she was going out with an architect from Girona, but I wasn't surprised (in fact I was flattered) when, as we entered the waiting room, she whispered, They'll probably think you're my husband. Once we went to Vilademuls together. Anne wanted me to meet Gloria, but Gloria didn't turn up that weekend. At Vilademuls, however, I discovered something that up until then I had only suspected: Anne could be different; she could be another person. It was a terrible weekend. Anne drank non-stop. Dan would occasionally emerge from his room and promptly disappear again (he was writing) and I had to endure the presence of one of Christine or Dan's ex-students, a brainless Catalan girl from Barcelona or Girona, the sort who's more American than the Americans.

The following year Anne travelled to the States. She was

going to Great Falls to see her parents and her sister, then on to Seattle to see Bill. I got a postcard from New York, and another from Montana, but nothing from Seattle. Later on I got a letter from San Francisco in which she told me that her time with Bill had been a disaster. I imagined her writing the letter in Linda's flat, or Paul's, drinking and maybe crying, although Anne rarely cried.

When she came back from the States she brought some packages with her. One afternoon she showed me: they were the diaries she had kept from shortly after her arrival in San Francisco up until her first meeting with Bill and Ralph. Thirty-four notebooks in all, just under a hundred pages each, each page covered with small, hurried writing, and quotations, drawings, and plans scattered throughout (plans of what? I asked her the first time I saw them: dream houses, imaginary cities or suburbs, the paths a woman's life should follow, though hers had not).

The diaries were kept in a box in the living room. I began to browse through them, in Anne's presence, and gradually my visits fell into a new and very peculiar pattern: I would arrive and sit down in the living room; Anne would put on some music or start drinking, while I resumed my perusal of her diaries. We hardly talked, except when I asked her about something I didn't understand, turns of phrase or words I didn't know. It could be painful, plunging into that writing in the presence of the author (sometimes I wanted to throw the notebook aside and go and hug her), but mostly it was stimulating, although I couldn't say exactly what it stimulated. It was like a fever rising imperceptibly. It made you want to scream or shut your eyes, but Anne's handwriting had the power to sew your lips shut and prop your eyes open, so you had no choice but to go on reading.

One of the early notebooks was entirely devoted to Susan, and the words 'horror' and 'sisterly love' give only the vaguest idea of its content. Two notebooks had been written after Tony's suicide; in these Anne reflected and discoursed on youth, love, death, the dimly recollected landscapes of Taiwan and the Philippines (where she had gone without Tony), the streets and cinemas of Seattle, and perfect evenings in Mexico. One notebook covered the early days of her relationship with Bill, but I couldn't bring myself to read it. My verdict was predictably uninspired. You should publish them, I said, and then I think I shrugged my shoulders.

At the time Anne had become preoccupied by her age, time slipping away, the few years left before she turned forty. At first I thought this was just a kind of coquetry (how could a woman like Anne Moore be worried about turning forty?), but soon I realised that her fear was real. Her parents came once, but I wasn't in Girona and when I got back Anne and her parents had gone off to travel in Italy, Greece, and Turkey.

Not long after this Anne and the architect parted on

the best of terms, and she started going out with one of her ex-students, a technician who worked for a company that imported machinery. He was a quiet sort of guy, and short, too short for Anne; the difference was not only physical, but also, to put it preciously, metaphysical, though I didn't tell her that – I felt it would have been rude. I think at this stage Anne was thirty-eight and the technician was forty, and that was the main thing he had going for him: being older than her. One day I moved away from Girona, and when I came back Anne was no longer living in the flat opposite the Opera cinema. I wasn't particularly worried; she had my new address, but I didn't hear from her for a long time.

During the months when I didn't see her, Anne went travelling in Europe and Africa, had a car accident, left the technician from the machinery-importing firm, saw Paul and Linda who came to visit her, started sleeping with an Algerian, developed a skin complaint on her hands and arms caused by nervous tension, read several books by Willa Cather, Eudora Welty, and Carson McCullers.

One day she finally turned up at my house. I was on the patio, pulling up weeds when suddenly I heard steps, turned around and there was Anne.

That afternoon we made love to hide the sheer joy of seeing each other again. Some days later I went to see her in Girona. She had moved to the new part of town and was living in a tiny attic room. She told me that her neighbour was an old Russian man, a guy called Alexei, the sweetest, most polite person she had ever met. Her hair was cut very short and she had done nothing to disguise the grey. I asked her what had happened to her beautiful hair. I looked like an old hippy, she said.

She was about to go to the States. This time the Algerian was going with her and I think they had problems getting him a visa at the consulate in Barcelona. So it's serious with him, I said. She didn't reply. She said that at the consulate they thought he wanted to go and live in the States for good. And doesn't he? I asked. No, he doesn't, she said.

I don't know where the rest of the time went. I can't remember what we said to each other, the stories we told, nothing important, anyway. Then I left and I never saw her again. A while later I got a letter from her, written in Spanish, from Great Falls. She told me that her sister Susan had killed herself with an overdose of barbiturates. Her parents and her sister's partner, a carpenter from Missoula, were devastated and simply couldn't understand why. I prefer not to say anything, she wrote, there's no point adding to the pain, or adding our own little mysteries to it. As if the pain itself were not enough of a mystery, as if the pain were not the (mysterious) answer to all mysteries. Shortly before leaving Spain, she added (having finished with the topic of Susan's death), Bill had called her several times.

According to Anne, Bill would ring her at all hours of

the day and night, and he almost always ended up insulting her. They almost always ended up insulting one another. The last few times, Bill had threatened to come to Girona and kill her. The funny thing, she said, was that she was saving him the trip, although she had hardly any friends left to visit in Seattle. She didn't mention the Algerian, but he must have been there with her, or so I preferred to assume, for my own peace of mind.

After that I had no more news of her.

Several months went by. I moved house. I went to live by the sea in a village that has acquired a legendary aura since Juan Marsé wrote about it in the seventies. I was too busy working and dealing with my own problems to do anything about Anne Moore. I think I even got married.

Finally, one day I caught a train, returned to grey Girona and climbed up to Anne's little attic room. As I had anticipated, a stranger opened the door. Of course she knew nothing about the previous tenant. Before turning to go I asked if there was a Russian gentleman living in the building, an elderly man, and the stranger said yes, and told me which door to knock at on the second floor.

A very old man came to the door, walking with great difficulty and the aid of a spectacular oak stick, which looked rather as if it had been designed for ceremonial occasions or combat. He remembered Anne Moore. In fact he remembered almost all of the twentieth century, but that, he admitted, was beside the point. I explained that I hadn't heard from her in a long time and had come to see if he had any news. Not much news, he said, just a few letters from America, a great country where I should have liked to stay longer. He took the opportunity to tell me briefly about the years he had spent in New York and his adventures as a croupier in Atlantic City. Then he remembered the letters, made me a cup of tea and went off to look for them. Finally he appeared with three post-cards. All from America, he said. I don't know exactly when I realised he was completely mad. It seemed logical, all things considered. It seemed appropriate, so I sat back and waited for the ending.

The Russian handed me the three cards over the steaming tea. They were arranged in order of arrival and written in English. The first was from New York. I recog-nised Anne's handwriting. She said the usual things and at the end she told him to take care of himself and to eat every day. She said she was thinking of him, with love. There was a photo of Fifth Avenue on the other side. The second postcard was from Seattle. A view of the port from the air. It was much briefer than the first, and harder to understand. There was something about exile and crime. The third postcard was from Berkeley: a quiet street in bohemian Berkeley, read the caption. I'm seeing my old friends and making new ones, said Anne's clear hand-writing. And it ended like the first card, advising dear

Alexei to look after himself and eat every day, if only a little.

Sadly, curiously, I looked at the Russian. He looked back at me kindly. Have you been following her advice? I asked. Of course, he replied, I always follow a lady's advice.

Mauricio 'The Eye' Silva

*for Rodrigo Pinto
and María and Andrés Braithwaite*

MAURICIO SILVA, ALSO KNOWN AS 'THE Eye', always tried to avoid violence, even at the risk of being considered a coward, but violence, real violence, is unavoidable, at least for those of us who were born in Latin America during the fifties and were about twenty years old at the time of Salvador Allende's death. That's just the way it goes.

The case of The Eye is paradigmatic and exemplary, and it may well be worth recalling, especially now that so many years have passed.

In January 1974, four months after the military coup, The Eye left Chile. First he went to Buenos Aires, but then the ill winds blowing in the neighbouring republic sent him to Mexico, where he lived for a couple of years. That is where I met him.

He wasn't like most of the Chileans living in Mexico City at the time: he didn't brag about his role in the largely phantasmal resistance; he didn't frequent the various groups of Chileans in exile.

We became friends and used to meet at least once a week at the Café La Habana in the Avenida Bucareli or at my house in the Calle Versalles, where I lived with my mother and sister. For the first few months, The Eye scraped by doing odd jobs, before finding work as a photographer for a newspaper. I can't remember which one it was, maybe *El Sol*, if such a newspaper ever existed in Mexico, or *El Universal*; I would like to think it was *El Nacional*, whose cultural supplement was edited by the old Spanish poet Juan Rejano, but it can't have been, because I worked there and I never saw him at the office. Anyway, he worked for one of the Mexico City papers, I'm quite sure of that, and his financial situation improved, imperceptibly to start with, because The Eye had grown accustomed to a spartan way of life, but if you looked carefully, you could detect unequivocal signs of an economic upturn.

For example, during the early months I remember him wearing sweatshirts. Towards the end of his time in Mexico City he had bought himself a pair of shirts with collars and once I even saw him in a tie, an item of apparel quite foreign to me and my poet friends. In fact the only person wearing a tie who ever sat down at our table in the Café La Habana was Mauricio (The Eye) Silva.

At the time, The Eye was reputed to be homosexual. By which I mean that a rumour to that effect was circulating in the various groups of Chileans in exile, who made it their business partly for the sheer pleasure of denigration and partly to add a little spice to their rather boring lives. In spite of their left-wing convictions, when it came to sexuality, they reacted just like their enemies on the right, who had become the new masters of Chile.

The Eye came to dinner at my house once. My mother liked him and The Eye returned her affection by taking family photos from time to time: my mother and one of her friends, my sister and me. Everyone likes to be photographed, he once told me. At the time I thought, I don't care one way or the other, but on reflection I decided he was right. The only people who don't like it are certain Indians, he said. My mother thought he was talking about the Mapuche, but in fact he meant Indians from India, a country that was to play a major part in his life.

One night I ran into him in the Café La Habana. There was hardly anyone else there and The Eye was sitting by the windows that look out on to the Avenida Bucareli, with a white coffee in one of those big, thick glasses they used to have at La Habana (I've never come across them in any other café or restaurant). I sat down next to him and we talked for a while. He seemed translucent. That was the impression I had. The Eye seemed to be made of some vitreous material. His face and the glass of white coffee in front of him seemed to be exchanging signals: two incomprehensible phenomena whose paths had just crossed at that point in the vast universe, making valiant but probably vain attempts to find a common language.

That night he confessed to me that he was homosexual, just as the exiled Chileans had been whispering, and that he was leaving Mexico. For a moment I thought he was leaving *because* he was homosexual. But no, a friend had found him a job with a photographic agency in Paris, the sort of work he had always dreamed of. He was in the mood for talking and I listened. He said that for years he had felt guilty and hidden his sexuality, mainly because he considered himself a socialist and there was a certain degree of prejudice among his friends on the left. We talked about the antiquated word 'invert', which conjured up desolate landscapes, and the term 'ponce', which I would have written with a 'c', while The Eye thought it was spelt with an 's'.

I remember we ended up railing against the Chilean left, and at one point I proposed a toast to the 'wandering warriors of Chile', a substantial subset of the 'wandering warriors of Latin America', a legion of orphans, who, as the name suggests, wander the face of the earth offering their services to the highest bidder, who is almost always the lowest as well. But when we finished laughing, The Eye said violence wasn't for him. I'm not like you, he said, with a sadness I didn't understand at the time, I hate violence.

I assured him that I did too. Then we started talking about other things: books and films, and after that we didn't see each other again.

One day I heard that The Eye had left Mexico. One of his former colleagues from the newspaper told me. I wasn't surprised that he hadn't said goodbye. The Eye never said goodbye to anyone. I never said goodbye to anyone either. None of my Mexican friends ever did. For my mother, however, it was a clear case of bad manners.

Two or three years later, I left Mexico, too. I went to Paris, where I tried (not very hard, admittedly) to find The Eye, without success. As time went by I began to forget what he looked like, although I still had a vague sense of his bearing and his manner. There was a certain way of expressing opinions, as if from a distance, sadly but gently, that I went on associating with The Eye, and even when his face had disappeared or receded into shadow, that essence lingered in my memory: a way of moving, an almost abstract entity in which there was no place for calm.

Years went by. Many years. Some friends died. I got married, had a child, published some books.

At one point I had to go to Berlin. On my last night there, after dinner with Heinrich von Berenberg and his family, I took a taxi to my hotel (as a rule Heinrich drove me back at night) and told the driver to stop before we got there, because I felt like a walk. The driver (an elderly Asian man who was listening to Beethoven) dropped me about five blocks from the hotel. It wasn't very late, but there was hardly anyone about. I walked across a square. The Eye was sitting on a bench. I didn't recognise him until he spoke to me. He called my name and asked me how I was. I turned around and looked at him for a few moments without realising who it was. He remained seated on the bench, looking at me, then he glanced down at the ground or to the side, at the huge trees crowding that little square in Berlin and at the shadows that surrounded him more densely than me (or so I thought). I took two steps towards him and asked who he was. It's me, Mauricio Silva, he said. The Eye, I asked, from Chile? He nodded, and only then did I see him smile.

That night we talked almost until dawn. The Eye had been living in Berlin for some years and knew where to find the bars that stayed open all night. I asked him about his life. He gave me a general idea of the freelance photographer's lot. He had lived in Paris, Milan, and now Berlin, in small flats, where his books kept each other company much of the year. It was only when we went into the first bar that I could tell how much he had changed. He was a lot thinner, his hair was going grey, and wrinkles had creased his face. I also noticed that he drank much more than he used to in Mexico. He wanted to know about me. Our meeting had not been a coincidence, of course. My name had been in the newspapers, and The Eye had seen it, or someone had told him that one of his compatriots was giving a reading or a talk, which he couldn't attend, but he rang the organisers and found out where I was staying. He told me he'd been sitting there in the square thinking while he waited for me to turn up.

I laughed. I was very glad to have met him again. The Eye was the same as ever: an odd person, but good-natured and unassuming. You felt you could say goodbye to him at any time of the night and he would simply say good-bye, without reproach or ill feeling. He was the ideal Chilean, stoic and amiable, a type that has never been very numerous in Chile but cannot be found anywhere else.

Reading over the previous sentence I realise that it is not strictly true. The Eye would never have made such a sweeping generalisation. In any case, the conversation we had, sitting in various bars, he with his whisky and I with my non-alcoholic beer, was made up essentially of recollections; it was, in other words, a confessional and melancholic dialogue. But the most interesting part for me, which was more like a monologue, came as we were returning to my hotel, around two in the morning, and coincidentally it began just as we were crossing the square in which we had met a few hours before. I remember that it was cold and that suddenly The Eye started talking, saying he wanted to tell me something he had never told anyone else. I looked at him. His gaze was fixed on the paved path winding across the square. I asked him what he wanted to tell me about. A trip, he replied immediately. And what happened on this trip? I asked. Then The Eye stopped and for a few moments nothing seemed to exist for him except the tops of the tall German trees and, above them, the fragments of sky and silently seething clouds.

Something terrible, said The Eye. Do you remember a conversation we had in the Café La Habana before I left Mexico? Yes, I said. Did I tell you I was gay? asked The Eye. You said you were homosexual, I said. Let's sit down, said The Eye.

He sat down on the very same bench as before, I swear, as if I still hadn't arrived, as if I hadn't yet started to cross the square and he was still waiting for me and thinking about his life and the story that he was compelled, by history or destiny or chance, to tell me. He turned up the collar of his coat and began to talk. I remained standing and lit a cigarette. The Eye's story was set in India. He had gone there for work, not as a tourist, and he had two assignments. The first was typical third world photo-journalism, a mixture of Marguerite Duras and Hermann Hesse (we smiled); there are people who like to imagine India as a cross between *India Song* and *Siddhartha*, he said, and we have to give the editors what they want. So the first assignment consisted of photos of colonial houses, derelict gardens, all sorts of restaurants, especially the seedier kind (or rather restaurants that looked seedy but were in fact normal Indian family restaurants); photos of the city outskirts, the really poor areas, then the country and the transport system: roads, railway junctions, buses and trains arriving and departing; and nature of course, in a dormant state quite unlike Western hibernation, trees that were clearly non-European, rivers and streams, bare fields and fields sown with crops, the Land of Holy Men, said The Eye.

The second assignment took him to the prostitutes' district in an Indian city whose name I will never know.

And that was where The Eye's story really began. He was still living in Paris at the time and had been commissioned to take photos to illustrate a text written by a well-known French writer who had become a specialist in the underworld of prostitution. In fact, the assignment was only the first of a series, which would cover red-light districts around the world, each one shot by a different photographer, but all described by the same writer.

I don't know which city The Eye flew into, Bombay maybe, or Calcutta, perhaps Benares or Madras; I remember I asked him, but he ignored my question. Anyway, he arrived in India on his own, because the Frenchman had already written his text and he simply had to illustrate it, so he went to the districts mentioned in the text and started taking photographs. According to his plans – and the plans of his publisher – the work, and consequently his visit to India, shouldn't have lasted more than a week. He stayed in a hotel in a quiet part of town. His room was air-conditioned and the window looked on to a garden that didn't belong to the hotel, where he could see two trees on either side of a fountain and part of a terrace on which two women would sometimes appear, followed or preceded by several little boys. The women were dressed in what The Eye took to be traditional Indian style, but not the boys; once he even saw them wearing ties. In the afternoons he went to the red-light district, took photos and talked to the prostitutes, some of whom were very young and beautiful, while others were older or more faded, with the air of sceptical, laconic matrons. He came to like the smell, which had bothered him at first. The pimps (whom he rarely saw) were friendly and carried themselves like Western pimps or perhaps (but this thought only occurred to him later, in his air-conditioned hotel room) it was the other way around: Western pimps had adopted the body language of their Indian counterparts.

One afternoon he was invited to have sexual intercourse with one of the prostitutes. He refused politely. The pimp understood immediately that The Eye was homosexual and the next night took him to a brothel where there were young male prostitutes. That night The Eye fell sick. It was only then, he said, examining the shadows in that Berlin square, that I really knew I was in India. What did you do? I asked. Nothing. I looked and smiled. And did nothing. Then it occurred to one of the boys that perhaps their guest would like to visit another kind of establishment. Or that is what The Eye supposed, because they didn't speak English amongst themselves. So they left the brothel and walked through narrow, filthy streets until they came to a building with a small façade, behind which lay a labyrinth of dim passages and tiny rooms, with altars and shrines emerging here and there from the gloom.

It is customary in some parts of India, said The Eye, looking at the ground, to offer a young boy to a deity whose name I can't remember. I regret to say that here I interrupted to point out that as well as having forgotten the name of the deity, he couldn't remember the name of the city or any of the people in his story. The Eye looked at me and smiled. I've tried to forget, he said.

At that point I started to fear the worst. I sat down beside him and for a while we remained there in silence with our coat collars turned up. After looking around the square as if he were afraid a stranger might be lurking in the shadows, he resumed his story. They make an offering of this boy and he becomes the incarnation of the god, for a time, I couldn't say how long. Maybe only as long as the procession lasts, maybe a week, a month, a year, I don't know. It's a barbaric ceremony, forbidden by Indian law, but that doesn't stop it happening. During the festival the boy is showered with gifts, which his parents, who are generally poor, are only too glad to accept. When the festival is over the boy is sent back to his house, or the filthy hovel he lives in, and in a year's time it all begins again.

Outwardly the ceremony is like a Latin American pilgrimage, but perhaps more joyful, more turbulent, and for the participants, those who know what they're participating in, the experience is probably more intense. But there is one major difference. A few days before the festivities begin, they castrate the boy. The god whose incarnation he is to be during the festival requires a male body – although the boys are usually no more than seven years old – purified of the male sexual organs. So the parents hand him over to the festival doctors, or barbers, or priests, and they emasculate him, and when the boy has recovered from the operation, the festival begins. Weeks or months later, when it is all over, the boy goes home, but now he is a eunuch and his parents reject him. So he ends up in a brothel. These brothels vary; there are all sorts, said The Eye with a sigh. That night, they took me to the very worst.

For a while we said nothing. I lit a cigarette. Then The Eye described the brothel for me and it was as if he were describing a church. Covered interior courtyards. Open galleries. Cells from which hidden eyes watch your every move. They brought him a eunuch who couldn't have been more than ten years old. He looked like a terrified little girl, said The Eye. Terrified and taunting at the same time. Do you understand what I'm saying? Sort of, I said. We fell silent again. When I was finally able to speak I said, No, I have no idea. Neither do I, said The Eye. No one can have any idea. Not the victim. Not the people who did it to him. Not the people who watched. Only a photo . . .

You took a photo of him? I asked. A shiver seemed to run down The Eye's spine. I got out my camera, he said, and I took a photo of him. I knew I was condemning myself for all eternity, but I did it.

I don't know how long we sat there in silence after that. I know it was cold and at one point I began to shiver. Once or twice I heard The Eye sob beside me, but I didn't want to look at him. I saw the headlights of a car driving down one side of the square. Through the foliage I saw a light come on in a window.

Then The Eye went on with his story. He said the boy smiled, then quietly slipped away down one of the passages of that baffling edifice. At some point a pimp suggested that if none of the boys took his fancy, he should go. But The Eye said no. He couldn't leave. That's what he said to him: I can't leave yet. And it was true, though he didn't know what was stopping him from walking straight out of that lair. The pimp, however, seemed to understand and ordered tea or some such beverage. The Eye remembers that they sat down on the floor, on mats or worn-out rugs. The room was lit by a pair of candles. A poster of the god hung on a wall.

For a while The Eye looked at the god and at first he felt fear, but then he felt something like rage, or perhaps hate.

I have never hated anyone, he said, lighting a cigarette and blowing the first breath of smoke out into the Berlin night.

At one point, while The Eye was staring at the image of the god, the others disappeared, leaving him alone with a male prostitute about twenty years old, who spoke English. Then, summoned by a couple of claps, the eunuch reappeared. I was crying, or thought I was, said The Eye, or maybe that's what the prostitute thought, poor kid, but none of it was true. I tried to keep a smile on my face (although it wasn't *my* face any more, I could feel it drifting away from me like a leaf on the wind), and all this time, underneath, I was scheming. Not that I had a plan, or any idea of redress, just a blind determination.

The Eye, the prostitute, and the eunuch stood up and walked down a dimly lit corridor, then another more dimly lit still (the eunuch at The Eye's side, watching him and smiling, the prostitute smiling at him too, as The Eye nodded and emptied the money from his pockets into their hands) until they reached a room in which the doctor was dozing beside a boy who was younger than the eunuch, maybe six or seven years old, and had darker skin, and The Eye listened to the doctor's long-winded explanations, invoking tradition, ritual, privilege, communion, elation, and saintliness, and he could see the surgical instruments with which the child would be castrated the following morning or the morning after, in any case the child had come to the temple or the brothel that day, he gathered – a preventive or hygienic measure – and had eaten well, as if he were already the god's incarnation, although what The Eye saw was a drowsy, tearful child, and the eunuch, who was still at his side, with a half-amused half-terrified look on his face. Then The Eye was transformed into something else, although the expression he used was not 'something else' but 'mother'.

Mother, he said and sighed. At last. Mother.

What happened next is all too familiar: the violence from which there is no escape. The lot of Latin Americans born in the fifties. Naturally, The Eye tried to negotiate, bribe, and threaten, without much hope of success. All I know for certain is that there was violence and soon he was out of there, leaving the streets of that district behind, as if in a dream, drenched with sweat. He vividly remembers the feeling of exaltation welling up inside him, stronger and stronger, a joy that felt dangerously like lucidity, but wasn't (couldn't have been). Also, the shadows they cast on to the peeling walls, he and the two boys he was leading by the hand. Anywhere else he would have attracted attention. There, at that time of night, no one took any notice of him.

The rest is more an itinerary than a story or a plot. The Eye went back to the hotel, packed his suitcase and left with the boys. First they took a taxi to a town or a suburb on the outskirts. Then a bus to another town, where they caught a second bus that took them to yet another town. At some point in their flight they boarded a train and travelled all night and part of the following day. The Eye remembered the faces of the boys looking out at a landscape frayed by the morning light, as if all that had ever really existed were the stately and humble scenes framed by the window of that mysterious train.

Then they took another bus, a taxi, a bus again, another train; they even hitch-hiked, said The Eye, gazing at the silhouettes of the German trees but seeing, beyond them, the silhouettes of other trees, countless and incomprehensible. Finally they came to rest in a village somewhere in India, where they rented a house.

After two months The Eye's money ran out and he walked to a neighbouring village, where he sent a letter to the friend he had left behind in Paris. A fortnight later he received a bank draft. To cash it he had to go to a town bigger than the village where he had gone to send the letter and much bigger than the one where he lived. The boys were well. They played with other children but did not go to school, and sometimes they came back to the house with food: vegetables the neighbours had given them. Instead of calling him father, he had the boys call him The Eye, as we used to; he thought it safer, less likely to attract the attention of the curious. He did, however, tell the villagers that they were his sons. His story was that the boy's mother, an Indian woman, had recently died, and he didn't want to go back to Europe. It was believable. Yet The Eye had nightmares about the Indian police coming to arrest him, making shameful accusations. He would wake up trembling. He would go over to the mats where they boys were sleeping, and the sight of them gave him the strength to carry on, to sleep, get up and face another day.

He became a farmer. He tended a small orchard and occasionally worked for the richer farmers in the village. They too were poor, of course, but not as poor as the others. He spent the rest of his time teaching the boys English and a little maths, and watching them play. He could not understand a word of the language they spoke to each other. Sometimes, when he was watching them play, they would stop and wander off across the fields like sleepwalkers. He would call out to them. Sometimes the boys pretended not to hear and kept walking until they disappeared. Other times they turned back and smiled at him.

How long were you in India? I asked, getting worried.

About a year and a half, said The Eye, I'm not exactly sure.

Once his friend from Paris came to the village. He still loved me, said The Eye, although in my absence he had set up house with an Algerian mechanic who worked for Renault. Telling me this, he laughed. So did I. It was all so sad, said The Eye. His friend arriving in the village in a taxi covered with red dust, the boys chasing after an insect in the dry scrub, the wind, it seemed, bearing good news and bad.

In spite of his friend's entreaties, he did not return to Paris. Months later a letter arrived from France informing him that he was not wanted by the Indian police. Apparently no one had reported the incident at the brothel. This news did not put an end to The Eye's nightmares. The characters who came to arrest and brutalise him simply changed their clothes: instead of policemen, now they were thugs from the sect of the castrated god. Which turned out to be even more horrifying, The Eye confessed, although by then he was used to the nightmares and at some level always knew that he was dreaming, that it wasn't real.

Then the disease came to the village and the boys died. I wanted to die too, said The Eye, but I wasn't that lucky.

After convalescing in a hut that was steadily being destroyed by the rain, The Eye left the village and returned to the city where he had met his children. He was somewhat surprised to discover that it was not nearly as far away as he had thought; his flight had followed a spiral path and the return journey was relatively short. On the afternoon of his return, he went to see the brothel where boys used to be castrated. Its rooms had been converted into lodgings for entire families. The corridors he remembered as lonely and funereal were now swarming with life, from toddling children to old men and women who could barely drag themselves along. To him it was an image of paradise.

That night when he went back to his hotel, he wept for his dead children and all the other castrated boys, for his own lost youth, for those who were young no longer and those who died young, for those who fought for Salvador Allende and those who were too scared to fight. Unable to stop crying, he called his French friend, who was now living with a former weightlifter from Bulgaria, and asked him to send an air ticket and some money for the hotel.

And his friend said yes, of course he would, straight away, and then: What's that sound? Are you crying? And The Eye said yes, he couldn't stop crying, he didn't know what was happening to him, he had been crying for hours. His French friend told him to calm down. At this The Eye, still crying, laughed, said he would do that and hung up. But he went on crying, and couldn't stop.

Gómez Palacio

I WENT TO GÓMEZ PALACIO DURING ONE OF THE worst phases of my life. I was twenty-three years old and I knew that my days in Mexico were numbered.

My friend Montero, who worked for the Arts Council, had found me a job teaching a writing workshop in that town, with its hideous name. First, to warm up, so to speak, I had to do a tour of the writing workshops the Arts Council had established in various places throughout the region. A bit of a holiday in the north to start off, said Montero, then you can get down to work in Gómez Palacio and forget all your problems. I don't know why I accepted. I knew that under no circumstances would I settle down in Gómez Palacio. I knew I wouldn't stay long running a writing workshop in some godforsaken town in northern Mexico.

One morning I left Mexico City in a bus packed to capacity and began my tour. I went to San Luis Potosí, Aguascalientes, Guanajuato, León – not necessarily in that order; I can't remember which town came first or how long I spent in each. Then Torreón and Saltillo. I went to Durango as well.

Finally I arrived in Gómez Palacio and visited the Arts Council offices, where I met my future students. I couldn't stop shivering in spite of the heat. The director, a plump, middle-aged woman with bulging eyes, wearing a large dress of printed fabric featuring almost all of the state's native flowers, took me to my lodgings: a frightful motel on the edge of town, beside a highway leading nowhere.

She used to come and pick me up herself mid-morning. She had an enormous, sky-blue car, which she drove perhaps rather too boldly, although generally speaking she wasn't a bad driver. It was an automatic and her feet hardly reached the pedals. Invariably, the first thing we did was to stop at a roadside restaurant that was visible in the distance from the motel, a reddish bump on the blue and yellow horizon. There we breakfasted on orange juice and Mexican-style eggs, followed by several cups of coffee, all paid for (I presume) with Arts Council vouchers – not cash, in any case.

Then she would lean back on her chair and start talking about her life in that northern town, her poetry, which had been published by a small local press subsidised by the Arts Council, and her husband, who didn't understand the poet's calling or the suffering it entailed. Meanwhile I chain-smoked Bali cigarettes, looking out of the window at the highway and thinking about the disaster that was my life. Then we'd get back into her car and head off to the main office of the Arts Council in Gómez Palacio, a two-storey building whose only redeeming feature was an unpaved yard with a grand total of three trees and an abandoned or unfinished garden, swarming with zombie-like adolescents who were studying painting, music, or literature. The first time I hardly noticed the yard. The second time it made me shudder. None of this makes any sense, I thought, but deep down I knew it did make sense and that was what I found unbearably sad, to use a rather hyperbolic expression, though it seemed perfectly accurate at the time. Maybe I was confusing sense with necessity. Maybe I was just a nervous wreck.

I found it hard to get to sleep at night. I had nightmares. Before going to bed, I would make sure the door and windows of my room were securely and tightly shut. My throat kept feeling dry and the only solution was to drink water. I was continually getting up and going to the bathroom to refill my glass. Since I was up, I would check the door and windows again to see that they were properly shut. Sometimes I forgot my fears and stayed by the window, looking out at the desert stretching away into the dark. Then I went back to bed and closed my eyes, but having drunk so much water I soon had to get up again to urinate. And since I was up, I would check all the locks and then stand still listening to the distant sounds of the desert (the muffled hum of cars heading north or south) or looking out of the window at the night. And so on until dawn, when I could finally get some unbroken sleep, two or three hours at most.

One morning while we were having breakfast, the director asked about my eyes. It's because I don't sleep much, I said. Yes, they're bloodshot, she said, and changed the subject. That afternoon, as she was taking me back to the motel, she asked if I would like to drive for a bit. I don't know how to drive, I said. She burst out laughing and pulled up on the shoulder. A white refrigerated truck went past. I managed to read what was written on the side in large blue letters: THE WIDOW PADILLA'S MEAT. The truck had Monterrey number plates and the driver stared at us with a curiosity that struck me as excessive. The director opened her door and got out. Get in the driver's seat, she said. I obeyed. As I gripped the wheel I saw her walk around the back of the car. Then she got into the passenger seat and ordered me to get going.

For a long time I drove along the grey strip connecting Gómez Palacio and the motel. When I reached the motel I didn't stop. I looked at the director; she was smiling, she didn't mind me driving a bit further. To begin with, both of us had stared at the highway in silence. But when we passed the motel she started talking about her poetry, her work, and her insensitive husband. When she had said her piece, she put a cassette into the player and turned it on:

a woman singing *rancheras*. She had a sad voice that was always a couple of notes ahead of the orchestra. I'm her friend, said the director. I didn't understand. What? I said. She's a close friend of mine, said the director. Ah. She's from Durango, she said. You've been there, haven't you? Yes, I've been to Durango, I said. And what were the writing workshops like? Worse than the ones here, I replied, meaning it as a compliment, although she didn't seem to take it that way. She's from Durango, but she lives in Ciudad Juárez, she said. Sometimes, when she's going back home to see her mother, she rings me and I reorganise things so I can go to Durango and spend a few days with her. That's nice, I said, keeping my eyes on the road. I stay at her house – her mother's house, actually, said the director. The two of us sleep in her room, and spend hours talking and listening to records. Every now and then one of us goes to the kitchen to make coffee. I usually take biscuits with me, La Regalada biscuits, her favourite. And we drink coffee and eat biscuits. We've known each other since we were fifteen. She's my best friend.

On the horizon I could see the highway disappearing into a range of hills. The night was beginning to approach from the east. Days before, at the motel, I had asked myself, What colour is the desert at night? A stupid rhetorical question, yet somehow I felt it held the key to my future, or perhaps not so much my future as my capacity for suffering. One afternoon, at the writing workshop in Gómez

Palacio, a boy asked me how I came to start writing poetry and how long I thought I would go on doing it. The director wasn't present. There were five other people in the workshop, the five students: four boys and a girl. You could tell from the way they dressed that two of them were very poor. The girl was short and thin and her clothes were rather garish. The boy who asked the question should have been studying at a university; instead of which he was working in a factory, the biggest and probably the only soap factory in the state. Another boy was a waiter in an Italian restaurant, the remaining two were at college, and the girl was neither studying nor working.

By chance, I replied. For a while none of us said anything. I considered the possibility of taking a job in Gómez Palacio and staying there for the rest of my life. I had noticed a couple of pretty girls among the painting students in the yard. With a bit of luck I might have been able to marry one of them. The prettier one also seemed to be the more conventional. I imagined a long, complicated engagement. I imagined a dark, cool house and a garden full of plants. And how long do you think you'll go on writing? asked the boy who worked in the soap factory. I could have said anything, but opted for simplicity: I don't know, I said. What about you? I started writing because poetry sets me free, sir, and I'm never going to stop, he said with a smile that barely hid his pride and determination. As an answer it was too vague and declamatory to be convincing, yet somehow it gave me a glimpse of the factory worker's life, not as it was then, but the life he had led at the age of fifteen, or maybe twelve. I saw him running or walking through the out-skirts of Gómez Palacio, under a sky that looked like a rockslide. I saw his friends and wondered how they could possibly survive. Yet, one way or another, they probably had.

Then we read some poems. The only one who had any talent was the girl. But by then I wasn't sure of anything. When we came out of the room, the director was waiting with two guys who turned out to be civil servants employed by the state of Durango. For some reason my first thought was, They're policemen, here to arrest me. The kids said goodbye and off they went, the skinny girl with one of the boys, and the other three on their own. I watched them walk down the hallway with its peeling walls. I followed, as if I had forgotten to say something to one of them. And from the door I saw them disappear at opposite ends of that street in Gómez Palacio.

The director said: She's my best friend. That was all. The highway was no longer a straight line. In the rear-view mirror I could see an enormous wall rising beyond the town. It took me a while to realise it was the night. The singer on the cassette began to warble another song. The lyrics were about a remote village in the north of Mexico where everyone was happy, except her. I had the impression the director was crying. Silent, dignified, unstoppable tears. But I couldn't confirm this impression. I had to keep my eyes on the road. The director took out a handkerchief and blew her nose. Switch the headlights on, I heard her say in a barely audible voice. I kept on driving.

Switch on the headlights, she repeated, and without waiting for an answer she leant forward and did so herself. Slow down, she said after a while, her voice stronger now, as the singer reached the final notes of her song. What a sad song, I said, just for something to say.

The car came to a halt by the side of the road. I opened the door and got out. It wasn't yet completely dark, but it was no longer day. The land all around us and the hills into which the highway went winding were a deep, intense shade of yellow that I have never seen anywhere else. As if the light (though it seemed to me not so much light as pure colour) were charged with something, I didn't know what, but it could well have been eternity. I was immediately embarrassed to have had such a thought. I stretched my legs. A car whizzed past honking its horn. I told him where to go with a gesture. Maybe it wasn't just a gesture. Maybe I yelled, Go fuck yourself, and the driver saw or heard me. But it's unlikely, like most things in this story. In any case, when I think about the driver, all I can see is my own image frozen in his rear-view mirror: my hair is still long; I'm thin, wearing a denim jacket and a pair of awful, oversize glasses.

The car pulled up several metres in front of us. The driver didn't get out, or reverse, or honk the horn again, but his mere presence seemed to distend the space that we were now, in some sense, sharing with him. Cautiously, I walked around to the director's side of the car. She wound down her window and asked me what had happened. Her eyes were bulging more than ever. I said I didn't know. It's a man, she said, and slid across into the driver's seat. I got into the seat she had left empty. It was hot and moist, as if the director had a fever. Through the windscreen I could see the man's silhouette, the nape of his neck; like us he was looking ahead, at the line of the highway beginning to wind its way towards the hills.

It's my husband, said the director, her eyes fixed on the stationary car, as if she were talking to herself. Then she flipped the cassette over and turned up the volume. Sometimes my friend rings me up, she said, when she's touring in towns she doesn't know. Once she rang from Ciudad Madero. She'd been singing all night at the Oil Workers' Union building and she rang me at four in the morning. Another time she rang from Reinosa. That's nice, I said. Not especially, said the director. She just rings. Sometimes she needs to talk. If my husband answers, she hangs up.

For a while neither of us said anything. I imagined the director's husband with the telephone in his hand. He picks up the telephone, says, Hello, who is it? Then he hears someone hang up at the other end and he hangs up too, almost by reflex. I asked the director if she wanted me to get out and say something to the driver of the other car. There's no need, she said. Which seemed a reasonable answer to me, although in fact it was mad. I asked her what her husband was going to do, if it was really her husband. He'll stay there until we go, said the director. Then we'd better go straight away, I said. The director seemed to be lost in thought, although much later I surmised that, in fact, all she was doing was shutting her eyes and listening to her friend from Durango, drinking that song down to the very last drop. Then she switched on the ignition, pulled out slowly and passed the car parked several metres ahead. I looked through the window as we went past, but the driver turned his back to us and I couldn't see his face.

Are you sure it was your husband? I asked as we sped off again towards the hills. No, said the director, and started laughing. I don't think it was. I started laughing too. The car was like his, she said, almost choking with laughter, but it probably wasn't him. So it might have been? I said. Not unless he's changed his number plates, said the director. At which point I understood that the whole thing had been a joke. I shut my eyes. Then we came out of the hills and into the desert: a plain swept by the headlights of cars heading north or back towards Gómez Palacio. It was already night.

Now we're coming to a very special place, said the director. Those were her words. Very special.

I wanted you to see this, she said proudly, this is one of my favourite things. She pulled over and stopped in a sort of rest area, although it was really no more than a patch of ground big enough for trucks to park on. Lights were sparkling in the distance: a town or a restaurant. We didn't get out. The director pointed in the direction of something. A stretch of highway that must have been about five kilometres from where we were, maybe less, maybe more. She even wiped the inside of the windscreen with a cloth so I could see better. I looked: I saw the headlights of cars. From the way the beams of light were swivelling, there must have been a bend in the highway. And then I saw some green shapes in the desert. Did you see? asked the director. Yes, lights, I replied. The director looked at me: her bulging eyes gleamed, as do, no doubt, the eyes of the small mammals native to the inhospitable environs of Gómez Palacio in the state of Durango. Then I looked again in the direction she had indicated: at first I couldn't see anything, only darkness, the sparkling lights of that restaurant or town, then some cars went past and the beams of their headlights carved the space in two.

Their progress was exasperatingly slow, but we were beyond exasperation.

And then I saw how the light, seconds after the car or truck had passed that spot, turned back on itself and hung in the air, a green light that seemed to breathe, alive and aware for a fraction of a second in the middle of the desert, set free, a marine light, moving like the sea but with all the fragility of earth, a green, prodigious, solitary light, that must have been produced by something near that curve in the road – a sign, the roof of an abandoned shed, huge sheets of plastic spread on the ground – but that, to us, seeing it from a distance, appeared to be a dream or a miracle, which comes to the same thing, in the end.

Then the director started the car, turned it around and drove back to the motel.

I was to leave for Mexico City the next day. When we arrived at the motel, the director got out of the car and came with me part of the way. Before we reached my room she held out her hand and said goodbye. I know you'll forgive my eccentricities, she said, after all we both read poetry. I was grateful she hadn't said we were both poets. When I got to my room I switched on the light, took off my jacket, and drank some water straight from the tap. Then I went to the window. Her car was still in the parking lot. I opened the door and was hit in the face by a gust of desert air. The car was empty. A little further off, beside the highway, I saw the director, who looked as if she were contemplating a river or the landscape of another planet. From the way she was standing with her arms slightly raised, she might have been talking to the air or reciting, or playing statues like a young girl.

I didn't sleep well. At dawn the director herself came to fetch me. She took me to the bus station and told me that if eventually I accepted the job, I would be very welcome at the workshop. I said I would have to think about it. She said that was fine, best to think things over. Then she said, A hug. I bent down and hugged her. The seat I had been given was on the other side of the bus, so I didn't see her leave. The last thing I remember, vaguely, is her standing there, looking at the bus or perhaps at her watch. Then I had to sit down so the other passengers could get past or settle into their seats, and when I looked again she was gone.

Last Evenings on Earth

THIS IS THE SITUATION: B AND HIS FATHER
are going to Acapulco on holiday. They are planning to leave very early, at six in the morning.
B sleeps the previous night at his father's house. He doesn't
dream or if he does he forgets his dreams as soon as he
opens his eyes. He hears his father in the bathroom. He
looks out of the window; it is still dark. He gets dressed
without switching on the light. When he comes out of his
room, his father is sitting at the table, reading the sports
news from the day before, and breakfast is ready. Coffee
and ranch-style eggs. B says hello to his father and goes
into the bathroom.

His father's car is a 1970 Ford Mustang. At six-thirty in
the morning they get into the car and head out of the city.
The city is Mexico City, and the year in which B and his
father leave Mexico City for a short holiday is 1975.

Overall, the trip goes smoothly. Leaving the city both
father and son feel cold, but as they leave the high valley

behind and begin to descend into the state of Guerrero, the temperature rises and they have to take off their sweaters and open the windows. B, who is inclined to melancholy (or so he likes to think), is at first completely absorbed in contemplating the landscape, but after a few hours the mountains and forests become monotonous and he starts reading a book instead.

Before they get to Acapulco, B's father pulls up in front of a roadside café. The café serves iguana. Shall we try it? he suggests. The iguanas are alive and they hardly move when B's father goes over to look at them. B leans against the mudguard of the Mustang, watching him. Without waiting for an answer, B's father orders a portion of iguana for himself and one for his son. Only then does B move away from the car. He approaches the open-air eating area – four tables under a canvas shade that is swaying slightly in the gentle breeze – and sits down at the table furthest from the highway. B's father orders two beers. Father and son have rolled up their sleeves and unbuttoned their shirts. Both are wearing light-coloured shirts. The waiter, by contrast, is wearing a black, long-sleeved shirt and doesn't seem bothered by the heat.

Going to Acapulco? asks the waiter. B's father nods. They are the only customers at the café. Cars whiz past on the bright highway. B's father gets up and goes out the back. For a moment B thinks his father is going to the toilet, but then he realises he has gone to the kitchen to see how they cook the iguanas. The waiter follows him without a word. Then B hears them talking. First his father, then the man's voice, and finally the voice of a woman B can't see. B's forehead is beaded with sweat. His glasses are misted and dirty. He takes them off and cleans them with the corner of his shirt. When he puts them back on he notices his father watching him from the kitchen. He can see only his father's face and part of his shoulder, the rest is hidden by a red curtain with black dots, and B has the intermittent impression that this curtain separates not only the kitchen from the eating area but also one time from another.

Then B looks away and his gaze returns to the book lying on the table. It is a book of poetry. An anthology of French surrealist poets translated into Spanish by the Argentine surrealist Aldo Pellegrini. B has been reading this book for two days. He likes it. He likes the photos of the poets. The photo of Unik, the one of Desnos, the photos of Artaud and Crevel. The book is thick and covered with transparent plastic. It wasn't covered by B (who never covers his books), but by a particularly fastidious friend. So B looks away from his father, opens the book at random and comes face to face with Gui Rosey, the photo of Gui Rosey and his poems, and when he looks up again his father's head has disappeared.

The heat is stifling. B would be more than happy to go back to Mexico City, but he isn't going back, at least not yet, he knows that. Soon his father is sitting next to him and they are both eating iguana with chilli sauce and drinking more beer. The waiter in the black shirt has turned on a transistor radio, and now some vaguely tropical music is blending with the noises of the jungle and the noise of the cars passing on the highway. The iguana tastes like chicken. It's tougher than chicken, says B, not entirely convinced. It's tasty, says his father, and orders another portion. They have cinnamon coffee. The man in the black shirt serves the iguana, but the woman from the kitchen brings out the coffee. She is young, almost as young as B; she is wearing white shorts and a yellow blouse with white flowers printed on it, flowers B doesn't recognise, perhaps because they don't exist. As they drink their coffee, B feels nauseous, but he says nothing. He smokes and looks at the canvas shade, barely moving, as if weighed down by a narrow puddle of rainwater from the last storm. But it can't be that, thinks B. What are you looking at? asks his father. The shade, says B. It's like a vein. But he doesn't say the bit about the vein, he only thinks it.

They arrive in Acapulco as night is falling. For a while they drive up and down the avenues by the sea with the windows wide open and the breeze ruffling their hair. They stop at a bar and go in for a drink. This time B's father orders tequila. B thinks for a moment. Then he orders tequila too. The bar is modern and has air-conditioning. B's father talks to the waiter and asks him about hotels near the beach. By the time they get back to the Mustang a few stars are visible and for the first time that day B's father looks tired. Even so, they visit a couple of hotels, which for one reason or another are unsatisfactory, before finding one that will do. The hotel is called La Brisa: it's small, a stone's throw from the beach, and has a swimming-pool. B's father likes the hotel. So does B. It's the off season, so the hotel is almost empty and the prices are reasonable. The room they are given has two single beds and a small bathroom with a shower. The only window looks on to the terrace, where the swimming-pool is. B's father would have preferred a sea view. The air-conditioning, they soon discover, is out of order. But the room is fairly cool, so they don't complain. They make themselves at home: each opens up his suitcase and puts his clothes in the wardrobe. B leaves his books on the bedside table. They change their shirts. B's father takes a cold shower while B just washes his face, and when they are ready they go out to dinner.

The reception desk is manned by a short guy with teeth like a rabbit. He's young and seems friendly. He recommends a restaurant near the hotel. B's father asks if there's somewhere lively nearby. B understands what his father means. The receptionist doesn't. A place with a bit of action, says B's father. A place where you can find girls, says B. Ah, says the receptionist. For a moment B and his father stand there, without speaking. The receptionist crouches down, disappearing behind the counter, and re-appears with a card, which he holds out. B's father looks at the card, asks if the establishment is reliable, then extracts a note from his wallet, which the receptionist is quick to intercept.

But after dinner, they go straight back to the hotel.

The next day, B wakes up very early. As quietly as possible he takes a shower, brushes his teeth, puts on his bathing suit, and leaves the room. There is no one in the hotel dining room, so B decides to go out for breakfast. The hotel is on a street that runs straight down to the beach, which is empty except for a boy hiring out paddle boards. B asks him how much it costs for an hour. The boy quotes a price that sounds acceptable, so B hires a board and pushes off into the sea. Opposite the beach is a little island, towards which he steers his craft. At first he has some trouble, but soon he gets the hang of it. At this time of day the sea is crystal clear and B thinks he can see red fishes under the board, about a foot and a half long, swimming towards the beach as he paddles towards the island.

It takes exactly fifteen minutes for him to get from the beach to the island. B doesn't know this, because he is not wearing a watch, and for him time slows down. The crossing seems to last an eternity. At the last minute, waves rear unexpectedly, impeding his approach. The sand is noticeably different from that of the hotel beach; back there it was a golden, tawny colour, perhaps because of the time of day (though B doesn't think so), while here it is a dazzling white, so bright it hurts your eyes to look at it.

B stops paddling and just sits there, at the mercy of the waves, which begin to carry him slowly away from the island. By the time he finally reacts, the board has drifted halfway back. Having ascertained this, B decides to turn around. The return is calm and uneventful. When he gets to the beach, the boy who hires out the boards comes up and asks if he had a problem. Not at all, says B. An hour later B returns to the hotel without having had breakfast and finds his father sitting in the dining room with a cup of coffee and a plate in front of him on which are scattered the remains of toast and eggs.

The following hours are hazy. They drive around aimlessly, watching people from the car. Sometimes they get out to have a cold drink or an ice cream. In the afternoon, on the beach, while his father is stretched out asleep in a deck chair, B rereads Gui Rosey's poems and the brief story of his life or his death.

One day a group of surrealists arrives in the south of France. They try to get visas for the United States. The north and the west of the country are occupied by the Germans. The south is under the aegis of Pétain. Day after day, the US Consulate delays its decision. Among the members of the group are Breton, Tristan Tzara, and

Péret, but there are also less famous figures. Gui Rosey is one of them. In the photo he has the look of a minor poet, thinks B. He is ugly, he is impeccably dressed, he looks like an unimportant public servant or a bank clerk. Up to this point, a few disagreements, but nothing out of the ordinary, thinks B. The surrealists gather every afternoon at a café by the port. They make plans and chat; Rosey is always there. But one day (one afternoon, B imagines), he fails to appear. At first, he isn't missed. He is a minor poet and no one pays much attention to minor poets. After a few days, however, the others start to worry. At the *pension* where he is staying, no one knows what has happened; his suitcases and books are there, undisturbed, so he clearly hasn't tried to leave without paying (as guests at certain *pensions* on the Côte d'Azur are prone to do). His friends try to find him. They visit all the hospitals and police stations in the area. No one can tell them anything. One morning the visas arrive. Most of them board a ship and set off for the United States. Those who remain, who will never get visas, soon forget about Rosey and his disappearance; people are disappearing all the time, in large numbers, and they have to look out for themselves.

That night, after dinner at the hotel, B's father suggests they go and find a bit of action. B looks at his father. He is blond (B is dark), his eyes are grey, and he is still in good shape. He looks happy and ready to have a good time. What sort of action? asks B, who knows perfectly well what his father is referring to. The usual kind, says B's father. Drinking and women. For a while B says nothing, as if he were pondering a reply. His father looks at him. The look might seem inquisitive, but in fact it is only affectionate. Finally B says he's not in the mood for sex. It's not just about getting laid, says his father, we'll go and see, have a few drinks, and enjoy ourselves with some friends. What friends, says B, we don't know anyone here. You always make friends when you're out for a ride. The expression 'out for a ride' makes B think of horses. When he was seven his father bought him a horse. Where did my horse come from? asks B. This takes his father completely by surprise. What horse? he asks. The one you bought me when I was a kid, says B, in Chile. Ah, Hullabaloo, says his father, smiling. He was from the island of Chiloé, he says, then after a moment's reflection he starts talking about brothels again. The way he talks about them, they could be dance halls, thinks B. Then they both fall silent.

That night they don't go anywhere.

While his father is sleeping, B goes out on to the terrace to read by the swimming-pool. There is no one there apart from him. The terrace is clean and empty. From his table B can see part of the reception area, where the receptionist from the night before is standing at the counter reading something or doing the accounts. B reads the

French surrealists, he reads Gui Rosey. To tell the truth, Gui Rosey doesn't interest him much. He is far more interested in Desnos and Éluard, and yet he always ends up coming back to Rosey's poems and looking at his photo, a studio portrait, in which he has the air of a solitary, wretched soul, with his large, glassy eyes and a dark tie that seems to be strangling him.

He must have committed suicide, thinks B. He knew he was never going to get a visa for the States or Mexico, so he decided to end his days there and then. B imagines or tries to imagine a town on the Mediterranean coast of France. He still hasn't been to Europe. He has been all over Latin America, or almost, but he still hasn't set foot in Europe. So his image of a Mediterranean town is derived from his image of Acapulco. Heat, a small, cheap hotel, beaches of golden sand and beaches of white sand. And the distant sound of music. B doesn't realise that there is a crucial element missing from the soundtrack of this scene: the rigging of the small boats that throng the ports of all the towns on the Mediterranean coast, especially the smaller ones. The sound of the rigging at night, when the sea is as still as a mill pond.

Suddenly someone comes on to the terrace. The silhouette of a woman. She sits down at the farthest table, in a corner, near two large urns. A moment later the receptionist appears, bringing her a drink. Then, instead of going back to the counter, he comes over to B, who is sitting by the edge of the pool, and asks if he and his father are having a good time. Very good, says B. Do you like Acapulco? asks the receptionist. Very much, says B. How was the San Diego? asks the receptionist. B doesn't understand the question. The San Diego? For a moment he thinks the receptionist is referring to the hotel, but then he remembers that the hotel is called something else. Which San Diego? asks B. The receptionist smiles. The club with the hookers. Then B remembers the card the receptionist gave his father. We still haven't been, he says. It's a reliable place, says the receptionist. B moves his head in a way that could mean almost anything. It's on Constituyentes, says the receptionist. There's another club on the avenue, the Ramada, but I wouldn't recommend it. The Ramada, says B, watching the woman's motionless figure in the corner of the terrace and the apparently untouched glass in front of her, between the enormous urns, whose shadows stretch and taper off under the neighbouring tables. Best to steer clear of the Ramada, says the receptionist. Why? asks B, for something to say, although he has no intention of visiting either club. It's not reliable, says the receptionist, and his bright little rabbit-like teeth shine in the semi-darkness that has suddenly submerged the terrace, as if someone at reception had switched off half the lights.

When the receptionist goes away, B opens his book of poetry again, but the words are illegible now, so he leaves the book open on the table, shuts his eyes and, instead of the faint chimes of rigging, he hears an atmospheric sound, the sound of enormous layers of hot air descending on the hotel and the surrounding trees. He feels like getting into the pool. For a moment he thinks he might.

Then the woman in the corner stands up and begins to walk towards the stairs that lead from the terrace to the reception area, but she stops midway, as if she felt ill, resting one hand on the edge of a raised bed in which there are no longer flowers, only weeds.

B watches her. The woman is wearing a loose, light-coloured summer dress, cut low, leaving her shoulders bare. He expects her to start walking again, but she stands still, her hand still gripping the edge of the raised bed, looking down, so B gets up with the book in his hand and goes over to her. The first thing that surprises him is her face. She must be about sixty years old, B guesses, although from a distance, he wouldn't have said she was more than thirty. She is North American, and when B approaches she looks up and smiles at him. Good night, she says, rather incongruously, in Spanish. Are you all right? asks B. The woman doesn't understand and B has to ask again, in English. I'm just thinking, says the woman, smiling at him fixedly. For a few seconds B considers what she has said to him. Thinking, thinking, thinking. And suddenly it seems to him that this declaration conceals a threat. Something approaching over the sea. Something advancing in the wake of the dark clouds invisibly crossing the Bay of Acapulco. But he doesn't move or make any attempt to break the spell that seems to be holding him captive. Then the woman looks at the book in B's left hand and asks him what he is reading, and B says: poetry. I'm reading poems. The woman looks him in the eye, with the same smile on her face (a smile at once bright and faded, thinks B, feeling more uneasy by the moment), and says that she used to like poetry, once. Which poets? asks B, keeping absolutely still. I can't remember them now, says the woman, and again she seems to lose herself in the contemplation of something visible only to her. B assumes she is making an effort to remember and waits in silence. After a while she looks at him again and says: Longfellow. And straight away she starts reciting lines with a monotonous rhythm that sound to B like a nursery rhyme, a far cry, in any case, from the poets he is reading. Do you know Longfellow? asks the woman. B shakes his head, although in fact he has read some Longfellow. We did it at school, says the woman, with her immutable smile. And then she adds: It's too hot, don't you think? It is very hot, whispers B. There could be a storm coming, says the woman. There is something very definite about her tone. At this point B looks up: he can't see a single star. But he can see lights in the hotel. And, at the window of his room, a silhouette watching them, which makes him start, as if struck by the first, sudden drops of a tropical downpour.

For a moment he is bewildered.

It's his father, on the other side of the glass, wrapped in a blue dressing-gown that he must have brought with him (B hasn't seen it before and it certainly doesn't belong to the hotel), staring at them, although when B notices him, he steps back, recoiling as if bitten by a snake, lifts his hand in a shy wave, and disappears behind the curtains.

The Song of Hiawatha, says the woman. B looks at her. The Song of Hiawatha, the poem by Longfellow. Ah, yes, says B.

Then the woman says good night and makes a gradual exit: first she goes up the stairs to reception, where she spends a few moments chatting with someone B can't see, then, in silence, she sets off across the hotel lobby, her slim figure framed by successive windows, until she turns into the corridor that leads to the inside stairs.

Half an hour later, B goes back to the room and finds his father asleep. For a few seconds, before going to the bathroom to brush his teeth, B stands very straight at the foot of the bed, gazing at him, as if steeling himself for a fight. Good night, dad, he says. His father gives not the slightest indication that he has heard.

On the second day of their stay in Acapulco, B and his father go to see the cliff divers. They have two options: they can watch the show from an open-air platform or go to the bar-restaurant of the hotel overlooking the precipice. B's father asks about the prices. The first person he asks doesn't know. He persists. Finally an old ex-diver who is hanging around doing nothing tells him what it costs: six times more to watch from the hotel bar. Let's go to the bar, says B's father without hesitating. We'll be more comfortable. B follows him. The other people in the bar are North American or Mexican tourists wearing what are obviously holiday clothes; B and his father stand out. They are dressed as people dress in Mexico City, in clothes that seem to belong to some endless dream. The waiters notice. They know the sort, no chance of a big tip, so they make no effort to serve them promptly. To top it off, B and his father can hardly see the show from where they are sitting. We would have been better off on the platform, says B's father. Although it's not bad here either, he adds. B nods. When the diving is over, having drunk two highballs each, they go outside and start making plans for the rest of the day. Hardly anyone is left on the platform, but B's father recognises the old ex-diver sitting on a buttress and goes over to him.

The ex-diver is short and has a very broad back. He is reading a cowboy novel and doesn't look up until B and his father are at his side. He recognises them and asks what they thought of the show. Not bad, says B's father, although in precision sports you need experience to be able to judge properly. Would I be right in guessing you were a sportsman yourself? asks the ex-diver. B's father looks at him for a few moments and then says, You could say that. The ex-diver gets to his feet with an energetic movement as if he were back on the edge of the cliff. He must be about fifty, thinks B, so he's not much older than my father, but the wrinkles on his face, like scars, make him look much older. Are you gentlemen on holiday? asks the ex-diver. B's father nods and smiles. And what was your sport, sir, if I might ask? Boxing, says B's father. How about that, says the ex-diver, so you must have been a heavyweight? B's father smiles broadly and says yes.

Before he knows what is going on, B finds himself walking with his father and the ex-diver towards the Mustang, and then all three get into the car and B hears the directions the ex-diver is giving his father as if they were coming from the radio. For a while the car glides along the Avenida Miguel Alemán, but then it turns and heads inland and soon the tourist hotels and restaurants give way to an ordinary cityscape with tropical touches. The car keeps climbing, heading away from the golden horseshoe of Acapulco, along badly paved or unpaved roads, until it pulls up beside the dusty pavement in front of a cheap restaurant, a fixed-menu place (although, thinks B, it's really too big for that). The ex-diver and B's father get out of the car immediately. They have been talking all the way and while they wait for him on the pavement, they continue their conversation gesturing incomprehensibly. B takes his time getting out of the car. We're going to eat, says his father. So it seems, says B.

The place is dark inside and only a quarter of the space is occupied by tables. The rest looks like a dance floor, with a stage for the band, surrounded by a long balustrade made of rough wood. At first, B can't see a thing, until his eyes adjust to the darkness. Then he sees a man coming over to the ex-diver. They look alike. The stranger listens attentively to an introduction that B doesn't catch, shakes hands with his father and a few seconds later turns to B. B reaches out to shake his hand. The stranger says a name and his handshake, which is no doubt meant to be friendly, is not so much firm as violent. He does not smile. B decides not to smile either. B's father and the ex-diver are already sitting at a table. B sits down next to them. The stranger, who looks like the ex-diver and turns out to be his younger brother, stands beside them, waiting for instructions. The gentleman here, says the ex-diver, was heavyweight champion of his country. So you're foreigners? asks his brother. Chileans, says B's father. Do you have red snapper? asks the ex-diver. We do, says his brother. Bring us one, then, a red snapper Guerrero-style, says the ex-diver. And beers all round, says B's father, for you too. Thank you, murmurs the brother, taking a notebook from his pocket and painstakingly writing down an order that, in B's opinion, a child could easily remember.

Along with the beers, the ex-diver's brother brings them

some savoury crackers to nibble and three rather small plates of oysters. They're fresh, says the ex-diver, putting chilli sauce on all three. Funny, isn't it. This stuff's called chilli and so's your country, says the ex-diver, pointing to the bottle full of bright red chilli sauce. Yes, intriguing, isn't it, admits B's father. Like the way the sauce is the opposite of chilly, he adds. B looks at his father with barely veiled incredulity. The conversation revolves around boxing and diving until the red snapper arrives.

Later, B and his father leave the premises. The hours have flown without them noticing and by the time they climb into the Mustang, it is already seven in the evening. The ex-diver comes with them. For a moment, B thinks they'll never get rid of him, but when they reach the centre of Acapulco the ex-diver gets out in front of a billiard hall. When he has gone, B's father comments favourably on the service at the restaurant and the price they paid for the red snapper. If we'd had it here, he says, pointing to the hotels along the beachfront boulevard, it would have cost an arm and a leg. When they get back to their room, B puts on his bathing suit and goes to the beach. He swims for a while and then tries to read in the fading light. He reads the surrealist poets and is completely bewildered. A peaceful, solitary man, on the brink of death. Images, wounds. That is all he can see. And the images are dissolving little by little, like the setting sun, leaving only the wounds. A minor poet disappears while waiting for a visa to admit him to the New World. A minor poet disappears without leaving a trace, hopelessly stranded in some town on the Mediterranean coast of France. There is no investigation. There is no corpse. By the time B turns to Daumal, night has already fallen on the beach; he shuts the book and slowly makes his way back to the hotel.

After dinner, his father proposes they go out and have some fun. B declines this invitation. He suggests to his father that he go on his own, says he's not in the mood for having fun, he'd prefer to stay in the room and watch a film on TV. I can't believe it, says his father, you're behaving like an old man, at your age! B looks at his father, who is putting on clean clothes after a shower, and laughs.

Before his father goes out, B tells him to take care. His father looks at him from the doorway and says he's only going to have a couple of drinks. You take care yourself, he says, and gently shuts the door.

Once he's on his own, B takes off his shoes, looks for his cigarettes, switches on the TV, and collapses on to the bed again. Without intending to, he falls asleep. He dreams that he is living in (or visiting) the city of the Titans. All there is in the dream is an endless wandering through vast dark streets that recall other dreams. And in the dream his attitude is one that he knows he doesn't have in waking life. Faced with buildings whose voluminous shadows seem to be knocking against each other, he is, if not exactly courageous, unworried or indifferent.

A while later, just after the end of the programme, B wakes up with a jolt, and, as if responding to a summons, switches off the TV and goes to the window. On the terrace, half-hidden in the same corner as the night before, the North American woman is sitting with a cocktail or a glass of fruit juice in front of her. B observes her indifferently, then walks away from the window, sits on the bed, opens his book of surrealist poets, and tries to read. But he can't. So he tries to think, and to that end he lies down on the bed again, with his arms outstretched, and shuts his eyes. For a moment he thinks he is on the point of falling asleep. He even catches an oblique glimpse of a street from the dream city. But soon he realises that he is only remembering the dream, opens his eyes and lies there for a while contemplating the ceiling. Then he switches off the bedside lamp and goes back over to the window.

The North American woman is still there, motionless. The shadows of the urns stretch out and touch the shadows of the neighbouring tables. The reception area, fully lit, unlike the terrace, is reflected in the swimming-pool. Suddenly a car pulls up a few yards from the entrance of the hotel. His father's Mustang, thinks B. But no one appears at the hotel gate for a very long time and B begins to think he must have been mistaken. Then he makes out his father's silhouette climbing the stairs. First his head, then his broad shoulders, then the rest of his body, and finally the shoes, a pair of white moccasins that B, as a rule, finds profoundly disgusting, but the feeling they provoke in him now is something like tenderness. The way he came into the hotel, he thinks, it was like he was dancing. The way he made his entrance, it was as if he had come back from a wake, unconsciously glad to be alive. But the strangest thing is that, after appearing briefly in the reception area, his father turns around and heads towards the terrace: he goes down the stairs, walks around the pool and sits at a table near the North American woman. And when the guy from reception finally appears with a glass, his father pays and, without even waiting for him to be gone, gets up, glass in hand, goes over to the table where the North American woman is sitting and stands there for a while, gesticulating and drinking, until, at the woman's invitation, he takes a seat beside her.

She's too old for him, thinks B. Then he goes back to the bed, lies down, and soon realises that all the sleepiness weighing him down earlier has evaporated. But he doesn't want to turn on the light (although he feels like reading); he doesn't want his father to think (even for a moment) that he is spying on him. He thinks about women; he thinks about travel. Finally he goes to sleep.

Twice during the night he wakes up with a start and his father's bed is empty. The third time, day is already dawning and he sees his father's back: he is sleeping deeply.

B switches on the light and stays in bed for a while, smoking and reading.

Later that morning B goes to the beach and hires a paddle board. This time he has no trouble reaching the island opposite. There he has a mango juice and swims for a while in the sea, alone. Then he goes back to the hotel beach, returns the board to the boy, who smiles at him, and takes a roundabout way back to the hotel. He finds his father in the restaurant drinking coffee. He sits down beside him. His father has just shaved and is giving off an odour of cheap aftershave that B finds pleasant. On his right cheek there is a scratch from ear to chin. B considers asking him what happened last night, but in the end decides not to.

The rest of the day goes by in a blur. At some point B and his father walk along a beach near the airport. The beach is vast, and it is lined with numerous wattle-roofed shacks where the fishermen keep their gear. The sea is choppy; for a while B and his father watch the waves breaking in the bay of Puerto Marqués. A fisherman tells them it's not a good day for swimming. You're right, says B. His father goes in for a swim anyway. B sits down on the sand, with his knees up, and watches him advance to meet the waves. The fisherman shades his eyes and says something that B doesn't catch. For a moment the head and arms of his father swimming out to sea vanish from his visual field. Now there are two children with the fisherman. They are all standing, looking out to sea, except for B, who is still sitting down. A passenger plane appears in the sky, curiously inaudible. B stops looking at the sea and watches the plane until it disappears behind a rounded hill covered with vegetation. He remembers waking up, exactly a year ago, in Acapulco airport. He was returning from Chile, on his own, and the plane stopped in Acapulco. He remembers opening his eyes and seeing an orange light with blue and pink overtones, like the fading colours of an old film, and knowing then that he was back in Mexico and safe at last, in a sense. That was in 1974 and B had not yet turned twenty-one. Now he is twenty-two and his father must be about forty-nine. B closes his eyes. Because of the wind, the fisherman's and the boys' cries of alarm are almost unintelligible. The sand is cold. When he opens his eyes he sees his father coming out of the sea. He shuts his eyes and doesn't open them again until he feels a large wet hand grip his shoulder and hears his father's voice proposing they go and eat turtle eggs.

There are things you can tell people and things you just can't, thinks B disconsolately. From this moment on he knows the disaster is approaching.

In spite of which the next forty-eight hours go by in a placid sort of daze that B's father associates with 'The Idea of the Holiday' (B can't tell whether his father is serious or pulling his leg). They go to the beach, they eat at the hotel or at a reasonably priced restaurant on the Avenida López Mateos. One afternoon they hire a boat, a tiny plastic rowing-boat, and follow the coastline near their hotel, along with the trinket vendors who peddle their wares from beach to beach, upright on paddle boards or in very shallow-bottomed boats, like tightrope walkers or the ghosts of drowned sailors. On the way back they even have an accident.

B's father takes the boat too close to the rocks and it overturns. In itself, this is not dramatic. Both of them can swim quite well and the boat is built to float when overturned; it isn't hard to right it and climb in again. And that is what B and his father do. Not the slightest danger at any point, thinks B. But then, when both of them have climbed back into the boat, B's father realises that he has lost his wallet. Tapping his chest, he says: My wallet, and without a moment's hesitation he dives back into the water. B can't help laughing, but then, stretched out in the boat, he looks down, sees no sign of his father, and for a moment imagines him diving, or worse, sinking like a stone, but with his eyes open, into a deep trench, over which, on the surface, in a rocking boat, his son has stopped laughing and begun to worry. Then B sits up and, having looked over the other side of the boat and seen no sign of his father there either, jumps into the water, and this is what happens: as B goes down with his eyes open, his father, open-eyed too, is coming up (they almost touch), holding his wallet in his right hand. They look at each other as they pass, but can't alter their trajectories, or at least not straight away, so B's father keeps ascending silently while B continues his silent descent.

For sharks, for most fish in fact (flying fish excepted), hell is the surface of the sea. For B (and many, perhaps most, young men of his age) it sometimes takes the form of the sea bed. As he follows in his father's wake, but heading in the opposite direction, the situation strikes him as particularly ridiculous. On the bottom there is no sand, as he had for some reason imagined there would be, only rocks, piled on top of each other, as if this part of the coast were a submerged mountain range and he were near the top, having hardly begun the descent. Then he starts to rise again, and looks up at the boat, which seems to be levitating one moment and about to sink the next, and in it he finds his father sitting right in the middle, attempting to smoke a wet cigarette.

Then the lull comes to an end, the forty-eight hours of grace in the course of which B and his father have visited various bars in Acapulco, lain on the beach and slept, eaten, even laughed, and an icy phase begins, a phase which appears to be normal but is ruled by deities of ice (who do not, however, offer any relief from the heat that reigns in Acapulco), hours of what, in former days, when he was an adolescent perhaps, B would have called *boredom*, although he would certainly not use that word now, *disaster*

187

he would say, a private disaster whose main effect is to drive a wedge between B and his father: part of the price they must pay for existing.

It all begins with the appearance of the ex-diver, who, as B realises straight away, has come looking for his father, and not the family unit, so to speak, constituted by father and son. B's father invites the ex-diver to have a drink on the hotel terrace. The ex-diver says he knows a better place. B's father looks at him, smiles, and says OK. As they go out into the street, the light is beginning to fade. B feels an inexplicable stab of pain and thinks that perhaps it would have been better to stay at the hotel and leave his father to his own devices. But it's already too late. The Mustang is heading up the Avenida Constituyentes and from his pocket B's father takes the card that the receptionist gave him days ago. The nightspot is called the San Diego, he says. In the ex-diver's opinion, it's too expensive. I've got money, says B's father; I've been living in Mexico since 1968, and this is the first time I've taken a holiday. B, who is sitting next to his father, tries to see the ex-diver's face in the rear-view mirror, but can't. So first they go to the San Diego and for a while they drink and dance with the girls. For each dance they have to give the girl a ticket bought beforehand from the bar. To begin with, B's father buys only three tickets. There's something unreal about this system, he says to the ex-diver. But then he starts enjoying himself and buys a whole bundle. B dances too. His first dance partner is a slim girl with Indian features. The second is a woman with big breasts who, for a reason that B will never discover, seems to be preoccupied or cross. The third is fat and happy, and after dancing for a little while, she whispers into B's ear that she's high. What did you take? asks B. Magic mushrooms, says the woman, and B laughs. Meanwhile B's father is dancing with a girl who looks like an Indian and B is glancing across at him from time to time. Actually, all the girls look like Indians. The one dancing with his father has a pretty smile. They are talking (they haven't stopped talking, in fact) although B can't hear what they are saying. Then his father disappears and B goes to the bar with the ex-diver. They start talking too. About the old days. About courage. About the narrow coves where the ocean waves break. About women. Subjects that don't interest B, or at least not at the moment. But they talk anyway.

Half an hour later his father comes back to the bar. His blond hair is wet and freshly combed (B's father combs his hair back) and his face is red. He smiles and says nothing; B observes him and says nothing. Time for dinner, says B's father. B and the ex-diver follow him to the Mustang. They eat an assortment of shellfish in a place that's long and narrow, like a coffin. As they eat, B's father watches B as if he were searching for an answer. B looks back at him. He is sending a telepathic message: There is no answer because it's not a valid question. It's an idiotic question.

Then, before he knows what is going on, B is back in the car with his father and the ex-diver, who talk about boxing all the way to a place in the suburbs of Acapulco. It's a brick and wood building with no windows and inside there's a juke-box with songs by Lucha Villa and Lola Beltrán. Suddenly B feels nauseous. He leaves his father and the ex-diver and looks for the toilet or the back yard, or the door to the street, belatedly realising that he has had too much to drink. He also realises that apparently well-meaning hands have prevented him from going out into the street. They don't want me to get away, thinks B. Then he vomits several times in the yard, among piles of beer boxes, under the eye of a chained dog, and having relieved himself, gazes up at the stars. A woman soon appears beside him. Her shadow is darker than the darkness of the night. Were it not for her white dress, B could hardly make her out. You want a blow-job? she asks. Her voice is young and husky. B looks at her, uncomprehending. The whore kneels down beside him and undoes his fly. Then B understands and lets her proceed. When it's over he feels cold. The whore stands up and B hugs her. Together they gaze at the night sky. When B says he's going back to his father's table, the woman doesn't follow him. Let's go, says B, but she resists. Then B realises that he has hardly seen her face. It's better that way. I hugged her, he thinks, but I don't even know what she looks like. Before he goes in he turns around and sees her walking over to pat the dog.

Inside, his father is sitting at a table with the ex-diver and two other guys. B comes up to him from behind and whispers in his ear: Let's go. His father is playing cards. I'm winning, he says, I can't leave now. They're going to steal all our money, thinks B. Then he looks at the women, who are looking at him and his father with pity in their eyes. They know what's going to happen to us, thinks B. Are you drunk? his father asks him, taking a card. No, says B, not any more. Have you taken any drugs? asks his father. No, says B. Then his father smiles and orders a tequila. B gets up and goes to the bar, and from there he surveys the scene of the crime with manic eyes. It is clear to B now that he will never travel with his father again. He shuts his eyes; he opens his eyes. The whores watch him curiously; one offers him a drink, which B declines with a gesture. When he shuts his eyes, he keeps seeing his father with a pistol in each hand, entering through an impossibly situated door. In he comes, impossibly, urgently, with his grey eyes shining and his hair ruffled. This is the last time we're travelling together, thinks B. That's all there is to it. The juke-box is playing a Lucha Villa song and B thinks of Gui Rosey, a minor poet who disappeared in the south of France. His father deals the cards, laughs, tells stories, and listens to those of his companions, each more sordid than the last. B remembers going to his father's house when he returned from Chile in 1974. His father had broken his foot and was in bed reading a sports magazine. What was it like? he asked, and B recounted his adventures. An episode from the chronicle of Latin America's doomed revolutions. I almost got killed, he said. His father looked at him and smiled. How many times? he asked. Twice, at least, B replied. Now B's father is roaring with laughter and B is trying to think clearly. Gui Rosey committed suicide, he thinks, or got killed. His corpse is at the bottom of the sea.

A tequila, says B. A woman hands him a half-full glass. Don't get drunk again, kid, she says. No, I'm all right now, says B, feeling perfectly lucid. Then two other women approach him. What would you like to drink? asks B. Your father's really nice, says the younger one, who has long, black hair. Maybe she's the one who gave me the blowjob, thinks B. And he remembers (or tries to remember) apparently disconnected scenes: the first time he smoked in front of his father; he was fourteen, it was a Viceroy cigarette, they were sitting in his father's truck waiting for a goods train to arrive, and it was a very cold morning. Guns and knives, family stories. The whores are drinking tequila with Coca-Cola. How long was I outside vomiting? wonders B. You were kind of jumpy before, says one of the whores. You want some? Some what? says B. He is shaking and his skin is cold as ice. Some weed, says the woman, who is about thirty years old and has long hair like the other one, but dyed blonde. Acapulco Gold? asks B, taking a gulp of tequila, while the two women come a little closer and start stroking his back and his legs. Yep, calms you down, says the blonde. B nods and the next thing he knows there is a cloud of smoke between him and his father. You really love your dad, don't you, says one of the women. Well, I wouldn't go that far, says B. What do you mean? says the dark woman. The woman serving at the bar laughs. Through the smoke B sees his father turn his head and look at him for a moment. A deadly serious look, he thinks. Do you like Acapulco? asks the blonde. Only at this point does he realise that the bar is almost empty. At one table there are two men drinking in silence, at another, his father, the ex-diver, and the two strangers playing cards. All the other tables are empty.

The door to the patio opens and a woman in a white dress appears. She's the one who gave me the blow-job, thinks B. She looks about twenty-five, but is probably much younger, maybe sixteen or seventeen. Like almost all the others, she has long hair, and is wearing shoes with very high heels. As she walks across the bar (towards the bathroom) B looks carefully at her shoes: they are white and smeared with mud on the sides. His father also looks up and examines her for a moment. B watches the whore opening the bathroom door, then he looks at his father. He shuts his eyes and when he opens them again the whore is gone and his father has turned his attention back to the game. The best thing for you to do would be to get your father out of this place, one of the women whispers in his ear. B orders another tequila. I can't, he says. The woman slides her hand up under his loose-fitting Hawaiian shirt. She's checking to see if I have a weapon, thinks B. The woman's fingers climb up his chest and close on his left nipple. She squeezes it. Hey, says B. Don't you believe me? asks the woman. What's going to happen? asks B. Something bad, says the woman. How bad? I don't know, but if I was you, I'd get out of here. B smiles and looks into her eyes for the first time: Come with us, he says, taking a gulp of tequila. Not in a million years, says the woman. Then B remembers his father saying to him, before he left for Chile: 'You're an artist and I'm a worker.' What did he mean by that? he wonders. The bathroom door opens and the whore in the white dress comes out again, her shoes immaculate now, goes across to the table where the card game is happening, and stands there next to one of the strangers. Why do we have to go? asks B. The woman looks at him out of the corner of her eye and says nothing. There are things you can tell people, thinks B, and things you just can't. He shuts his eyes.

As if in a dream, he goes back out to the patio. The woman with the dyed-blonde hair leads him by the hand. I have already done this, thinks B, I'm drunk, I'll never get out of here. Certain gestures are repeated: the woman sits on a rickety chair and opens his fly, the night seems to float like a lethal gas among the empty beer boxes. But some things are missing: the dog has gone, for one, and in the sky, to the east, where the moon hung before, a few filaments of light herald dawn. When they finish, the dog appears, perhaps attracted by B's groans. He doesn't bite, says the woman, while the dog stands a few yards away, baring its teeth. The woman gets up and smoothes her dress. The fur on the dog's back is standing up and a string of translucent saliva hangs from his muzzle. Stay, Fang, stay, says the woman. He's going to bite us, thinks B as they retreat towards the door. What happens next is confused: at his father's table, all the card players are standing up. One of the strangers is shouting at the top of his voice. B soon realises that he is insulting his father. As a precaution he orders a bottle of beer at the bar, which he drinks in long gulps, almost choking, before going over to the table. His father seems calm. In front of him are a considerable number of banknotes, which he is picking up one by one and putting into his pocket. You're not leaving here with that money, shouts the stranger. B looks at the ex-diver, trying to tell from his face which side he will take. The stranger's probably, thinks B. The beer runs down his neck and only then does he realise he is burning hot.

B's father finishes counting his money and looks at the three men standing in front of him and the woman in white. Well, gentlemen, we're leaving, he says. Come over here, son, he says. B pours what is left of his beer on to the floor and grips the bottle by the neck. What are you doing, son? says B's father. B can hear the tone of reproach in his voice. We're going to leave calmly, says B's father, then he turns around and asks the women how much they owe. The woman at the bar looks at a piece of paper and reads out a sizeable sum. The blonde woman, who is standing halfway between the table and bar, says another figure. B's father adds them up, takes out the money and hands it to the blonde: What we owe you and the drinks. Then he gives her a couple more bills: the tip. Now we're going to leave, thinks B. The two strangers block their exit. B doesn't want to look at her, but he does: the woman in white has sat down on one of the vacant chairs and is examining the cards scattered on the table, touching them with her fingertips. Don't get in my way, whispers his father, and it takes a while for B to realise that he is speaking to him. The ex-diver puts his hands in his pockets. The one who was shouting before starts insulting B's father again, telling him to come back to the table and keep playing. The game's over, says B's father. For a moment, looking at the woman in white (who strikes him now, for the first time, as very beautiful), B thinks of Gui Rosey, who disappeared off the face of the earth, quiet as a lamb, without a trace, while the Nazi hymns rose into a blood-red sky, and he sees himself as Gui Rosey, a Gui Rosey buried in some vacant lot in Acapulco, vanished for ever, but then he hears his father, who is accusing the ex-diver of something, and he realises that unlike Gui Rosey he is not alone.

Then his father walks towards the door, stooping slightly, and B stands aside to give him room to move. Tomorrow we'll leave, tomorrow we'll go back to Mexico City, thinks B joyfully. And then the fight begins.

Days of 1978

ONE DAY B GOES TO A PARTY ORGANISED BY a group of Chileans exiled in Europe. He has recently arrived from Mexico and knows very few of the people there. He is surprised to discover that it is a family gathering: the guests are united by blood ties as well as ties of friendship. Brothers dance with cousins, aunts with nephews,.and wine flows in abundance.

At one point, possibly at dawn, a young man starts quarrelling with B on some pretext or other. The argument is regrettable and predictable. The young man, U, shows off his crackpot erudition: he confuses Marx with Feuerbach, Che Guevara with Frantz Fanon, Rodó with Mariátegui and Mariátegui with Gramsci. It is not a good time to start an argument, to say the least: in Barcelona the light of dawn can drive people mad if they've been up all night, or turn them cold and hard like executioners. That's not my comment; that's what B thinks, and consequently his replies are icy and sarcastic, more than enough provocation for U, who is positively spoiling for a fight. But when the fight seems imminent, B stands up and refuses to have it out. U insults and challenges him, hits the table (or maybe the wall) with his fist. All in vain.

B ignores him and leaves.

The story could end there. B hates the Chilean exiles who live in Barcelona, although he is one of them and there's not a thing he can do about it. The poorest and probably the loneliest of them all. Or so he believes. The way he remembers the incident, it was really like a schoolboys' scrap. But U's violence is bitterly disappointing to B, because U was, and possibly still is, an active member of the left-wing party to which he himself, at this point in his life, is most sympathetic. Once again reality has proven that no particular group has a monopoly over demagogy, dogmatism, and ignorance.

But B forgets the incident, or tries to, and gets on with his life.

Periodically he hears U mentioned, in a vague sort of way, as if he were dead. B would really prefer not to know, but when you associate with certain people, you can't avoid hearing what has happened in their circle of friends, or what they think has happened. In this way, B discovers that U has become a Spanish citizen or that U was seen with his wife at a concert given by a Chilean folk group. For a moment, B even imagines U and U's wife sitting in a theatre as it gradually fills with people, waiting for the curtain to go up revealing the folk group, guys with long hair and beards, more or less like U, and he imagines U's wife, whom he has seen only once and remembers as beautiful but with something odd about her, a woman who is absent, elsewhere, who says hello (as she said hello to B at that party) from elsewhere; he imagines her looking at the curtain, which still hasn't been raised, and looking at her husband from elsewhere, from a shapeless place dimly visible in her large, calm eyes. But how, wonders B, could that woman possibly have calm eyes? There is no answer.

One night, however, the answer presents itself, though it is not the answer that B was expecting. Over dinner with a Chilean couple, B discovers that U has been interned in a psychiatric hospital after having tried to kill his wife.

Perhaps B has had too much to drink that night. Perhaps the Chilean couple's version of the events is grossly exaggerated. In any case B listens to the story of U's misfortunes with considerable pleasure, which imperceptibly gives way to a feeling of triumph, an irrational, small-minded triumph, hailed by all the shadows of his bitterness and disenchantment. He imagines U running down a vaguely Chilean, vaguely Latin American street, howling or shouting, while smoke begins to emerge steadily from the buildings on either side, although at no point can any flames be seen.

From then on, whenever B sees the Chilean couple, he makes a point of asking about U and that is how he discovers, little by little, as if the news were being served up to him once a fortnight or once a month for his secret delectation, that U has left the psychiatric hospital, that U is out of work, that U's wife has not left him (which strikes B as truly heroic on her part), that sometimes U and his wife talk about returning to Chile. Naturally, the Chilean couple find the idea of returning to Chile attractive. B finds it horrific. But wasn't U a revolutionary? he asks. Wasn't U a member of the MIR?

Although he doesn't say so, B feels sorry for U's wife. How could a woman like her fall in love with a guy like that? At some point he even imagines them making love. U is tall and blond and his arms are strong. If we had fought that night, he thinks, I would have lost. U's wife is slim; she has narrow hips and black hair. What colour are her eyes? B wonders. Green. Very pretty eyes. Sometimes it infuriates B to think of U and his wife, and if only he could, he would forget them for ever (after all, he has only seen them once!), but the image of the couple against the background of that awful party has a mysterious purchase on his memory, as if it held some meaning for him, an important meaning, but one that B, though he keeps coming back to it, cannot decipher.

One night as he is walking down the Ramblas, he happens to run into his Chilean friends. They are with U and his wife. U's wife smiles and greets him in what could be described as an effusive manner. U, by contrast, barely says a word to him. For a moment B thinks that U is pretending to be shy or distracted. Yet nothing in his behaviour indicates the slightest hostility. In fact, it is as if U were seeing him for the first time. Is it an act? Is this disinterest natural or a result of the psychotic episode? U's wife talks about a book she has just bought at one of the newspaper stands in the Ramblas, as if she were trying to attract B's attention. She takes out the book, shows it to him, asks what he thinks of the author. B is obliged to confess that he has not read the author in question. You have to, says U's wife, adding: If you like, when I finish it, I'll lend it to you. B doesn't know what to say. He shrugs his shoulders. He mumbles a non-committal yes.

When they say goodbye, U's wife kisses him on the cheek. U gives him a firm handshake. See you soon, he says.

When they are gone, it strikes B that U is not as tall or as strong as he remembered from the party; in fact he is only slightly taller than B. His wife, by contrast, has grown and taken on a singular radiance in B's imagination. For reasons unrelated to this encounter, B has trouble getting to sleep that night and at some point his insomniac ruminations return to U.

He imagines him in the Sant Boi psychiatric hospital; he sees him tied to a chair, writhing in fury while doctors (or the shadows of doctors) attach electrodes to his head. Maybe that sort of treatment can make a tall person shorter, he thinks. It all seems absurd. Before falling asleep he realises that he has settled his score with U.

But that is not the end of the story.

And B knows it. He also knows that the story of his relationship with U is not the story of a banal grudge.

The days go by. At first, impelled by a somewhat self-destructive urge, B tries to find U and his wife, and to that end he starts visiting the Chilean exiles he knows in Barcelona far more assiduously than before, and listens to their problems and commentaries on daily life with a mixture of horror and indifference, but U and his wife are never there; no one has seen them, although everyone, of course, has an anecdote to recount or an opinion about their dreadful situation, which can only get worse. After a string of such visits and monologues, B is obliged to conclude that U and his wife are avoiding the company of their compatriots. B's urge to see them wanes and dies, and he goes back to his old ways.

One day, however, he runs into U's wife in the Boquería market. He sees her from a distance. She is with a young woman he doesn't know. They have stopped in front of a stall selling tropical fruit. As he approaches them, B notices that there is something different about U's wife, a new depth to her face. She is not just a pretty woman any more; now she is interesting as well. He says hello to them. U's wife responds rather coldly, as if she didn't recognise him. Which is what B thinks has happened at first, so he proceeds to explain who he is. He reminds her of the last time they saw each other, the book she recommended; he even mentions the ill-fated party at which they first met. U's wife keeps nodding, but it is clear that she is increasingly ill at ease, as if she were wishing she could somehow make him vanish. Although he is disconcerted, and knows deep down that the best thing to do would be to say goodbye immediately and go, he stays. What he is really waiting for is something – a signal, a word – to make it quite clear that his presence is unwelcome. But no such signal is forthcoming. U's wife is simply trying not to see him. Her friend, by contrast, is observing him carefully, and B clings to her gaze as if it were a lifeline. Her name is K and she is Danish, not Chilean. Her Spanish is bad but comprehensible. She hasn't been living in Barcelona for long and hardly knows the city. B offers to show her around. K accepts.

So that night B meets the Danish woman and they walk around the Gothic quarter (Why am I doing this? he wonders, while she is happy and slightly drunk – they have already visited a couple of old taverns), and they talk and K points out the shadows their bodies are throwing on the old walls and the paving stones. These shadows have a life of their own, says K. At first B thinks nothing of her remark. But then he observes his shadow, or perhaps it is hers, and for a moment that elongated silhouette seems to be looking askance at him. It gives him a start. Then all three or four of them are swallowed up by shapeless darkness.

That night he sleeps with K. She is studying anthropology with U's wife and although they are not what you would call close friends (in fact they are only classmates), as dawn begins to break, K starts talking about her, perhaps because she is their only mutual acquaintance. B can't make much sense of what she says; it is full of commonplaces. U's wife is a good person, always ready to do you a favour, a bright student (What does that mean? wonders B, who has never been to university), although – and this she states without any evidence, relying solely on her female intuition – she has lots of problems. What kind of problems? asks B. I don't know, says K, all sorts.

The days go by. B has stopped visiting Barcelona's Chilean exiles in the hope of finding U and his wife. Every two or three days he sees K and they make love, but they don't talk about U's wife, or if, occasionally, K mentions her, B pretends not to notice or listens in a deliberately distant, indifferent manner, trying to be objective (and succeeding without too much effort), as if K were talking about social anthropology or the little mermaid of Copenhagen. He returns to his old routines, that is, to his own madness or his own boredom. His relationship with K involves no socialising, so he is spared any unwelcome or chance encounters.

One day, long after his last visit, he happens to drop in on his friends the Chilean couple.

B is not expecting them to have company. B is expecting

to have dinner with them, so he comes bearing a bottle of wine. But on arrival he finds the house virtually overrun. His friends are at home, but there is also another Chilean woman, about fifty years old, a tarot reader by trade, and a pale, surly girl, about seventeen, who has a reputation (undeserved, as it will turn out) among the exiled Chileans as something of a prodigy (she is the daughter of a union leader killed under the dictatorship), along with her boyfriend, a Catalan Communist Party official at least twenty years older than she is, together with U's wife, who has been crying, to judge from her eyes and the colour of her cheeks, while in the living room, apparently oblivious to what is going on around him, U sits in an armchair.

B's first impulse is to take his bottle of wine and leave immediately. But he reconsiders, and although he is unable to come up with a single good reason to stay, he does.

The atmosphere at his friends' house is funereal. The mood and the observable activity suggest a secret meeting, but not just one inclusive affair, rather a series of mini- or splinter-meetings, as if a conversation involving everyone were prohibited by an unstated but universally respected rule. The tarot reader and the hostess shut themselves in the host's study. The pale girl, the host, and U's wife shut themselves in the kitchen. The pale girl's boyfriend and the hostess shut themselves in the bedroom. U's wife and the pale girl shut themselves in the bathroom. The tarot reader and the host shut themselves in the corridor, which is no mean feat. With all the coming and going, B even finds himself shut in the guest room with the hostess and the pale girl, listening through the wall to the high-pitched voice of the tarot reader addressing or solemnly admonishing U's wife, the pair having shut themselves in the rear courtyard.

Meanwhile, the only person to remain quite still, as if the agitation had nothing to do with him or were taking place in a world of illusions is U in his armchair in the living room. Which is where B goes after being subjected to a flood of vague if not contradictory reports, from which only one thing emerges clearly: that U tried to kill himself that morning.

In the living room, U greets him with an expression that could hardly be called friendly, but is not aggressive. B sits down in an armchair opposite U. For a while, they both remain silent, looking at the floor or watching the others come and go, until B realises that U has the television on, with no sound, and seems to be interested in the programme.

Nothing in U's face indicates suicidal tendencies, thinks B. On the contrary, there are signs of what could reasonably be interpreted as a new calm, new to B in any case. When he thinks of U, he sees his face as it was at the party: flushed, caught between fear and malice; or the day they met in the Ramblas: an expressionless mask (although it is hardly more expressive now) behind which lurked monsters of fear and malice. The new face has a freshly washed look. As if U had spent hours or maybe days submerged in the waters of a strongly flowing river. Were it not for the soundless television and U's dry eyes carefully following every movement on the screen (while the house is alive with the whispers of the Chileans, engaged in pointless discussions about the possibility of having him committed to Sant Boi again) B might not feel that something extraordinary is going on.

And then what appears at first to be an insignificant movement begins (or rather emerges), a kind of ebbing or backwash: without budging from his armchair, B watches as all the guests (who up to a moment before were conferring or confabulating in little groups) file towards the hosts' bedroom, all except the pale girl, the daughter of the assassinated union leader, who comes into the living room (is it rebellion or boredom, he wonders, or is she just keeping an eye on us?) and sits herself down on a chair not far from the armchair in which U is ensconced, watching television. The bedroom door closes. The muffled sounds cease.

This might be a good moment to leave, thinks B. But instead he opens the bottle and offers them a glass of wine, which the pale girl accepts without batting an eyelid, as does U, although he seems unwilling or unable to drink and takes only a sip, as if not to offend B. And as they drink, or pretend to drink, the pale girl starts talking, telling them about the last film she saw; it was awful, she says, and then she asks them if they have seen anything good, anything they could recommend. The question is, in fact, rhetorical. By posing it the pale girl is tacitly establishing a hierarchy in which she occupies a position of supremacy. Yet she observes a certain queenly decorum, for the question also implies a disposition (on her part, but also on the part of a higher agency, moved by its own sovereign will) to grant both B and U places in the hierarchy, which is a clear indication of her desire to be inclusive, even in circumstances such as these.

U opens his mouth for the first time and says it's a long while since he went to the cinema. To B's surprise, his voice sounds perfectly normal. A well-modulated voice, with a tone that betrays a certain sadness, a Chilean, bottom-heavy tone, which the pale girl does not find unpleasant, nor would the people shut in the bedroom, were they there to hear it. Not even B finds it unpleasant, although for him that tone of voice has strange associations: it conjures up a silent black-and-white film in which, all of a sudden, the characters start shouting incomprehensibly at the top of their voices, while a red line appears in the middle of the screen and begins to widen and spread. This vision, or premonition, perhaps, makes B so nervous that in spite of himself he opens his mouth and says he has seen a film recently and it was a very good film.

And straight away (though what he would really like to

do is extract himself from that armchair, and put the room, the house, and that part of town behind him) he begins to tell the story of the film. He speaks to the pale girl, who listens with an expression of disgust and interest on her face (as if disgust and interest were inextricable), but he is really talking to U, or that, at least, is what he believes as he rushes through his summary.

The film is scored into his memory. Even today he can remember it in detail. At the time he had just seen it, so his account must have been vivid if not elegant. The film tells the story of a monk who paints icons in medieval Russia. B's words conjure up feudal lords, Orthodox priests, peasants, burnt churches, envy and ignorance, festivals and a river at night, doubt and time, the certainty of art and the irreparable spilling of blood. Three characters emerge as central, if not in the film itself, in the version of this Russian film recounted by a Chilean in the house of his Chilean friends, sitting opposite a frustrated Chilean suicide, one beautiful spring evening in Barcelona: the first of these characters is the monk and painter, who unintentionally brings about the arrest, by soldiers, of the second character, a satirical poet, a goliard, a medieval beatnik, poor and half-educated, a fool, a sort of Villon wandering the vast steppes of Russia; the third character is a boy, the son of a bell caster, who, after an epidemic, claims to have inherited the secrets of his father's difficult art. The monk represents the Artist wholly devoted to his art. The wandering poet is a Fool, with all the fragility and pain of the world written on his face. The adolescent caster of bells is Rimbaud, in other words the Orphan.

The ending of the film, drawn out like a birth, shows the process of casting the bell. The feudal lord wants a new bell, but a plague has decimated the population and the old caster has died. The lord's men go looking for him but all they find is a house in ruins and the sole survivor, the caster's adolescent son. He tries to convince them that he knows how to cast a bell. The lord's henchmen are dubious at first, but finally take him with them, having warned that he will pay with his life if there is anything wrong with the bell.

From time to time, the monk, who has renounced painting and sworn a vow of silence, walks through the countryside, past the place where workers are building a mould for the bell. Sometimes the boy makes fun of him (as he makes fun of everything). He taunts the monk by asking him questions and laughs at him. Outside the city walls, as the construction of the mould progresses, a kind of festival springs up in the shadow of the scaffolding. One afternoon, as he is walking past with some other monks, the former painter stops to listen to a poet, who turns out to be the beatnik, the one he unwittingly sent to prison many years ago. The poet recognises the monk and confronts him with his past action, tells him, in brutal, childish language, about the hardships he had to bear, how close he came to dying, day after day. Faithful to his vow of silence, the monk does not reply, although by the way he gazes at the poet you can tell he is taking responsibility for it all, including what was not his fault, and asking forgiveness. The people look at the poet and the monk and are completely bewildered, but they ask the poet to go on telling them stories, to leave the monk alone, and make them laugh again. The poet is crying, but when he turns back to his audience he recovers his spirits.

And so the days go by. Sometimes the feudal lord and his nobles visit the makeshift foundry to see how work on the bell is progressing. They do not talk to the boy, but to one of the lord's henchmen, who serves as intermediary. The monk keeps walking past, watching the work with growing interest. He doesn't know himself why he is so interested. Meanwhile, the tradesmen who are working under the boy's orders are worried about their young master. They make sure he eats. They joke with him. Over the weeks they have become fond of him. And finally the big day arrives. They hoist up the bell. Everyone gathers around the wooden scaffolding from which the bell hangs to hear it ring for the first time. Everyone has come out of the walled city: the feudal lord and his nobles and even a young Italian ambassador, for whom the Russians are barbarians. Everyone is waiting. Lost in the multitude, the monk is waiting too. They ring the bell. The chime is perfect. The bell does not break, nor does the sound die away. Everyone congratulates the feudal lord, including the Italian.

The celebrations begin. When they are over, in what had seemed a fairground and is now a wasteland scattered with debris, only two people remain beside the abandoned foundry: the boy and the monk. The boy is sitting on the ground crying his eyes out. The monk is standing beside him, watching. The boy looks at the monk and says that his father, drunken pig that he was, never taught him the art of casting bells and would have taken his secrets to the grave; he taught himself, by watching. And he goes on crying. Then the monk crouches down and, breaking what was to be a lifelong vow of silence, says, Come with me to the monastery. I'll start painting again and you can make bells for the churches. Don't cry.

And that is where the film ends.

When B stops talking, U is crying.

The pale girl is sitting on her chair looking at something out the window, perhaps just the night. Sounds like a good film, she says, and keeps looking at something that B can't see. U drinks his glass of wine in a single gulp and smiles at the pale girl, then at B, and hides his head in his hands. Silently, the pale girl gets up, leaves the room, and comes back with U's wife and the hostess. U's wife kneels down beside him and strokes his hair. The host and the tarot reader appear in the corridor and stand there in silence, until the tarot reader sees the bottle of wine left on the table and goes to pour herself a glass.

This has the effect of a starting gun. They all proceed to help themselves to the wine. The tarot reader proposes a toast. The host proposes a toast. The pale girl proposes a toast. When B goes to refill his glass there is no wine left. Goodbye, he says to his hosts. And off he goes.

It is only when he reaches the entrance hall (the dark entrance hall and the street awaiting him beyond) that he realises he didn't recount the film for U's benefit but for his own.

This is where the story should end, but life is not as kind as literature.

B does not see U or his wife again. In fact, B no longer needs U or the radiant ghost he used to imagine when he thought of U's life in ruins. One day, however, he hears of U's trip to Paris to visit an old friend from the MIR. U travels with another Chilean. They take a train. Shortly before arriving in Paris, U gets up, leaves the compartment without saying anything, and doesn't come back. His friend wakes up as the train begins to move again. He looks for U but can't find him. After talking to the ticket inspector he concludes that U has got off at the station they have just left. At the same moment, in the early hours of the morn-ing, the telephone rings in U's house. By the time his wife has woken up, got out of bed, and walked to the living room, the phone has stopped ringing. Shortly afterwards, the telephone rings in the house of a friend, who does pick up the receiver in time and is able to speak to U. U says that he is in some French village, that he was going to Paris, but suddenly, inexplicably, changed his mind, and is now on his way back to Barcelona. The friend asks him if he has enough money. U replies in the affirmative. According to the friend, U seems calm and even relieved to have made this decision. So the train in which U was travelling continues on its way north to Paris, while U starts walking through the village, southwards, as if he had fallen asleep and set off sleepwalking back to Barcelona.

He makes no more telephone calls.

Beside the village there is a wood. At some point during the night U leaves the path and enters the wood. The next day a farmer finds him: he has hanged himself from a tree with his own belt, not as simple a task as it might seem at first. The gendarmes find U's passport and his other papers, his driver's licence and social security card, scattered far from the corpse, as if U had thrown them away as he walked through the wood, or tried to hide them.

Vagabond in France
and Belgium

B HAS CROSSED THE BORDER INTO FRANCE. IN five months of wandering he will spend all the money he has. Ritual sacrifice, gratuitous act, boredom. Sometimes he takes notes, but as a rule he limits himself to reading. What does he read? Detective novels in French, a language he hardly understands, which makes the novels more interesting. Even so, before the last page he always guesses who the murderer is. France is not as dangerous as Spain and B needs to feel that he is in a low-danger zone. B has crossed the border with money to spend because he has received an advance from his publisher and, after putting sixty per cent of the sum in his son's bank account, he has gone to France because he likes France. Simple as that. He took the train from Barcelona to Perpignan, spent half an hour walking around Perpignan station, until he felt he had understood what there was to understand; he ate in a restaurant in the city, saw an English film at a cinema, and then, as night was falling, took another train, direct to Paris.

In Paris, B stays in a little hotel in the rue Saint-Jacques. The first day he visits the Luxembourg Gardens, sits on a park bench and reads, then goes back to the rue Saint-Jacques, finds a cheap restaurant and eats there.

The second day, after finishing a novel in which the killer lives in an old people's home (which resembles the world beyond Lewis Carroll's looking glass), he sets off in search of second-hand bookshops and finds one in the rue du Vieux Colombier, where he discovers an old copy of the magazine *Luna Park*, number 2, a special issue on writing and graphics, with texts or drawings (the texts are drawings and vice versa) by Roberto Altmann, Frédéric Baal, Roland Barthes, Jacques Calonne, Carlfriedrich Claus, Mirtha Dermisache, Christian Dotremont, Pierre Guyotat, Brion Gysin, Henri Lefebvre and Sophie Podolski.

The magazine, edited by Marc Dachy, which comes out or used to come out three times a year, was published in Brussels by TRANSédITION, and has or had its registered office at number 59, rue Henry van Zuylen. At one time Roberto Altmann was a famous artist. Who remembers Roberto Altmann now? wonders B. The same goes for Carlfriedrich Claus. Pierre Guyotat was a notable author. But there is a difference between notable and memorable. In fact, B once thought he wanted to be like

Guyotat, in days gone by, when as a young man he was reading Guyotat's work. That bald, massive individual, Pierre Guyotat, ready to take on all comers and eat them alive in the darkness of a mansard room. He doesn't know who Mirtha Dermisache was, but her name rings a bell: possibly a beautiful woman, and almost certainly elegant. Sophie Podolski was a poet whom he and his friend L admired (adored even) back in Mexico, when they were little more than twenty years old. Roland Barthes, well, everyone knows who he is. B has seen Dotremont's name somewhere else, perhaps he once read some of his poems, in a forgotten anthology. Brion Gysin was a friend of Burroughs, the one who gave him the idea for his cutups. And that leaves Henri Lefebvre. The name means nothing to B. And suddenly, in the second-hand bookshop, that name, the only one that means nothing to B, lights up like a match struck in a dark room. Or that is how it feels to B. He would have preferred it to light up like a lamp. And in a cave rather than a dark room, but the fact is that Lefebvre, the name Lefebvre, flares briefly like a match.

So B buys the magazine and loses himself in the streets of Paris, where he has gone precisely to lose himself, to watch the days slip away, and although he'd been imagining the lost days as sunny, as he walks along with the issue of *Luna Park* in a plastic bag dangling lazily from his hand, that sunny image is cast into shade, as if the old magazine (which is beautifully produced, by the way, and in almost perfect condition in spite of the years and the dust that builds up in second-hand bookshops) had triggered or provoked an eclipse. The eclipse, as B knows, is Henri Lefebvre. It is Henri Lefebvre's relationship with literature. Or more precisely: his relationship with *writing*.

After walking aimlessly for many hours, B arrives at his hotel. He feels well. He is relaxed and feels like reading. Earlier, on a bench in the square Louis XVI, he tried to decipher Lefebvre's graphic script. A difficult undertaking. Lefebvre draws his words as if the letters were blades of grass. The words seem to be shifting in the wind, an easterly wind; a field, grass of uneven height, a cone unravelling. As he watches the words (because the first thing he has to do is to *watch* them) B remembers – as if he were seeing it all on a cinema screen – faraway fields in the southern hemisphere where his adolescent self is searching desultorily for a four-leafed clover. Then it occurs to him that this memory may actually come from a film and not his real life. The real life of Henri Lefebvre, it seems, was touchingly simple: he was born in Masnuy Saint-Jean in 1925. He died in Brussels in 1973. In other words he died in the year of the military coup in Chile. B tries to remember the year 1973. It is no use. He has walked too far and although he feels relaxed, in fact he is tired, and what he needs is food or sleep. But B can't sleep so he goes out to eat. He gets dressed (he is naked though he can't remember taking off his clothes), combs his hair, and goes down to the street. He eats in a restaurant in the rue des Écoles.

At the next table is a woman who is also eating on her own. They smile at each other and leave the restaurant together. He invites her up to his room. The woman accepts spontaneously. They talk and B observes her as if through a curtain. Although he is listening carefully, he cannot understand much. The woman refers to unrelated events: children playing on swings in a park, an old woman knitting, moving clouds, the silence that reigns, so the physicists tell us, in outer space. A world without noises, she says, in which even death is silent. At some point, just to keep the conversation going, B asks her what her job is, and she replies that she is a prostitute. Ah, good, says B. But just for something to say. In fact he doesn't mind one way or the other. When the woman finally falls asleep, he looks for *Luna Park*, which is lying on the floor, almost under the bed. He reads that Henri Lefebvre, who was born in 1925 and died in 1973, spent his childhood and adolescence in the country. In the deep green fields of Belgium. Then his father died. His mother, Julia Nys, remarried when he was eighteen. His stepfather, a jovial fellow, used to call him Van Gogh. Not because he liked Van Gogh, of course, but to make fun of his stepson. Lefebvre moved out to live on his own. But he soon came back to his mother's house and there he stayed until she died in June 1973.

Two or three days after the death of his mother, Henri's body was found beside his desk. Cause of death: a massive overdose of prescribed drugs. B gets out of bed, opens the window and looks at the street. After Lefebvre's death, fifteen kilos of manuscripts and drawings were discovered. 'Very few publishable texts,' says the brief note on the author. In fact, the only thing that Lefebvre published in his lifetime was a critical essay entitled "Phases de la poésie d'André du Bouchet", under the pseudonym Henri Demasnuy, in *Synthèses*, number 190, March 1962. B imagines Lefebvre in his home town of Masnuy Saint-Jean. He imagines him at the age of sixteen, looking at a German army truck, in which there are only two German soldiers, smoking and reading letters. Henri Demasnuy, Henri of Masnuy. When he turns around, the woman is leafing through the magazine. I have to go, she says, without looking at him, still flicking the pages. You can stay here, says B, knowing it's not likely. The woman says neither yes nor no, but after a while she stands up and starts getting dressed.

B spends the following days wandering around the streets of Paris. Sometimes he comes to the entrance of a museum, but he never goes in. Sometimes he comes to a cinema and stands there examining the photos at length, then walks on. He buys books, which he browses through but never reads to the end. He eats in a different restaurant every time and lingers after his meals, as if he were not in Paris but out in the country and had nothing better to do than smoke and drink camomile tea.

One morning, after a couple of hours' sleep, B takes a train to Brussels. He has a friend there, a black girl, the daughter of a Chilean exile and a Ugandan woman, but he can't bring himself to ring her. He walks around central Brussels for hours and then into the northern suburbs until he finds a little hotel in a street where there is virtually nothing else. Next to it is a fenced-off vacant lot where grass and garbage are thriving. Opposite is a row of mostly unoccupied houses that look as if they have been bombed. Some have broken windows and shutters hanging precariously as if the wind had unhinged them, but there is practically no wind in this street, thinks B, looking out of the window of his room. He also thinks: I should hire a car. And: I don't know how to drive. The next day he goes to see his friend. Her name is M and she is living on her own now. He finds her at home, wearing jeans and a T-shirt. She is barefoot. When she sees him, for the first few seconds she can't remember who he is. She speaks to him in French and looks at him as if she knows that he is going to do her harm, but doesn't care.

After a moment's hesitation, B says his name. He speaks in Spanish. I'm B, he says. Then M remembers him and smiles, though not because she is particularly happy to see him; it is more that B's sudden appearance, something she hadn't even considered as a possibility, comes as an amusing if perplexing surprise. In any case, she invites him in and offers him a drink. They talk for a while, seated opposite each other. B asks about her mother (her father died a while ago), her studies, her life in Belgium. M replies obliquely and asks about B's health, his books, his life in Spain.

Finally they run out of things to say and sit there in silence. Silence suits M. She is tall, slim, and about twenty-five. Her eyes are green, the same colour as her father's. Even the rings under her eyes, which are very pronounced, remind B of the exiled Chilean he met many years ago (he can't remember how many years, nor does it matter) when M was a little girl, about two, and her parents (her mother was studying politics, though she didn't finish the degree) were travelling through France and Spain on a shoestring, staying with friends.

For a moment he imagines the three of them, M's father, her mother, and M at the age of two or three, with her green eyes, surrounded by precarious suspension bridges. Her father was never really a close friend of mine, thinks B. There were never really any bridges, not even precarious ones.

Before leaving, he gives her the name and the telephone number of his hotel. When night comes he walks through the centre of Brussels in search of a woman, but all he can see are ghostly figures; it's as if the bureaucrats and bank clerks had all worked late and were just leaving their offices. When he returns to his hotel he has to wait a long time before someone comes to the door. The porter is a haggard young man. B gives him a tip and climbs the dark staircase to his room.

The next morning he is woken by a phone call from M. She invites him to breakfast. Where? asks B. Wherever, says M. I'll come and pick you up and then we can go somewhere. As he is getting dressed, B thinks of Julia Nys, Lefebvre's mother, who illustrated some of her son's last texts. They lived here, he thinks, in Brussels, in a house somewhere in this part of the city. A gust of wind is blowing in his memory, blurring the houses he has seen. After shaving, B looks out of the window at the façades of the neighbouring houses. Everything is the same as yesterday. A middle-aged woman, perhaps only a few years older than B, is walking down the street, dragging an empty shopping trolley. A few yards in front of her, a dog has stopped, with his muzzle raised and his eyes, like slots in a money box, fixed on one of the hotel's windows, perhaps the one from which B is looking out. Everything is the same as yesterday, thinks B as he puts on a white shirt, a black jacket, and a pair of black trousers. Then he goes downstairs to wait for M in the lobby.

What do you make of this? B asks M, once they are in

the car, showing her Lefebvre's pages in *Luna Park*. It looks like bunches of grapes, says M. Can you read the writing? No, says M. Then she looks at Lefebvre's scribbles again and says that maybe he is talking about existence . . . maybe. But in fact she is the one who talks about existence that morning. She says her life is one error after another; she tells him that she has been very ill (what with, she doesn't say) and describes a trip to New York that sounds more like a descent into hell. M's Spanish is larded with French and her face remains expressionless throughout the monologue, except when she allows herself a smile to underline the farcical nature of this or that situation, as she sees it, although nothing, thinks B, could be further from farce.

They have breakfast together in a café on the rue de l'Orient, near the church of Notre-Dame l'Immaculée, a church M seems to know well, as if she had recently converted to Catholicism. Then she says she's going to take him to the Natural History Museum, next to Leopold Park and the European Parliament, a location that strikes B as paradoxical – though he can't say why when pressed to explain – but first, M informs him, she has to go home and get changed. B has no desire to visit a museum of any sort. And he can't see why M needs to change her clothes. He says so. M bursts out laughing. I look like a junkie, she says.

While M gets changed, B sits in an armchair and starts

leafing through *Luna Park*, but soon he gets bored, as if *Luna Park* and M's small flat were incompatible, so he gets up and starts looking at the photos and pictures on the wall, and then the single, sparsely laden bookshelf and the few Spanish books on it, among which he recognises the works of M's father, which M, in all likelihood, has never read: political essays, a history of the coup, a book about the Mapuche communities, and B smiles, taken aback, feeling a slight twinge of emotion, though what it is he doesn't know, tenderness perhaps or disgust or simply a warning that something is wrong. Then suddenly M appears in the room, or rather she walks across it from her bedroom to what must be the bathroom door, unless it's the laundry where her clothes are hanging, and B watches her cross the room half naked or half clothed, a sight which along with her dead father's old books seems to constitute a sign. A sign of what? He doesn't know. An ominous sign, in any case.

When they leave the flat M is wearing a dark, close-fitting, knee-length skirt, a white shirt with the top buttons undone, showing some cleavage, and high-heeled shoes that make her at least two centimetres taller than B. As they head towards the museum, M talks about her mother and points to a building, which they pass without stopping. B doesn't understand until the building is five blocks behind them: M's mother, the widow of the exiled Chilean, lives there, in one of the flats. Instead of asking about her, as he would like to, he says he really doesn't feel like visiting a museum, and especially not some awful Natural History Museum, of all things. But his feeble resistance is no match for M, who has suddenly become energetic while retaining a certain frosty air, and he lets himself be dragged along.

Another surprise is waiting for him. When they reach the museum, M pays for the tickets, then sits down to wait for him in the café with a newspaper and a cappuccino, her legs crossed in a pose that is at once elegant and solitary, and the sight makes B (who has turned back to look at her) feel old, in a rather abstract way. Then B walks from room to room until he comes to one in which he finds several curvilinear machines. What is going to happen to M? he wonders as he sits down, resting his hands on his knees, with a slight twinge of pain in his chest. He feels like a cigarette, but smoking is prohibited. The pain grows stronger. B shuts his eyes but can still see the silhouettes of the machines, persisting like the pain in his chest, although perhaps they are not machines but bewildering figures, the human race suffering and laughing as it marches towards the void.

When he returns to the museum café M is still sitting there with her legs crossed, underlining something in the newspaper with a silver ballpoint pen, probably an ad for a job. As soon as B appears she discreetly folds the paper away. They eat at a restaurant in the rue des Béguines. M

227

hardly touches her food. She hardly talks either, and when she does, it is to suggest they visit the cemetery together. I often come down this way, she says. B looks at her and makes it clear that he has no desire at all to visit a cemetery. On the way out of the restaurant, however, he asks where the cemetery is. M does not reply. They get into the car and less than three minutes later her hand (a slender and elegant hand, thinks B) is pointing out the Du Karreveld castle, the Demolenbeek cemetery, and a sports complex with tennis courts. B laughs. M's face, by contrast, remains hieratic and impassive. But underneath, thinks B, she is laughing too.

What are you going to do tonight? she asks as she drops him off at his hotel. I don't know, says B, read maybe. For a moment B thinks that M has something to say to him, but she says nothing. That night B does in fact lie down and try to read one of the novels he didn't leave behind in Paris, but after a few pages he gives up and tosses it to the floor. He leaves the hotel. After walking aimlessly for a long time he comes to a part of the city in which there are many coloured people. That is what he thinks, that is how he articulates his thought as he sees himself walking through those streets. He has never liked the expression 'coloured people'. So why did that form of words cross his mind? Black people, Asians, North Africans, yes, but not coloured people, he thinks. Soon after, he goes into a topless bar. He orders camomile tea. The waitress looks at him and laughs. She is pretty, about thirty years old, tall and blonde. B laughs too. I'm not well, he says, still laughing. The waitress makes his camomile tea. B spends the night with a black girl who talks in her sleep. Her voice, which B remembers as soft and musical, has become hoarse and querulous, as if at some point during the night, unbeknownst to B, her vocal cords had undergone a transformation. It is, in fact, her voice that wakes him, with the effect of a hammer blow, and then, once he is over the shock, he lies there propped up on one elbow listening for a while, until he decides to wake her up. What were you dreaming about? he asks her. The girl replies that she was dreaming about her mother, who died not long ago. The dead are at peace, thinks B, stretching out in the bed. As if she had read his mind, the girl says that no one who has passed through this world is at peace. Not any more, not ever, she says with total conviction. B feels like crying, but instead he falls asleep. When he wakes up the following morning, he is alone. He does not have breakfast. He stays in his room reading until the cleaning lady asks if she can make the bed. While he is waiting in the lobby, M rings for him. She asks him what he is planning to do. Before he knows it, M has arranged to come and pick him up.

That day, they visit another museum, as B suspected they might, and then they eat at a restaurant next to a park in which a crowd of children and adolescents are skating. How long are you going to stay here? asks M. B says he is thinking of leaving the next day. And going to Masnuy Saint-Jean, he adds, anticipating M's question. M has no idea what part of Belgium the village is in. Nor do I, says B. If it isn't too far I could take you in my car, says M. Do you have friends there? B replies in the negative. When they finally go their separate ways outside the hotel, B walks around the district until he finds a pharmacy. He buys condoms. Then he heads towards the topless bar where he went the night before, but although he searches street after street (and gets lost several times in the process) he cannot find it. The next day he has breakfast with M in a roadside restaurant. M tells him that sometimes when she is sad she gets into her car and drives, without having a clear idea where she is going, just for the pleasure of being on the move. Once, she says, I got to Bremen and I didn't know where I was. All I knew was that I was in Germany, that I had left Brussels that morning and now it was night. And what did you do? asks B, who can guess the answer. I turned around and came back, says M.

In Masnuy Saint-Jean they see cows. Trees. Fallow fields. A pre-fab shed. Three-storey houses. At B's request, M asks an old woman who is selling vegetables and postcards how to get to Julia Nys's house. The old woman shrugs her shoulders, but then starts laughing and launches into a long speech, which B can hear from the car. M and the

230

old woman are both gesturing, as if they were talking about the rain or the weather, thinks B. The house is in the rue Colombier; it has a sizeable, neglected garden and a shed that has been turned into a garage. The walls of the house are yellow and the windowless left half is shaded by a large tree that has not been pruned for a long time. She was mad, that old bat, says M, it could be this house or any other house in the village. B rings the doorbell. Which sounds like a real bell with a clapper. After a while a girl appears, wearing jeans, with wet hair; she's about fifteen. M asks her if this is the house where Julia Nys and her son Henri used to live. The girl says Monsieur and Madame Marteau live here. Since when? asks B. Since always, says the girl. Were you washing your hair? asks M. I was dyeing it, says the girl. A short conversation follows, which B does not understand, and yet, for a moment, M with her high heels on one side of the fence and the girl in her tight jeans on the other seem to be the principal figures in a painting, which initially gives an impression of peace and balance, but then strikes him as deeply disturbing. Later, after exploring the village from north to south and south to north, they go into what seems to be the library. Is this where Henri of Masnuy came to read? It can't be. The library is new and Lefebvre must have frequented the old one, the one that was here before the war. There must have been at least two libraries between Henri's and this one, says M, who is better acquainted with her country's public institutions. For lunch, B has a steak and M a salad, half of which she leaves. I wasn't even born when your friend died, says M nostalgically. He wasn't my friend, says B. But *you* were alive, says M, with a gently mocking smile. I was travelling when he died, says B.

Later, when all the other customers have left the restaurant, and they are alone at their table by the window, M reads *Luna Park* 2 and stops at the last page, which announces the forthcoming contributions for *Luna Park* 3 or *Luna Park* 4, if the fourth number ever saw the light of day. She reads out the list of future contributors: Jean-Jacques Abrahams, Pierrette Berthoud, Sylvano Bussoti, William Burroughs, John Cage, and so on up to Julia Nys, Henri Lefebvre and Sophie Podolski. An all-star cast, says M with a mocking smile.

They're all dead, thinks B.

And then: What a pity M doesn't smile more often.

You have a beautiful smile, he says. She looks him in the eyes. Are you trying to seduce me? No, no, God forbid, murmurs B.

Late in the afternoon they leave the restaurant and go back to the car. Where to? asks M. Brussels, says B. M sits there pensively for a while, then says she doesn't think it's a good idea. All the same, she switches on the ignition. There's nothing more for me to do here, says B. This sentence will pursue him throughout the return journey like the headlights of a phantom car.

When they arrive in Brussels B wants to go back to his hotel. M thinks it's ridiculous to waste money on a couple of hours in a hotel when she has a sofa bed he can use. They sit talking in the car outside M's flat for a while. Finally B accepts her offer to put him up for the night. He is planning to leave very early the next day to catch the first train to Paris. They have dinner at a vegetarian restaurant run by a couple of Brazilians, which is open till three in the morning. Once again they are the last customers to leave the premises.

Over dinner M talks about her life. For a moment B is under the impression that she is analysing her life as a whole. But he is mistaken: M talks about her adolescence, her trips to New York and back, her sleepless nights. She doesn't mention boyfriends, or work, or madness. M drinks wine and B smokes one cigarette after another. Sometimes they look away from each other and watch a car go past outside the window. When they get back to M's flat she helps him open out the sofa bed, then goes into her bedroom and shuts the door. Still dressed, B falls asleep reading a novel that seems to be written in the language of another planet. He is woken by M's voice. Like the prostitute the other night, thinks B, the one who talked in her sleep. But before he can muster the willpower to get up, go into M's room, and wake her from her nightmare, he falls asleep again.

The following morning he takes a train to Paris.

He stays at the same hotel in the rue Saint-Jacques, but in a different room, and spends the first few days looking for something by André du Bouchet in the second-hand bookshops. He can't find anything. Like Henri of Masnuy, du Bouchet has disappeared from the map. On the fourth day he does not leave the hotel. He orders meals from room service, but hardly touches them. He finishes reading the last novel he bought and tosses it into the waste-paper basket. He sleeps and has nightmares, but when he wakes up he is sure he has not spoken in his sleep. The next day, after a long shower, he goes for a walk in the Luxembourg Gardens. Then he catches the métro and gets off at Pigalle. He eats at a restaurant on the rue La Bruyère and sleeps with a prostitute in a little hotel on the rue Navarin. Her hair is shaved at the back but very long on top of her head. She tells him she lives on the fourth floor. There is no lift. And it is clear that nobody lives there. It is just a room she uses for work, she and her friends.

While they make love the prostitute tells him jokes. B laughs. In his pidgin French he tries to tell her a joke too, but she doesn't understand. When they are finished, the prostitute goes to the bathroom and asks B if he wants a shower. B says no, he had a shower that morning, but all the same he goes into the bathroom to smoke a cigarette and watch her shower.

He is not surprised (or at least he doesn't let it show)

when she takes off her wig and leaves it on the toilet lid. Her head is clean-shaven and he can see two relatively recent scars on her scalp. He lights a cigarette and asks how she got them. But the prostitute is already in the shower and doesn't hear him. B doesn't repeat his question. Nor does he leave the bathroom. On the contrary, he makes himself at home; he lies down on the white tiles, feeling placid and relaxed, contemplating the steam billowing out from behind the shower curtain until he can no longer see the wig, or the toilet, or the cigarette in his hand.

By the time they leave, night has fallen, and after saying goodbye he walks unhurriedly but almost without stopping from the Montmartre cemetery to the Pont Royal, by a vaguely familiar route, via the Gare Saint-Lazare. When he gets back to his hotel he looks at himself in a mirror. He is expecting a hangdog look, but what he sees is a thinnish, middle-aged man, sweating slightly from the walk, who seeks, finds, and flees his own gaze, all in a fraction of a second. The next morning he rings M in Brussels. He is not expecting her to be there. He is not expecting anyone to be there. But someone picks up the phone. It's me, says B. How are you? asks M. Well, says B. Have you found Henri Lefebvre? asks M. She must be still half asleep, thinks B. Then he says no. M laughs. She has a pretty laugh. Why are you so interested in him? she asks, still laughing. Because nobody else is, says B. And because he was good. Straight away he thinks: I shouldn't have said that. And he thinks: M is going to hang up. He clenches his teeth and an involuntary grimace tenses his face. But M doesn't hang up.

Dentist

H E WASN'T RIMBAUD, HE WAS JUST AN INDIAN
boy.

I met him in 1986. That year, for reasons
that are neither particularly germane to this story nor, it
strikes me now, particularly interesting, I spent a few days
in Irapuato, the strawberry capital, where I stayed with a
dentist friend who was going through a rough patch. I
thought I was in a mess (my girlfriend had recently decided
to put an end to our long-term relationship), but when I
arrived in Irapuato, intending to take some time out,
recover my peace of mind and think about my future, I
found my dentist friend, normally so discreet and com-
posed, in a state bordering on desperation.

Ten minutes after I arrived he told me he had killed a
patient. Since I didn't see how a dentist could possibly kill
anyone, I begged him to calm down and tell me the whole
story. The story was simple, in as much as a story of this
sort can be, and from his rather disjointed telling of it I

deduced that in no way could he be held responsible for anybody's death.

The story also struck me as strange. On top of his day job in a private dental clinic, which provided a more than comfortable living, my friend worked for a kind of medical cooperative for the poor and needy, categories that might appear to be synonymous, but for my friend, and above all for the ideologues who had established the charitable organisation in question, there was, it seems, some kind of difference. Only two dentists had volunteered their services and there was a great deal to do. As the cooperative did not possess a dental surgery, the dentists saw patients at their respective clinics, outside business hours (as my friend put it), mainly at night, when they were assisted by volunteers: dentistry students with a social conscience, keen to refine their skills.

The patient who had died was an old Indian woman who had turned up one night with an abscessed gum. The operation on the abscess had not been performed by my friend but by a student working at his clinic. The woman passed out and the student panicked. Another student rang my friend. When he arrived at the clinic and tried to find out what was going on, he was confronted with a cancerous gum, clumsily incised, and soon realised there was nothing to be done. They sent the woman to the Irapuato General Hospital, where she died a week later.

Such cases were, he told me, quite rare, roughly one in a hundred thousand, and a dentist could reasonably expect never to encounter one in the course of his career. I said I understood, although in fact I didn't understand at all, and that night we went out drinking. As we proceeded from bar to bar (they were more or less middle-class bars) I kept thinking about the old Indian woman and the cancer gnawing at her gums.

My friend told me the story again, with a number of significant changes, which I attributed to the quantity of alcohol we had absorbed by that stage, after which we got into his Volkswagen and went to eat at a cheap restaurant on the outskirts of Irapuato. It was a striking change of scene. Before we had been rubbing shoulders with professional people, public servants, and businessmen, now we were surrounded by labourers, the unemployed, and beggars.

Meanwhile, my friend's melancholy was becoming more pronounced. At midnight he began railing against Cavernas. The painter. A few years before, my friend had bought two of his engravings, which had pride of place on his living room wall. One day, at a party thrown by one of his colleagues, a dentist who lived in the Zona Rosa and, if I remember the story rightly, devoted his talents to repairing the smiles of Mexico's screen idols, my friend had tried to engage the prolific artist, who happened to be present, in conversation.

239

At first, Cavernas had been willing not only to converse but also to confide, revealing, without any prompting from my friend, certain intimate details of his life. At one point Cavernas proposed they share the favours of a young girl who, inexplicably, seemed to fancy the dentist rather than the painter. My friend made it clear that he didn't give a damn about the girl. He wasn't interested in a threesome; what he wanted was to buy another engraving, directly, without middle men; he didn't mind which one, and the artist could name his price, as long as it was personally dedicated: 'For Pancho, in memory of a wild night' or something along those lines.

From that point on, Cavernas's attitude changed. He started to look askance at me, my friend recalled. What the fuck do dentists know about art? he said. He asked if I was an out-and-out faggot or if it was just a phase I was going through. Naturally it took my friend a while to realise he was being insulted. Before he could react and explain that what he felt for Cavernas was simply the admiration of an art lover for the work of a misunderstood genius, one of the world's truly great painters, the genius had made himself scarce.

It was a while before my friend found him again. As he searched, he rehearsed in his head what he would say. Finally, he spotted the painter on the balcony, with two guys who looked like gangsters. Cavernas saw him coming and said something to his companions. My friend the dentist smiled. Cavernas's companions smiled too. My friend was probably rather more drunk than he realised, or than he cared to remember. In any case the painter greeted him with an insult and the two heavies grabbed him by his arms and his waist and dangled him over the balcony. My friend passed out.

He vaguely remembered Cavernas calling him a faggot again, and the men laughing as they dangled him, cars parked in the sky, a grey sky like the Calle Sevilla. Knowing for certain that he was going to die, and for nothing, or something completely stupid; knowing that his life, the life he was about to lose, had been one long series of stupidities – in other words, nothing. And there was not even any dignity in that certain knowledge.

He told me all this as we drank tequila in that cheap restaurant in one of the poor suburbs of Irapuato, which, needless to say, didn't have a licence to sell alcoholic beverages. Then he launched into an argument whose principal objective was to discredit art. Cavernas's engravings, I knew, were still hanging in my friend's living room and I had no reason to suspect that he had taken any steps to sell them. When I tried to point out that what had happened between him and Cavernas was an incident in his life story, not an episode in art history, so that it might be used to discredit certain persons, but not artists in general and certainly not art itself, my friend hit the roof.

But that's where art comes from, he said: life stories. Art history comes along only much later. That's what art *is*, he said, the story of a life in all its particularity. It's the only thing that really is particular and personal. It's the expression of and, at the same time, the fabric of the particular. And what do you mean by the fabric of the particular? I asked, supposing he would answer: Art. I was also thinking, indulgently, that we were pretty drunk already and that it was time to go home. But my friend said: What I mean is the secret story.

He stared at me for a moment, a gleam in his eye. The death of the Indian woman from gum cancer had obviously affected him more than I had realised at first.

So now you're wondering what I mean by the secret story? asked my friend. Well, the secret story is the one we'll never know, although we're living it from day to day, thinking we're alive, thinking we've got it all under control and the stuff we overlook doesn't matter. But every damn thing matters! It's just that we don't realise. We tell ourselves that art runs on one track and life, our lives, on another, we don't even realise it's a lie.

And what separates one track from the other? he asked me. I must have said something, although I can't remember what; in any case, at that point my friend saw someone he knew, turned away from me and started waving. I remember that the restaurant had been gradually filling up with people. I remember that there were green tiles on the walls, like a public urinal, and that the bar, deserted before, was now thronged with weary, jovial, or sinister-looking characters. I remember a blind man singing a song in the corner of the room or maybe the song was *about* a blind man. A cloud of smoke had accumulated over our heads. Then the object of my friend's attention approached our table.

He can't have been more than sixteen years old. He looked younger. He was rather short, and could have been strongly built, but he was filling out and losing definition. His clothes were cheap, yet there was something vaguely incongruent about them, as if they were sending an incomprehensible message from various places at once, and he was wearing a pair of worn-out tennis shoes, shoes that my friends and I, or rather the children of some of my friends, would have laid to rest long ago in a wardrobe or dispatched to the rubbish dump.

He sat down at our table and my friend told him to order whatever he liked. It was then that he smiled for the first time. It wasn't what you would call a pleasant smile; on the contrary, it was wary and suspicious, the smile of someone who expects little from others and all of it bad. Then, as the boy sat down with us and exhibited his wintry smile, it occurred to me that perhaps my friend, a confirmed bachelor who could have chosen to live in Mexico City years ago but had preferred to stay in his home town, Irapuato, had become, or had always been, a homosexual, and that for some obscure reason this fact, kept secret for years, had emerged in the course of our conversation that night about the Indian woman and her cancerous gum. But I soon discarded this idea and concentrated on the newcomer, or perhaps what happened was that his eyes, which I hadn't noticed until then, compelled me to put aside my fears (since in those days, even the remote possibility that my friend might be homosexual frightened me) and turn my full attention to the boy, who seemed to be suspended between adolescence and an appalling childhood.

His eyes were – I don't know how else to put it – forceful. That was the adjective that occurred to me at the time, and clearly it fell far short of capturing the palpable effect they had on the air, the impression they made when you met his gaze, like an ache between the eyebrows – but I still can't come up with a better word. Though his body, as I said, was filling out towards the ampler forms of years to come, his eyes were all sharpness, sharpness in movement.

My friend introduced him with undisguised pleasure. His name was José Ramírez. I held out my hand (I don't know why; I'm not normally so formal, at least not in bars, at night) and he hesitated for a moment. His handshake took me completely by surprise. His right hand, which I had expected to be smooth and indecisive, like that of a typical adolescent, was so covered in calluses it felt like iron. It was quite a small hand, and now that I think back to that night in the suburbs of Irapuato, the hand I see in my mind's eye is small, a small outstretched hand against a background of darkness and the bar's feeble gleams, a hand emerging from parts unknown, like the tentacle of a storm, but hard as iron, a hand forged in a smithy.

My friend was smiling. For the first time that day I saw a glimmer of happiness in his face, as if the physical presence of José Ramírez (with his round face, sharp eyes and hard hands) had dispelled both his guilt about the Indian woman with her cancerous mouth and the recurrent malaise caused by his memory of the painter Cavernas. As if in reply to a question that elementary good manners forbade me to ask, although I was tempted, my friend said that he had met José Ramírez through his work.

It took me a moment to realise that he was referring to his dental practice. Free treatment, said the boy, with a voice that, like his eyes and hands, was at odds with the rest of his body. At the cooperative, said my friend. Six fillings I did for him: a work of art. José Ramírez nodded and lowered his eyes. It was as if he had reassumed his true identity, that of a sixteen-year-old boy. Later on, I remember, we ordered more drinks and José Ramírez ate a helping of corn tortillas with chilli sauce (he didn't want anything more, although my friend kept saying, Order whatever you like, it's my treat).

Throughout the time we spent in the restaurant, they talked to each other; I didn't join in. Now and then I caught a few words of their conversation; it was about art. My friend had gone back to his story about Cavernas, which for some reason he seemed to be mixing up with the story of the Indian woman dying in a hospital bed, in terrible pain, or perhaps not, perhaps she had been anaesthetised, perhaps someone had given her regular doses of morphine, anyway that was the image I had: the Indian woman, a little bundle abandoned in a hospital bed in Irapuato, Cavernas laughing, and his impeccably framed engravings hanging in the dentist's living room, a room that the young José Ramírez, so I gathered from what my friend was saying, had visited (along with the rest of the house no doubt) and in which he had seen, and appreciated, the engravings, the pride of the dentist's art collection.

Eventually we left that restaurant. My friend paid and led the march towards the exit. He wasn't as drunk as I thought and there was no need to suggest that he let me drive. I vaguely remember some other places, where we didn't stay very long, and finally an enormous vacant lot, on a dirt road running out into the country, where José Ramírez got out of the car and said good night without shaking hands.

I said it seemed funny to drop him off there, with no houses in sight, only darkness and the contours of a hill in the background, dimly lit by the moon. I said we should go with him part of the way. Without turning to look at me, my friend (his hands on the wheel, tired but calm) replied that we couldn't go with him, there was no need to worry, the kid knew the way perfectly well. Then he started the engine, switched the headlights to full beam and, before the car started to reverse, I glimpsed an unreal landscape, in black and white, made up of stunted trees, weeds, a cart trail – a cross between a rubbish dump and an idyllic picture postcard of the Mexican countryside.

The boy had disappeared without a trace.

Back at the dentist's house, I had trouble getting to sleep. In the guest room there was a painting by a local artist: an impressionist landscape in which there seemed to be a city and a valley, rendered almost exclusively in a range of yellow tones. I believe there was something evil in that picture. I remember tossing and turning, exhausted but unable to sleep, while a feeble light from the window spread a rippling fire through the landscape. It was not a good picture. It wasn't the picture that was troubling me, stopping me from getting to sleep, filling me with a vague and irreparable sadness, although I was tempted to get up, take it down and turn it to the wall. I was tempted to go back to Mexico City that night.

The next day I got up late and didn't see my friend until lunchtime. I was alone in the house with the woman who came every day to clean, so I thought it would be best to go out for a walk. Irapuato is not a beautiful city, but there is, undeniably, a charm to its streets and the calm central district, where the locals busy themselves conspicuously with what in Mexico City would be considered mere distractions. Since I had nothing to do, after breakfast in a café (orange juice) I sat down on a bench to read the newspaper, while high school students and public servants strolled past, exercising their talents for leisure and idle chat.

For the first time since I had set out for Irapuato, my troubled love-life back in Mexico City seemed remote. There were even birds in the square where I was sitting. Later on I visited a bookshop (it took a while to find one), where I bought a book with illustrations by Emilio Carranza, a landscape painter born in El Hospital, a village or farming cooperative near Irapuato. I was planning to give it to my friend the dentist; I thought he would like it.

We were to meet at two in the afternoon. I went to his clinic. The secretary politely asked me to wait: at the last minute someone had turned up unannounced, but my friend would be free shortly. I sat down in the waiting room and started reading a magazine. I was alone in the room. The silence in my friend's clinic, indeed in the whole building, was almost absolute. For a moment I thought the secretary had lied to me: my friend wasn't there, something bad had happened and he had rushed off, leaving express instructions not to give me any cause for alarm. I stood up and started to walk back and forth in the waiting room; naturally I felt ridiculous.

The secretary had left the reception desk. I went to pick up the phone and make a call, but it was an absurd reflex, since I didn't know anyone to call in that city. I bitterly regretted having come to Irapuato, cursed my emotional susceptibility, swore that as soon as I got back to Mexico City I would find an intelligent, beautiful, and above all sensible woman, whom I would marry after a brief and drama-free engagement. I sat in the secretary's chair and tried to calm down. For a while I stared at the typewriter, the appointments book, a wooden container full of pencils, paperclips, and erasers, arranged in what seemed to be perfect order, which was incomprehensible to me, since no one in their right mind arranges paper-clips (pencils and erasers, yes, but not paperclips), until I noticed my hands trembling over the typewriter keys, which made me jump to my feet and set off resolutely in search of my friend with my heart thumping in my chest.

Even in the grip of a sudden panic attack, manners can sometimes prevail. While opening doors and barging through the clinic, calling out to my friend, I was, I remember, trying to think of a way to explain my behaviour when I found him, if I did. I still don't know what came over me that afternoon. It was probably the last outward manifestation of the anxiety or sadness I had brought with me from Mexico City and was to leave behind in Irapuato.

My friend, of course, was in his consulting room, and I found him with a patient, a distinguished-looking woman of about thirty, and his nurse, a short girl with mestizo features, whom I hadn't seen before. None of them seemed surprised by my sudden appearance. My friend smiled at me and said, I'll be finished in a minute.

Later, when I was trying to explain what I had felt in the waiting room (apprehension, anxiety, fear mounting uncontrollably), my friend declared that something similar often happened to him in buildings that seemed to be empty. Basically, I knew, he meant well. I tried to put it out of my mind. But once my friend got talking there was no stopping him, and during the meal, which lasted from three till six in the evening, he kept coming back to the subject of seemingly empty buildings, that is, buildings that you think are empty, because you can't hear a sound, but in fact they're not, and somehow you can tell, although your senses, your ears, your eyes, are telling you they are. So it's not that you feel anxious or afraid because you're in an empty building, or even because you might be trapped or locked inside an empty building, which is not beyond the realm of possibility, no, the reason you're anxious or afraid is that you know, deep down, that there is *no such thing* as an empty building; in every so-called empty building, someone is hiding, keeping quiet, and that's the terrifying thing: the fact that you are *not* alone, said my dentist friend, even when everything indicates that you are.

And then he said: You know when you really are alone? In a crowd, I said, thinking I was following his train of thought, but no, it wasn't in a crowd. I should have been able to guess the answer: When you die. Death: the only real solitude there is in Mexico; the only solitude in Irapuato.

That night we got drunk. I gave him my present. He said he didn't know Carranza's work. We went out to dinner and got drunk.

We started in the bars of the central district and then we returned to the outskirts, where we had been the night before, where we had met young Ramírez. I remember that at one point in our erratic journey I had the impression that my friend was looking for Ramírez. I said so. He said I was mistaken. I told him he could speak freely to me, anything he said would remain between us. He said he had always spoken freely to me and after a while he looked me in the eyes and added that he had nothing to hide. I believed him. But I still had the impression that he was looking for the boy. That night we didn't go to bed until around six in the morning. At one point the dentist started reminiscing about the old days, when we were both students at the UNAM and unconditional admirers of Elizondo. I was enrolled in the Faculty of Philosophy and Literature and he was studying dentistry. We met at a discussion organised by the university film society, after the screening of a film by a Bolivian director, who I guess must have been Sanjinés.

During the discussion my friend got up, and I don't know if he was the only one, but he was certainly the first to say he didn't like the film, and why. I didn't like it either, but at the time I would never have admitted it. We became friends immediately. That night I discovered that he shared my admiration for Elizondo, and during the second summer of our friendship, we attempted to emulate the characters in *Narda or Summer* by renting a shack by the sea in Mazatlán, not exactly the Italian coast, but, with a little imagination and goodwill, it was close enough.

Then we grew up and, looking back, our youthful adventures seemed rather contemptible. Young middle-class Mexicans are condemned to imitate Salvador Elizondo, who in turn imitated the inimitable Klossowski, or fatten slowly in business or bureaucratic suits, or flail around ineffectually in vaguely leftist, vaguely charitable organisations. Between them, Elizondo (whom I had stopped rereading) and the painter Cavernas just about sated our insatiable appetite for Culture, and each mouthful left us poorer, thinner, uglier, and more ridiculous than before. My friend went back to Irapuato and I stayed on in Mexico City and we both, in different ways, tried to distract ourselves from the gradual devastation of our lives, of the ethics and aesthetics we'd professed, the Mexican nation and our useless bloody dreams.

But we still had friendship and that was the main thing. So there we were, passably drunk by this stage, reminiscing about our youth, when suddenly my friend referred to the old Indian woman who had died of gum cancer and our conversation about art history and the particular; he mentioned the 'two tracks' (though I could barely remember what they were supposed to represent), and finally he started talking about the restaurant where we had met José Ramírez (all the rest had been a preamble) and he asked me what I thought of him, although from the way he put it I couldn't really tell if he was referring to the Indian boy or to himself, so to play safe, I said, Nothing much, or maybe I shrugged in a noncommittal way. My friend immediately asked me if I thought, if the thought had crossed my mind, that there might be something between him and José Ramírez (it was one of those awful, typically Mexican roundabout questions), and I said, No, of course not, mate . . . How could you think that? Come on, don't worry . . . Perhaps I'm exaggerating or my memory is playing tricks, but perhaps not – the real chasm may have opened at that moment, the chasm I had sensed in the seemingly empty building, the one I had glimpsed as the Indian boy walked over to us for the first time, just as my friend, as it happened, was talking or ranting about the Indian woman and her corpse that seemed to keep shrinking, and then, perhaps because I was drunk, it all swirled together in my mind: the memories of our youth, the books we read, *Narda or Summer* by Elizondo, a living national treasure, our aspiring, make-believe summer in Mazatlán, my girlfriend, who had decided out of the blue to make a new start, guided by her own sweet will, the years, Cavernas, my friend's art collection, the trip to Irapuato, its calm streets, my friend's mysterious decision to settle down and work there, in his home town, when the normal thing to do would have been . . .

And then he said: You have to get to know José. He stressed the verb *know*. You have to get to *know* him. And: I'm not . . . I'm not that way . . . you know . . . inclined. And then he talked about the dead Indian woman and the work of the cooperative. And he said: I'm not . . . you didn't think I was, did you? Of course not, I said. And then we went to a different bar, and on the way there he said: Tomorrow. And I knew it wasn't the drink talking; tomorrow he would remember because a promise is a promise, isn't it? Of course it is. Then, trying to change the subject, I started talking about something that had happened to me when I was a child: I got stuck in the lift of the building where we lived. Then I really *was* alone, I said. And my friend listened to me with a smile, as if he were thinking, What a jerk you've become, all those years in Mexico City, the stacks of books you've read and studied and taught, wherever it is you teach. But I went on: I was alone. For a long time. Sometimes (not often, to be perfectly honest) I still feel what I felt in that lift. And do you know why I felt like that? My friend shrugged as if to say he couldn't care less. But I told him anyway: Because I was a child. I remember his reaction. He turned away from me, trying to see where he had parked the car. Bullshit, he said. Tomorrow you're going to see the real thing.

And the next day he hadn't forgotten. On the contrary, he remembered more than I did. He talked about José Ramírez as if he were the boy's guardian. That night, I remember, we dressed as if we were going out to a singles bar or a brothel; my friend wore a brown corduroy jacket and I wore a leather jacket I had brought in case we went for a day trip into the country.

We began our tour with a couple of whiskies in a dim place near the centre that smelt of aftershave. Then we went straight to the suburb where José Ramírez hung out. We visited a pair of run-down cafés, the restaurant (where we tried to eat, although neither of us was hungry) and a bar called El Cielo. Not a trace of the Indian boy.

When it was starting to look as if we had wasted the

night, a curious night in the course of which we had hardly exchanged a word, we saw him, or thought we did, walking down a dimly lit footpath. My friend tooted the horn and executed a reckless U-turn. Ramírez was waiting for us quietly on a corner. I wound down the window and said hello. My friend leaned over in front of me and invited him to get in. The boy climbed into the car without a word. I remember the rest of the night as festive. Irrationally festive. It was as if we were celebrating the birthday of the young man in the back seat. As if we were his parents. As if we were his pimps. Or his minders: two sad white Mexicans protecting an enigmatic Indian compatriot. We laughed. We drank and laughed and everyone left us alone, sensing that to make fun of us would have been to risk life and limb.

We heard the story of José Ramírez, or fragments of it; my friend thought it was wonderful, and, after a moment of puzzlement, so did I, though later, as we approached the unknown slopes of the night, to quote Poe, the story began to blur, as if the Indian boy's words could find nowhere to settle in our memories, which must be why I can hardly remember a thing he said. I do remember him telling us that he had attended a poetry workshop, a free poetry workshop, the literary version of the medical cooperative, although he didn't write a single poem, and at this my friend burst out laughing, but I didn't understand; I couldn't see what was so funny, until they explained that Ramírez wrote fiction. Stories, not poems. Then I asked why he hadn't signed up for a fiction workshop. And my dentist friend said, Because there aren't any fiction workshops. Don't you see? In this shithole of a town the only thing they teach for free is poetry. Don't you see?

And then Ramírez started talking about his family, or maybe it was the dentist who told me about his family, but in any case there was nothing to say. Don't you see? Nothing. And I didn't really see, so just for something to say, I started talking about empty buildings and deception, but my friend silenced me with a gesture. There was *nothing* to say about them. Farmers. Dirt poor. Not the slightest indication. Don't you see? I nodded compliantly, but in fact I didn't see at all. And then my friend declared that there were very few writers alive on a par with the boy sitting there before us. I swear to God: Very few. At which point he launched into an explication of Ramírez's work that chilled me.

Better than the lot of them, he said. Mexico's famous writers were like babes in arms compared to this rather fat, inexpressive adolescent with his hands hardened by work in the fields. What fields? I asked. The fields all around us, said the dentist, moving his hand in a circular gesture, as if Irapuato were an outpost in the wilderness, a fort in the middle of Apache territory. I took a fearful, sidelong glance at the boy and saw that he was smiling.

Then my friend began to tell me about one of Ramírez's stories, a story about a child who had to look after his numerous younger brothers and sisters, that was the gist of it, the first part anyway, because then the plot swung around and smashed itself to pieces, and it became a story about the ghost of a schoolmaster trapped in a bottle, and about individual freedom, and new characters appeared: a pair of shady faith-healers, a twenty-year-old girl on drugs, a guy reading a book by de Sade and living in a wrecked car beside the highway. All this in one story, said my friend.

And although the good-mannered thing to say would have been Mmm, sounds interesting, I said I couldn't really express an opinion without reading it for myself. That's how I let myself in for it, when good manners could have saved me. My friend stood up and said to Ramírez, Let's go and get the stories. I remember Ramírez looked up at him, then across at me, and finally stood up without a word. I could have protested. I could have said there was no need. But by then I was already chilled through and nothing mattered to me any more, although from somewhere deep inside I was watching our movements, which seemed to be orchestrated with an almost supernatural precision, and although I knew that those movements were not leading us towards any physical risk, I was also aware that in another sense we were venturing into dangerous territory, from which we would not be allowed to return without having paid a toll of pain or estrangement, a toll that we would eventually come to regret.

But I said nothing. We left the bar, got into my friend's car, and proceeded to lose our way among the streets on the outskirts of Irapuato, where the only other vehicles were police cars and the odd bus, streets that young Ramírez walked, so my friend told me as he drove on in a state of rapture, every night or every morning, returning from his forays into the city. I chose not to make any further comment and looked out at the feebly lit streets and the shadow of the car, intermittently projected on to the high walls of factories or abandoned warehouses, vestiges of a former time, already consigned to oblivion, when attempts had been made to industrialise the city. Then we emerged into a kind of suburb attached to that jumble of obsolete buildings. The street narrowed. There were no street lamps. I heard dogs barking. Like something from *The Children of Sánchez*, isn't it, said the dentist. I didn't reply. Behind me I heard Ramírez's voice saying to turn right, then keep going straight ahead.

The headlights swept across a dirt road and lit up two wretched shacks behind a fence made of wood and wire, and then we emerged suddenly into what seemed to be open country, although it could equally have been a rubbish dump. From there we continued on foot, Indian file, Ramírez leading the way, followed by the dentist and me.

In the distance I could see headlights gliding along a highway: another world, and yet I felt those distant moving lights were somehow – horribly – emblematic of our destiny. I saw the silhouette of a hill. I sensed a movement in the darkness, among the bushes, and immediately assumed it was rats, although it could just as well have been birds. Then the moon came out and I saw little houses scattered over the lower slopes of the hill and, further off, a dark, ploughed field, stretching away to a bend in the highway, where a wood jutted up like a construction. Suddenly I heard the boy's voice saying something to my friend and we stopped. His house had appeared from nowhere; the walls were yellow and white, and it had a low roof, like all the other wretched houses holding out against the night on the outskirts of Irapuato.

For a moment the three of us stood there in silence, spellbound, contemplating the moon or looking sadly at the boy's cramped dwelling or trying to make sense of the objects piled up in the yard: the only thing I could identify with any certainty was a crate. Then we went into a room with a low ceiling that smelt of smoke and Ramírez switched on a light. I saw a table, farm tools leaning against the wall, and a child asleep in an armchair.

The dentist looked at me. His eyes were gleaming with excitement. But I felt we should have been ashamed of what we were doing: rounding off a night on the town with a bit of schadenfreude. Except that we would be contemplating our own misfortune as well, I thought. Ramírez brought over two wooden chairs before disappearing through a doorway that seemed to have been hacked out with an axe. I soon realised that the room in which we were standing was a new addition to the house. We sat down and waited. When Ramírez reappeared he was carrying a stack of papers more than five centimetres thick. With an intent expression he sat down and handed it to us. Read whatever you like, he whispered. I looked at my friend. He had already taken a story from the pile and was carefully arranging the pages. I said I thought the best thing to do would be to borrow the stories, take them back to my friend's house and read them at our leisure. Or maybe I didn't actually say that, probably not. But thinking about it now, I can't imagine the scene any other way: me saying, Let's take them back and read them later, we'll be more receptive, and the dentist looking at me with something hard in his gaze, like a man condemned to death, ordering me to pick a story at random and read it, for Christ's sake.

So I did. I lowered my eyes, ashamed, chose a story and began to read. The story was four pages long; maybe that's why I chose it, because it was short, but when I got to the end, I felt as if I had read a novel. I glanced across at Ramírez. He was sitting in front of us, nodding off. My friend followed my gaze and told me in a whisper that the young writer got up very early in the morning. I nodded and chose another story. When I looked at

Ramírez again he was slumped forward, sleeping with his head on his arms. Earlier, I had been almost falling asleep myself, but now I felt wide awake and absolutely sober. My friend passed me another story. Read this one, he whispered. I put it aside and finished the one I was reading before starting it.

As I was coming to the end of the third story, the other door opened and a man appeared who must have been about our age, but seemed much older. He smiled at us before walking quietly out into the yard. José's father, said my friend. Outside I heard tin cans knocking, quickening steps, and the sound of someone urinating on to the ground. In a different situation, this would have been enough to put me on my guard; I would have been straining to interpret those noises, preparing to avert a potential danger, but instead I went on reading.

We never stop reading, although every book comes to an end, just as we never stop living, although death is certain. But, to put it in plain terms and make myself clear, at a certain point I decided that I had read enough. My friend had stopped a while before. He was visibly tired. I suggested we leave. Before standing up, both of us looked at Ramírez, who was sleeping peacefully. When we went outside, day was dawning. There was no one in the yard and the fields all around seemed barren. I wondered where the father had gone. My friend pointed to his car and remarked how strange it was that the car didn't seem strange in those surroundings. Some surroundings! he added, no longer whispering. His voice sounded odd to me: hoarse, as if he had spent the night shouting. Let's go and have some breakfast, he said. I nodded. He said, We can talk about what's happened to us.

But as we left that godforsaken place I realised there was very little we could say about the events of the previous night. Both of us felt happy, but we knew, without a shadow of doubt, and without having to put it into words, that we would not be able to ascertain or reflect on the nature of what we had experienced.

When we got back to the house I poured us out a whisky each, as a nightcap, and my friend lapsed into silent contemplation of the engravings by Cavernas hanging on the wall. I put his glass on the table and stretched out in an armchair without saying a word. The dentist scrutinised his engravings, first with his hands on his hips, then resting his chin on one hand and finally ruffling his hair. I laughed. So did he. For a moment I thought he was going to take one of the pictures down and proceed to destroy it methodically. But instead he sat next to me and drank his whisky. Then we turned in.

We didn't get much sleep. About five hours. I dreamt of young Ramírez's house. I saw it standing in the middle of Mexico's wastelands, plains and rubbish dumps, exactly as it was, bare of all ornamentation. Just as I had seen it, a few hours before, at the end of that supremely literary night. And for barely a second I understood the mystery of art and its secret nature. But then somehow the corpse of the old Indian woman who had died of gum cancer came into the dream, and that's the last thing I can remember. I think her wake was being held in Ramírez's house.

When I woke up I told the dentist about my dream, or what I could remember of it. You're not looking too good, he said. He wasn't looking too good himself, although I chose not to point this out. I soon realised that he needed some time on his own. When I announced that I was going for a walk around the city, I saw the relief on his face. That afternoon I went to the cinema and fell asleep halfway through the film. I dreamed that we were committing suicide or forcing others to commit suicide. When I got back to my friend's house, he was waiting for me. We went out to dinner and tried to talk about what had happened the night before. It was useless. We ended up talking about some friends from Mexico City, people we had thought we knew but who had in fact turned out to be perfect strangers. Surprisingly, it was a pleasant evening.

The next day, Saturday, I went with him to his clinic, where he had a couple of hours' work to do for the co-operative. Community service, he said in a resigned sort of way as we got into his car. I was thinking of returning to Mexico City on Sunday and my conscience was telling me I should spend as much time as possible with my friend because I didn't know how long it would be before I would see him again.

For a long time (I couldn't even hazard a guess at how long now) we waited for a patient to turn up, my friend the dentist, a dentistry student, and I, but no one came.

Dance Card

1. MY MOTHER READ NERUDA TO US IN QUILPUÉ, Cauquenes and Los Ángeles. **2.** A single book: *Veinte poemas de amor y una canción desesperada* (*Twenty Love Poems and a Song of Desperation*), Editorial Losada, Buenos Aires, 1961. On the title page, a drawing of Neruda and a note explaining that this edition commemorated the printing of the millionth copy. Had a million copies of *Veinte poemas* already been printed in 1961? Or did the note refer to all of Neruda's published works? The first, I fear, although both possibilities are disturbing, and unimaginable now. **3.** My mother's name is written on the second page of the book: María Victoria Ávalos Flores. A somewhat hasty examination of the handwriting leads me to the improbable conclusion that someone else wrote her name there. It is not my father's handwriting, or that of anyone I know. Whose is it then? After closely scrutinising the signature blurred by the years, I am obliged to admit, albeit sceptically, that it is my mother's. **4.** In 1961 and 1962, my mother was not as old

266

as I am now; she hadn't turned thirty-five, and was working in a hospital. She was young and full of life. **5.** This copy of *Veinte poemas*, my copy, has travelled a long way. From town to town in southern Chile, from house to house in Mexico City, and then to three cities in Spain. **6.** The book didn't always belong to me, of course. First it was my mother's. She gave it to my sister, and when my sister left Girona and went to Mexico, she passed it on to me. Of the books my sister left me, my favourites were the science fiction and the complete works (up to that point) of Manuel Puig, which I had given her, and reread after she went. **7.** By that stage I didn't like Neruda any more. Especially not *Veinte poemas de amor*! **8.** In 1968, my family moved to Mexico City. Two years later, in 1970, I met Alejandro Jodorowski, who, for me, was the Archetype of the Artist. I waited for him outside a theatre (he was directing a production of *Zarathustra*, with Isela Varga) and said I wanted him to teach me how to make films. I then became a frequent visitor at his house. I don't think I was a good student. Jodorowski asked me how much I spent a week on cigarettes. Quite a bit, I said (I've always smoked like a chimney). He told me to stop smoking and spend the money on Zen meditation classes with Ejo Takata. All right, I said. I went along for a few days, but during the third session I decided it wasn't for me. **9.** I parted company with Ejo Takata in the middle of a Zen meditation session. When I tried to slip away he came at me brandishing a wooden stick, the one he used on the students. What he would do was hold out the stick; the students would say yes or no, and if the response was affirmative, he'd let them have a couple of whacks, and the sound would echo in the dim room hazy with incense. **10.** On this occasion, however, he didn't ask me first. His attack was precipitate and stentorian. I was sitting next to a girl, near the door, and Ejo was at the back of the room. I thought he had his eyes shut and wouldn't hear me leaving. But the bastard heard and threw himself at me shouting the Zen equivalent of *banzai*. **11.** My father was a heavyweight amateur boxing champion. His unchallenged reign was restricted to southern Chile. I never liked boxing, but had been taught since I was a kid; there was always a pair of boxing gloves in the house, whether in Chile or in Mexico. **12.** When Master Ejo Takata threw himself at me shouting, he probably didn't mean to do me any harm, or expect me to defend myself automatically. Normally when he whacked his followers with that stick it was to dissipate their nervous tension. But I wasn't suffering from nervous tension; I just wanted to get out of there once and for all. **13.** If you think you're being attacked, you defend yourself; it's only natural, especially when you're seventeen, especially in Mexico City. Ejo Takata was Nerudian in his ingenuity. **14.** Jodorowski was to thank for Ejo Takata's presence in Mexico, so he said. At one stage Takata used to go looking for drug addicts in the jungles of Oaxaca, mostly North Americans who had gone tripping and never found their way back. **15.** My experience with Takata, however, didn't make me give up smoking. **16.** One of the things I liked about Jodorowski was the way, whenever he talked about Chilean intellectuals (usually in critical terms), he would include me among them. That was a big boost to my confidence, although naturally I had no intention whatsoever of resembling the said intellectuals. **17.** One afternoon, I can't remember how, we got on to the topic of Chilean poetry. He said that the greatest Chilean poet was Nicanor Parra. He recited one of Nicanor's poems straightaway, and another, and then one more. Jodorowski recited well, but I wasn't impressed by the poems. At that stage I was a highly sensitive young man, as well as being ridiculous and full of myself, and I declared that Chile's finest poet was, without any doubt, Pablo Neruda. All the rest, I added, are midgets. The discussion must have lasted about half an hour. Jodorowski brandished arguments from Gurdjieff, Krishnamurti, and Madame Blavatsky, went on to talk about Kierkegaard and Wittgenstein, then Topor, Arrabal, and himself. I remember him saying that Nicanor, on his way somewhere, had stayed at his house. In this statement I glimpsed a childlike pride which I have since noticed again and again in the majority of writers. **18.** In one of his books Bataille says that tears are the ultimate form of communication. I started crying, not in a normal, ordinary way, letting the tears roll smoothly down my cheeks, but wildly, in spurts, more or less like Alice in Wonderland, wetting everything. **19.** As I left Jodorowski's house I realised I would never return, which hurt as much as what he had said, and I went on crying in the street. More dimly, I also realised that never again would I have a master as charming as that gentleman thief and consummate con-man. **20.** But what dismayed me most of all was my poorly argued, rather pathetic defence (a defence it was, nevertheless) of Pablo Neruda, when all I had read of his were the *Veinte poemas de amor* (which by that stage struck me as unintentionally funny) and *Crepusculario (Twilight)*, including the poem 'Farewell', to which I remain unshakeably faithful, though even then I saw it as the ultimate in schmaltz. **21.** In 1971 I read Vallejo, Huidobro, Martín Adán, Borges, Oquendo de Amat, Pablo de Rokha, Gilberto Owen, López Velarde, Oliverio Girondo. I even read Nicanor Parra. I even read Pablo Neruda! **22.** The Mexican poets I was hanging out and swapping books with at the time belonged for the most part to one of two camps: the Nerudians and the Vallejians. I was, unquestionably, Parrian in my isolation. **23.** But the fathers must be killed; poets are born orphans. **24.** In 1973 I went back to Chile: a long journey over land and sea, repeatedly delayed by hospitality. I met with revolutionaries of various stripes. The whirlwind of fire that would soon engulf Central America could already be glimpsed in the eyes of my friends, who spoke of death as if they were talking about a film. **25.** I reached Chile in August 1973. I wanted to help build socialism. The first book of poems I bought was Parra's *Obra Gruesa (Construction Work)*. The second was *Artefactos (Artifacts)*, also by Parra. **26.** I had less than a month in which to enjoy building socialism. At the time, of course, I didn't know that. I was Parrian in my ingenuity. **27.** I went to an exhibition and saw various Chilean poets; it was awful. **28.** On the eleventh of September I turned up at the only functioning party cell in the suburb where I was living and volunteered. The man in charge was a communist factory worker, chubby and perplexed, but willing to fight. His wife seemed to be more courageous than he was. We all piled into their little wooden-floored dining room. While the man in charge was speaking, I examined the books on the sideboard. There weren't many, mostly cowboy novels like the ones my father used to read. **29.** For me, the eleventh of September was a comic as well as a bloody spectacle. **30.** I kept watch in an empty street. I forgot my password. My comrades were fifteen years old, retired, or out of work. **31.** When Neruda died, I was already in Mulchén, with my uncles, aunts, and cousins. In November, while travelling from Los Ángeles to Concepción, I was arrested during a road check and taken prisoner. I was the only one they took from the bus. I thought they were going to kill me there and then. From the cell I could hear the officer in charge of the patrol, a fresh-faced policeman who looked like an arsehole (an arsehole wriggling around in a sack of flour) talking with his superiors in Concepción. He was saying he had captured a Mexican terrorist. Then he retracted and said: a foreign terrorist. He mentioned my accent, the dollars I was carrying, the brand of my shirt and trousers. **32.** My great-grandparents, the Flores and the Grañas, vainly attempted to tame the wilds of Araucanía (when they couldn't even tame themselves), so they were probably Nerudian in their excess. My grandfather, Roberto Avalos Martí, was a colonel, stationed at various forts in the south until his mysteriously early retirement, which leads me to suspect that he was Nerudian in his sympathy for the blue and white. My paternal grandparents came from Galicia and Catalonia, gave their lives to the province of Bío-Bío and were Nerudian in their landscape and laborious slowness. **33.** I was imprisoned in Concepción for a few days and then released. They didn't torture me, as I had feared; they didn't even rob me. But they didn't give me anything to eat either, or any kind of covering for the night, so I had to rely on the goodwill of the other prisoners, who shared their food with me. In the small hours I could hear them torturing others; I couldn't sleep and there was nothing to read except a magazine in English that someone had left behind. The only interesting article in it was about a house that had once belonged to Dylan Thomas. **34.** I got out of that hole thanks to a pair of detectives who knew me from high school in Los Ángeles, and my friend Fernando Fernández, who was twenty-one, just a year older than me, but possessed of a composure comparable to that of the idealised Englishman on whom Chileans were desperately and vainly trying to model themselves. **35.** In January 1974 I left Chile. I have never been back. **36.** Were the Chileans of my generation courageous? Yes, they were. **37.** In Mexico I heard the story of a young woman from the MIR who had been tortured by having live rats put into her vagina. This woman managed to get out of the country and went to Mexico City. There she lived, but each day she grew sadder, until one day the sadness killed her. That's what I heard. I didn't know her personally. **38.** The story isn't exceptional. We are told of peasant women in Guatemala being subjected to unspeakable humiliations. The amazing thing about the story is its ubiquity. In Paris I heard of a Chilean woman who had been tortured in the same way before emigrating to France. She too had been a member of the MIR; she was the same age as the woman in Mexico and, like her, had died of sadness. **39.** Some time later, I was told of a Chilean woman in Stockholm: she was young, a member or ex-member of the MIR; in November 1973 she had been tortured, using rats, and she had died, to the astonishment of the doctors who were treating her, of sadness, *morbus melancholicus.* **40.** Is it possible to die of sadness? Yes, it is. It is possible (though painful) to die of hunger. It is even possible to die of spleen. **41.** Was this anonymous Chilean, repeatedly subjected to torture and death, a single woman, or three different women who happened to share the same political affiliation and the same kind of beauty? According to a friend, it was one woman, who, as in Vallejo's poem 'Masa' multiplied in death without in any way surviving. (Actually, in Vallejo's poem, it is not the dead man who multiplies but the supplicants begging him not to die.) **42.** Once upon a time there was a Belgian poet called Sophie Podolski. She was born in 1953 and committed suicide in 1974. She published only one book, called *Le pays où tout est permis* (*The Country where Everything is Allowed*), Montfaucon Research Centre, 1970, 280 facsimile pages. **43.** Germain Nouveau (1852–1920), a friend of Rimbaud's, spent the last years of his life as a vagabond and beggar. He went by the name of Humilis (in 1910 he published *Les poèmes d'Humilis*) and lived on church porches. **44.** Everything is possible. Every poet *ought* to know that. **45.** I was once asked who were my favourite young Chilean poets. Maybe they didn't say 'young' but 'contemporary'. I said I liked Rodrigo Lira, although he can't really be called contemporary any more (though he is young, younger than any of us) because he's dead. **46.** Dance partners for the new Chilean poetry: the mathematical scions of Neruda and the cruel progeny of Huidobro, the comic followers of Mistral and the humble disciples of De Rokha, the heirs to Parra's bones and to Lihn's eyes. **47.** A confession: I cannot read Neruda's memoirs without feeling seriously ill.

What a mass of contradictions. All that effort to hide and beautify a thing with a disfigured face. So little generosity, so little sense of humour. **48.** During a period of my life, thankfully behind me now, I used to see Adolf Hitler in the corridor of my house. All Hitler did was walk up and down the corridor, without even looking at me when he passed the open door of my bedroom. At first I thought it was the devil (who else could it have been?) and feared I had gone irreversibly mad. **49.** After two weeks, Hitler disappeared, and I was expecting him to be replaced by Stalin. But Stalin didn't show. **50.** It was Neruda who took up residence in my corridor. Not for two weeks, like Hitler, but three days – the shorter stay seemed to indicate that my depression was easing. **51.** Neruda, however, made noises (Hitler had been as quiet as a block of drifting ice); he complained, murmuring incomprehensible words; his hands reached out and his lungs absorbed the air (the air of that cold European corridor) with relish. The pained gestures and beggar-like manner of the first night changed progressively, so that in the end the ghost seemed to have reconstituted himself as a grave and dignified courtier poet. **52.** On the third and final night, as he was going past my door, he stopped and looked at me (Hitler had never done that) and, this is the strangest part, he tried to speak but could not, expressed his impotence with gestures and finally, before disappearing with the first light of dawn, smiled at me (as if to say that communication is impossible, but one should still make an attempt?). **53.** Some time ago I met three Argentine brothers who later gave their lives for revolutionary causes in different Latin American countries. The mutual betrayal of the two elder brothers accidentally implicated the younger one, who hadn't betrayed anyone, and died, so I heard, calling out to them, although it is more likely that he died in silence. **54.** The children of the Spanish lion, said Rubén Darío, a born optimist. The children of Walt Whitman, José Martí, and Violeta Parra; torn apart, forgotten, in mass graves, at the bottom of the sea, the Trojan destiny of their mingled bones terrifying the survivors. **55.** I think of them this week as the veterans of the International Brigades visit Spain: little old men climbing down from the buses, brandishing their fists. There were 40,000 of them, and 350 or so have come back to Spain. **56.** I think of Beltrán Morales, I think of Rodrigo Lira, I think of Mario Santiago, I think of Reinaldo Arenas. I think of the poets who died under torture, who died of AIDS, or overdosed, all those who believed in a Latin American paradise and died in a Latin American hell. I think of their works, which may, perhaps, show the Left a way out of the pit of shame and futility. **57.** I think of our useless pointy heads and the abominable death of Isaac Babel. **58.** When I grow up I want to be Nerudian in my synergy. **59.** Questions to ponder before going to sleep. Why didn't Neruda like Kafka? Why didn't Neruda like Rilke? Why didn't Neruda like De Rokha? **60.** Did he like

Barbusse? Everything seems to suggest that he did. And Sholokov. And Alberti. And Octavio Paz. Odd companions for a voyage through Purgatory. **61.** But he also liked Éluard, who wrote love poems. **62.** If Neruda had been addicted to cocaine or heroin, if he had been killed by a piece of rubble during the siege of Madrid in 1936, if he had been Lorca's lover and committed suicide after Lorca was killed, it would be quite a different story. If Neruda had been the mystery that, deep down, he really is! **63.** In the basement of the edifice known as 'The Works of Pablo Neruda', is Ugolino lurking, waiting to devour his children? **64.** Without the slightest remorse! Innocently! Simply because he's hungry and doesn't want to die! **65.** He didn't have children, but the people loved him. **66.** Do we have to come back to Neruda as we do to the Cross, on bleeding knees, with punctured lungs and eyes full of tears? **67.** When our names no longer mean a thing, his will go on shining, his will go on soaring over an imaginary domain called *Chilean Literature*. **68.** By then all poets will live in artistic communities called jails or asylums. **69.** Our imaginary home, the home we share.

Discover more in **VINTAGE CLASSICS** red spine

Brave New World	Aldous Huxley
To Kill a Mockingbird	Harper Lee
Catch-22	Joseph Heller
Native Son	Richard Wright
The Handmaid's Tale	Margaret Atwood
The Gulag Archipelago	Aleksandr Solzhenitsyn
The Master and Margarita	Mikhail Bulgakov
Beloved	Toni Morrison
Stoner	John Williams
The Sailor Who Fell from Grace with the Sea	Yukio Mishima
The Savage Detectives	Roberto Bolaño
The Joy Luck Club	Amy Tan
Autobiography of Red	Anne Carson
I Who Have Never Known Men	Jacqueline Harpman
Oranges Are Not the Only Fruit	Jeanette Winterson
Disgrace	J. M. Coetzee
My Left Foot	Christy Brown
Sugar	Bernice L. McFadden
Death and the Penguin	Andrey Kurkov
Persepolis	Marjane Satrapi